# THE ETRUSCAN
# CONNECTION

DICK ROSANO

# CONTENTS

# PRAISE FOR DICK ROSANO'S BOOKS

DICK ROSANO'S BOOKS—PUBLISHED IN ENGLISH—HAVE also been translated into three languages: Italian, Spanish, and Portuguese, and continue to command attention around the world.

## Islands of Fire: The Sicily Chronicles, Part I

"An original and spellbinding novel rich in history and adventure... intimate and poignant... It is original, engaging, and features characters that are sophisticated and a setting that feels like a character in the story." (ReadersFavorite)

"Each prehistoric episode is told in omniscient third person, through the eyes of an individual, their family, and their village...The book is unique in that it gives life to a period of human history that is often overlooked." (GoodReads.com)

Crossroads of the Mediterranean: The Sicily Chronicles, Part II

"Dick Rosano's adroit research and storytelling continues in his second book, *Crossroads of the Mediterranean: The Sicily Chronicles, Part II...* replete with sharp and incisive dialogue, crucial historical episodes featuring a host of guileful rulers—kings, emperors and those with rebellion from freedom in their hearts." (Ambassador Magazine)

"Dick Rosano is not just a great storyteller; the reader is left in no doubt that they have been taught by a great researcher...a novel that brilliantly documents the history of a coveted piece of land and why it became the melting pot of civilizations...A breathtaking journey into history." (ReadersFavorite)

The Vienna Connection

"Rosano possesses quite an extensive knowledge regarding various fields like military, politics, architecture, wine, and even geology...his work shows his outstanding ability to depict graphic scenes which unfold the story right before your eyes." (Online Book Club)

"Fast paced and enthralling." (ReadersFavorite)

The Secret of Altamura: Nazi Crimes, Italian Treasure

"If you're a fan of Italy, this book is for you...Rosano skillfully blends all three themes into one well-written, emotionally engaging narrative that moves at a good pace." (ReadersFavorite.com)

## A Death in Tuscany

"If you want to read a book that introduces you to the culture of wine making, an appreciation of the countryside of Tuscany, and a lifestyle that appreciates good food and good wine, this book excels." (Five Stars). (Barnes & Noble)

"The book is as much a crime novel as it is an authoritative travelogue and wine tutorial, an enjoyable read for Tuscany aficionados in particular." (*Ambassador Magazine*)

## Hunting Truffles: A Mystery

"*Hunting Truffles* travels through the Piedmont region after the lucrative white truffle harvest has been stolen, the plot thickens as the bodies of truffle hunters are discovered! We can't wait for the movie!" (Bethesda Travel Magazine)

## Wine Heritage: The Story of Italian-American Vintners

"Original in conception, well-researched and deftly written, this book casts a long-overdue light on a fascinating corner aspect of America's wine history." (*The Washington Post*)

# KASAI RISTORANTE

## AMALFI COAST

IT COULD HAVE BEEN BETTER. IT SHOULD HAVE BEEN better.

Not the food. The food was terrific. A label-less carafe of local red wine, a basket of fresh bread still hot from the oven, and a plate of steaming *frutti di mare*—fried catch of the day—literally "set the table." The string of twinkling lights laced through the trellis overhead brought the stars in the heavens down to our table.

We were at Kasai, a restaurant perched on a ribbon of road in Praiano, a romantic and iconic little village on the Amalfi Coast. We sat at sidewalk tables overlooking the sea, but Kasai's small dining room inside the establishment was across this narrow roadway and pressed into the rocky rise of the mountain above. The tables there were snuggled close together between vases of lavender and an unkempt display of ceramics on the walls in a dimly lit scene that could have been a paragraph or two from a long-lost Hemingway novel.

But the sidewalk tables were infinitely better, lined up at

the railing overlooking the Mediterranean Sea in the cool evening air under a canopy of the sparkling night sky.

Waiters from the kitchen across the road showed no hesitation in dodging Vespas and tour buses careening around the curve to get to our table. The scent of fresh lemons—a staple of the Amalfi Coast—was in the air, and even the occasional squeal of tires as vehicles of all sizes rolled past in careless haste added to the operatic essence of the evening.

It was glorious.

But the call I got from Aggie earlier that afternoon could have been better.

"I need your help," was all he said.

Normally, I would have hoped for more detail than that. Even a "hello" or a simple, "How are you, Darren?" But Aggie didn't spin long sentences, for me or anyone else. Just "I need your help."

Seated across from me at Kasai, Alana paused with her fork held over the plate of steaming seafood and looked up at me. Even in the dim glow of the party lights overhead, her brown eyes sparkled and brought a pleasant thump to my heart.

"Everything alright?" she asked.

"Yeah. It's okay," I lied. Alana and I were celebrating our final evening in Praiano before returning home—she to Vienna, Austria, and me to Washington, D.C. The blissfully limpid night, the fragrance of summer flowers, and the aromas of seafood and fresh bread on the table made parting even harder. We never seemed to have enough time together, which is why I planned this week for us at the Villa Poesia just down the road.

We worked through our plate of seafood and shared glasses of wine and humorous recollections of our week together. The fried calamari had a hint of red spice, and the red wine was a welcome chaser for the oil-scented dressing that dappled the plate of tiny fish and mussels.

But I was a little distracted, and Alana could tell.

The waiter swung in our direction once again—mere seconds before a minibus sped down the road—and settled a plate of truffled pasta between us. The broad tagliatelle noodles glistened with a coating of melted butter and olive oil, and the shaved, paper-thin discs of black truffle gave off a savory aroma that trailed behind the waiter and turned heads from other tables. I lifted my fork to load some of it onto my plate as Alana watched.

"Is your friend okay?" she asked, pressing her point.

Alana knew of Aggie but had not met him. Not during our time in Vienna and not since then. But she knew that he was a part of my complicated history. Officer Alana Weber was an Austrian police investigator, and she was quick to pick up on telltale signals in my behavior.

Aggie Darwin was an old friend. We met at a rural commune just hours from Washington, D.C., after our tours of duty in Afghanistan. Tall Cedars was a way station for battered souls. Returning from the war zone where I served as a military intelligence interrogator, I needed the uncomplicated, undulating rhythms of the Tall Cedars lifestyle, a veritable wind chime for a settled life. There, I encountered Aggie, who was there in search of the same therapy.

"He said he needs help," I told Alana, turning the tagliatelle on my fork as I turned the conversation back to the phone call I got that afternoon. She and I had just risen from a pleasurable midday nap and moved lazily to the late-afternoon sunlight on the terrace when my cell phone had buzzed on the table beside me.

The terrace of the Villa Poesia—and the villa itself—offered numerous delights. Relaxing and sunburst in the afternoon, cooled with gentle Mediterranean breezes in the evening. The white-washed walls of the villa were brilliantly accented with ocean blue and green flourishes, a gorgeous palace on the edge of the coast. The vast terrazza provided privacy as well as views that seemed to stretch forever. Through long, languorous days and quiet evening hours, we sat there on the reclining lounges and gazed out at the endless sea.

"What kind of help?" she asked, bringing my attention back to Kasai, to Alana, and to the evening meal.

"He said a friend of his, a guy named Dielman or something, died in an archeological dig."

"Where?"

"In Tarquinia," I replied. "Don't know where that is, except Aggie said it's just north of Rome."

"How did he, this guy Dielman, die?"

"Not sure. Aggie didn't want to give too many details over the phone, but he was clearly in a bit of shock."

"And you can help with this?" Alana pursued.

"Aggie thinks it wasn't an accident."

Alana lifted some of the tagliatelle and truffles with a combination of fork and serving spoon and lowered the bundle onto her plate.

"You're not a bank examiner," she said with a wry smile. I, too, had to smile at her obvious jab.

When Alana and I had first met in Vienna, I was posing as a bank examiner, reluctant to give away my true identity, while I sorted out a strange series of coincidences for the American president.

Well, sorta true identity. After claiming to be a bank examiner to justify my interest in the DFR-Wien bank that was central to the President's concerns, I had to reset my bio to explain to her that I was actually a wine and food writer. True enough, since I had published articles for *The Wine Review* and was in Vienna at the time to attend a formal tasting of Italian wines. But when she doubted even that ruse, I realized that I wasn't far from admitting my even truer background. Her piercing gaze convinced me that her natural abilities or police training made Alana adept at divining the truth in a forest of lies. She saw through my layers of deception. Fortunately, our evolving personal relationship made her reluctant to force me to reveal more.

So, at dinner, I didn't have to reply to her comment. But I knew the time would come when I would have to tell her who I really was.

Darren Priest, my current name, served nicely as an adopted identity. As a writer, I could pass it off simply as a *nom de plume*. But I kept it for grander purposes, with a Social Security card in that name, tax records, and abundant other references—thanks to an assist from the U.S. government. I didn't have to return to my birth name, Armando Listrani, unless I wanted to. And with Alana—at least for now—I didn't want to.

And the U.S. government strongly agreed with that decision.

"Armando" might have been too much for Alana to handle at this point in our relationship. As him—or should I say, as the "really truly me"—I had worked in military intelligence, in a special squad used in the interrogation of particularly difficult subjects, from both sides of the conflict. Together with five other men who shared my odd ability to find truth amid a subject's lies, I had carried out interrogations in secret, weeks or months at a time as circumstances required. I had been able to break down the subjects with mind games and psychological tricks. No physical contact or threats; no menacing comments about their own lives or that of their family members. Just psy-ops—and what Sergeant Randall called "penetrating perceptions of nonverbal signals." Despite his penchant for obtuse verbiage, we got what Sarge was describing: the inexplicable talent for translating minor quirks, muscle twitches, dryness on the surface of the eyes, and skin temperature into signals that could be used against the subject and lead him to break down his defenses against the truth.

We didn't attempt to find out the truth about the subject; the truth was less important than knowing the lies. We only cared to know when he was being misleading or deceitful. Simply by leaning in or staring blankly at him, I could convey my skepticism about what he was saying. This, and a series of carefully worded questions, led him to worry that I knew more than he did and more than he was admitting to. Which in turn led him to expose everything he was trying to hide.

A rising pink glow on his forearms, an inconspicuous bristle of his eyebrows, a gulp or a stare that seemed forcibly non-blinking always gave him away.

It was called Operation Best Guess, a unit that foreswore the Medieval torture practices favored by misguided goons with rubber hoses and water buckets. Word play and a keen awareness of physical "tells" allowed us to peel back the layers of untruths to discover the nuggets of worthwhile information.

It worked every time.

But after separating from the U.S. Army, I was warned by the government officials to whom I reported that continuing as Armando Listrani might pose some difficulties that I would rather avoid. "You've been places that you should forget and dealt with people who won't forget," they told me. So, they offered help in abandoning that identity and assuming my new one, as Darren Priest.

That step was particularly hard on my family. With both mother and father deceased, I had only to break it to siblings. But they could only know that I was no longer Armando, not that I had become Darren Priest since they were not allowed to know where I had gone. I softened it a bit by maintaining regular communication, even occasional in-person visits, but generally had to divorce myself from my earlier life to remain safe.

Why safe? I had not committed any crimes while an interrogator. But I had spent too much time with too many people who wouldn't mind getting revenge for the role I played in their capture and imprisonment.

Some parts of the world were especially dangerous for me, so the Department of State flatly refused to let me travel there, even as a civilian. Fortunately, the Amalfi Coast was not one of those places.

But once you adopt a new identity, you can't keep changing it. I couldn't be Armando Listrani while at the Villa Poesia in Praiano, then resume Darren Priest when I returned to Washington.

So, Alana knew me as Darren Priest, the wine and food writer whose "cover" career she only barely believed. She easily discarded my ruse of being a bank examiner in Vienna and, when she found out I had posed as a journalist for *The Washington Post* at another point in time, she scoffed. I was convincing to most people; I knew a lot about the identities I assumed and the subjects they embodied. As a wine and food writer, I had published numerous articles and a few books, but anyone with Alana's perceptive skills—not to mention the emotional proximity I allowed her—would know that there lurked something else below the surface.

As the pistachio gelato and espresso appeared at the table, my mind went back to Alana's comment.

"No, I'm not a bank examiner," I smiled. I wanted to tell her more and knew that I would, in time, but not right now.

Alana smiled back and slipped a spoonful of gelato into her mouth.

"Aggie said he thinks Dielman's death was not an accident," I repeated.

"An archeological dig?" she asked with skepticism. "What kind of skullduggery goes on at those places?"

"Don't know," I replied. "And he's a little jumpy now and then. Aggie, I mean. But this sounded different."

"What do you want to do?"

"Well, the week at Villa Poesia ends tomorrow..." and this drew a sigh from Alana. It had been a spectacular escape for both of us. She from her duties as a police investigator; me from my double-life as a writer and as a too-often sought-after investigator for the American power center. In Praiano, and at Villa Poesia, we had forsaken all that, forgotten it all even. We had become Alana and Darren, lovers with only these infrequent getaways to remind us of our attraction to each other.

Work of the old kind had not intervened until Aggie's call.

Alana would be returning home to Vienna anyway, to work, and to her young daughter Kia. And I was returning to my condo in the suburbs of Washington. Aggie's call for help might create a detour for us, though, a delay in facing the real world again. So, I dipped my spoon into the gelato and turned my eyes toward Alana.

"Would you like to go to Tarquinia for a few days?" I asked.

"I would go to the Arctic with you," she said quickly but added, "well, maybe not there," and she smiled.

"But yes, I can spare a couple of days for that," she added. "It's only Friday, and I don't report back to work until Monday. If we check out tomorrow and head north, we'll have most of Saturday and all of Sunday. I can catch a train from Rome to Vienna on Monday morning."

"Okay. Done," I said with more confidence than I actually felt. Leaving the Amalfi Coast and heading toward Rome would not be as pleasant as days in the sun at Villa Poesia, but at least I'd still be with Alana.

# VILLA POESIA

WE SPENT THAT LAST EVENING AT VILLA POESIA SITTING
on the terrazza facing the sparkling waters of the Mediterranean a thousand feet below. White-hulled boats bobbed on
the soft ripples of the oncoming tide while lights blinked on
and off on the bow of small craft in the harbor, riding the surf
out into the bay below us.

The lights of the villa behind us were turned low, allowing
the twinkle of the heavens to show in all its glory. I held a glass
of Prosecco in one hand and cradled Alana's hand in a loose
embrace with my other, resting side-by-side on cushioned
recliners. The dinner at Kasai had worked its magic on us, and
all was wonderful—except that my thoughts occasionally went
back to Aggie.

"He died in a fall, he said," as I replayed Aggie's words from
memory. "Could've been pushed. I don't know. But Tesa is very
upset."

"Who's Tesa?" Alana asked.

I didn't know who Tesa was and didn't want to press Aggie
for details yet. After my conversation with Alana and our deci-

sion to go to Tarquinia to see what had happened, I placed a quick call to Aggie to reassure him that we would be there within the day, and he told me about her. Sounded like they were involved and that Tesa was part of the dig in Tarquinia.

But Alana and I wanted to spend our last evening in Praiano in the lap of the villa's grand hospitality, with no thought of accidents that weren't, or to archeological digs with unknown findings.

My hand jerked suddenly, and Alana turned her head to ask me what was the matter.

"Nothing," I said, not totally truthfully.

"Wrong," she replied. "I can tell whenever your squeeze your fingers a little that your attention has gone from me to something else."

I had to smile at her keen sense.

"I suppose it's about Aggie, right?" she asked.

"Yes."

I paused to gather my thoughts and try to come up with a brief sketch of the man for her. Too many words would confuse the description, and too few would alert Alana that I was holding back.

"Aggie served in Afghanistan, around the time I did, but we didn't meet until we were back in the States."

"Where?"

"It's called Tall Cedars. It's a refuge for people in search of peace, or a change of heart..."

"Or change of identity?" she pressed.

Alana was sharp enough to know that there were only two types of people who hide their true identities: Criminals and the people who chase them. I had not clarified this with Alana yet, but I hoped she took me to be the latter. But this wasn't the time to explain in greater detail, so I ignored her question about identity.

I checked my memory quickly before telling her more. Aggie was a drone pilot in the war—"Killing from a distance is worse than killing up close," he had said one afternoon. "You can't pay your respects to an enemy you never see." That information was not classified, so I explained his role to Alana.

"And what were you? In that war, I mean?"

A gentle breeze drifted across the terrazza, a pleasant physical sensation that seemed at odds with the knot that was developing in my stomach.

"We all had special roles." That sounded good in my head but came out sounding like a dodge.

"Uh, huh," she replied, recognizing my verbal gymnastics for what they were. "Did you go by Captain Priest? Major? Sergeant Priest?" After a pregnant pause, she added, "Or Sergeant somebody-else?"

Alana had access to Interpol data, but my identity would not have been revealed there. Only Darren Priest, the adopted identity, not Armando Listrani. But somehow, she pegged my rank, and that made me worry that she knew something—or was supernaturally good at guessing. Still, I didn't think she knew my name and, therefore, she probably didn't know my assignment.

I consciously softened my grip on her hand, trying to communicate through touch that I was relaxing. Alana smiled at me, sipped from her glass of Prosecco, and returned her gaze to the heavens above us.

———

When the morning sun flooded the bedroom with early light, we rose, showered, and arranged our bags in the large, brightly colored living area of the villa. We grazed on the remnants of food in the refrigerator, finding breakfast breads, espresso, and fresh fruit for a perfect meal, then Alana called Julietta to arrange for a cab to the train station in Sorrento.

"It's just as easy to get a cab direct to Roma," she had reminded me the day before, but I said we liked train travel. And this one would get us to Rome, where we would transfer to a rental car that was waiting at the Leonardo da Vinci airport.

Julietta had been part of the romance that was the Villa Poesia. As breathtaking as the villa was, her kind attention and personal touch made it feel like home.

The altitude of the Villa Poesia rewarded visitors with once-in-a-lifetime views, but it also required many steps up the terraced slope of Praiano to reach it. Every step was worth it when we arrived at the summit, so I tried not to think of that when we scaled them each day.

On that morning, hired hands helped us carry our bags down to the waiting cab. We followed along, Alana with her roller bag and me with my rucksack, past La Moressa, the ristorante that we had enjoyed several times during our week-long stay, and down to the little grocery store on the road below, *Tutto per Tutti*, which translated to "Everything for Everyone." When we first stopped in that store for provisions at the beginning of our weeklong sojourn, I saw shelves stocked with bread, cheese, fresh produce, wine, pasta, and more, and I understood the name.

The driver picked us up outside *Tutto* and loaded our bags into the back of the van-size taxi. It would be an hour and a half to Naples, and the views from the narrow road that hung onto the cliffside of the Amalfi Coast left us spellbound the entire trip. Alana and I were still in the *Amalfitani* spirit, and neither of us could close our eyes and miss the views that stretched out below as the soaring cliffs of the coast met the rippling waters of the Mediterranean.

We arrived at the train station in Naples just twenty

minutes before our scheduled departure. The train wasn't at the track yet; it was common in Italy with its bustling schedule of trains to arrange arrivals just minutes after another train cleared the track. Ours arrived about fifteen minutes later, leaving travelers only a handful of minutes to find their car, board, and settle in. We did so, in the throng of the morning crowd, and set our sights on Rome.

The club car offered some essentials for the trip, but our breakfast had filled our bellies, so I settled for espresso and Alana for a latte. Then we sat in our assigned seats and stared out the window as the Italian countryside slipped by.

I had tried to find a rental car company near Rome's main train station but settled for one about ten blocks away. We were traveling light, so after disembarking from the train, the short walk was no problem. In only a brief time, we were in the Hertz office and were assigned a small car for two days, enough to get us to Tarquinia and then back to Rome so that Alana and I could depart to our separate destinations on Monday.

———

While Alana drove, I read aloud from my phone.

"Tarquinia is more than a little village," I narrated from the Wikipedia references during the trip, "but in Etruscan times, it was a bustling metropolis that traded in many products brought from other shores as well as from the region of central Italy itself. Called Tarchon by the Etruscans, it was an important member of the Etruscan League in the 8th to 6th centuries BCE."

I was trying to understand the point of archeological digs in the area that Aggie was calling us to. Alana smiled back at my monologue without comment, but her impassive look revealed no great interest. Like many of her counterparts on the continent, I assumed that she was well educated in continental history, more so than most Americans, but I doubted that she knew that much about Etruscan history.

"Tarchon," I continued, "was connected by trade to the port city of Pyrgi, another Etruscan settlement on the western coastline of the Italian peninsula. Pyrgi was on the Tyrrhenian Sea and received imports from trade centers all around the Mediterranean, even ports as distant as modern-day Egypt, Turkey, and Israel."

"That's not right," she interjected.

"Yes, it is," I insisted, pointing to the screen of my phone as if this gave my comments more credibility.

"No, I mean that's not what Wikipedia says."

"I'm paraphrasing," I confessed but shrugged my shoulders as if it didn't really matter. "Besides, how do you know?"

"I read the entire section last night," Alana said with a grin.

"When?"

"After you dozed off on the terrazza."

"Oh, okay," I admitted sheepishly. "So, you know all this?"

"Most of it," she said, "but I like hearing you read it to me. Why is it called Tarchon?"

"Don't know. Let's see," I said, turning my focus back to the phone. The webpage offered too little detail on that, so I knew I'd have to dig a little deeper.

"And why the Tyrrhenian Sea?" she asked in a follow-up question. Alana seldom asked only one question at a time, a devilish technique for an inquisitor but hard to follow in a friendly conversation.

The green hills of Lazio rippled past us as we sped northward. I stared at the panorama spread out beside the roadway and gazed at an old stone castle on its hilltop perch, a romantic throwback to the warring times of Medieval Italy when city-states pitted their military might in an unrelenting series of conflict and conflagration.

"Don't know," I admitted. "Do you?"

"Not from Wikipedia," Alana responded. "But I have some vague memory of a mythical character, someone called Tyrrhenus ... maybe a son of some king. Might have been named after him."

"Do you know anything about him?"

"No. But I think it's way back."

She was cheating, leading me to make a guess about a guy named Tyrrhenus, whom I figured she already had researched. I saw her smile and decided I wasn't going to fall for the trap.

I didn't have anything to add and figured that Alana's factum would require some later research. So, I dropped it, laid my phone back down on the dashboard, and returned my gaze to the countryside speeding by.

# MONTEROZZI NECROPOLIS

ALANA AND I WENT DIRECTLY TO TARQUINIA. USING Aggie's rough directions to the archeological dig, we managed to arrive just after noon. We had no hotel arrangements yet but trusted that the nearby city of Civitavecchia would have accommodations for us when we were ready later in the day. Aggie told me that the team from the dig was staying in a little hotel in the city, so we hoped to find lodging there or nearby.

The dig was on a dusty plain east of Tarquinia and adjacent to an area circumscribed by fencing and signs that labeled it as the *Monterozzi Necropoli* in Italian. Back in the car, after we switched driving responsibilities about halfway through, I drove while Alana read descriptions of the area from her phone.

"'Tarquinia is a small city, but the local environs enjoy a vibrant culture. Despite the tourist attraction at the Monterozzi Necropolis where there are a series of funereal mounds built by the Etruscans from the 8th to the 6th centuries BC ...'" and here she paused to ad-lib for me. Turning in my direction to get my undivided attention, she continued:

"Many of the older books say BC, but ..."

"Yeah, I know," I interjected to defend my own knowledge of history. "Now we say BCE, 'before the common era' and CE to indicate the 'common era.'"

Scientists had abandoned BC—"before Christ" and AD— "Anno Domini" in favor of less-religiously-centered markers for history, and I wasn't about to let Alana get that one on me.

"Yes, well, hmmm. I'm impressed," Alana allowed, but it seemed more like a slap at American education than a compliment to me. I let it pass but smiled back to show my appreciation. At least she didn't pat me on the head.

"So, anyway," she continued, "'the funereal mounds —*tumuli* they're called—are evidence of Etruscan culture in the area near modern-day Tarquinia.'" Then, she lowered her phone and wondered aloud. "I guess that's where Aggie is."

I didn't know enough yet to respond, so I offered only the common Italian gesture, shrugging my shoulders.

Alana returned her attention to her phone, and I could see with my peripheral vision that she was swiping pages and changing reference works to dig deeper into this.

"Says here that there are archeological digs on the periphery of the necropolis—that's a prehistoric burial ground," she added, drawing an eye-roll from me, "which most scientists assume represent the actual settlement of the Etruscans during this period. 'The dig has produced an impressive amount of evidence,'" she read, "'suggesting not only that the Etruscans occupied the area but a site which also contributed significant clues about their origins.'"

For a moment, she paused and looked at me. "You think Aggie's dig is about the origins of the Etruscans?"

"First of all," I said, "Aggie is not an archeologist, he's a drone pilot. I suppose that this Tesa he mentioned might be involved, but we'll have to wait to find out."

Pulling off the main road through the countryside, we bumped along for a kilometer or so on rutted dirt roads before encountering a large, fenced-in property in a clearing among the trees. I pulled the rented Fiat to a stop at an opening in the fence-line where the chain link provided a gate just big enough for people to pass through, but not cars. There were two Jeep models parked on the perimeter and one Fiat 500, all dusty and dirty from months spent in this environment.

Alana and I stepped out of the air-conditioned comfort of the rental car into the dry heat of a Tuscan summer and headed through the gate toward the largest tent on the property. The size of the canvas covering suggested that the scientific team would be found there, and I hoped to find Aggie and Tesa among them.

It was an open tent, which is to say that it had no sides, but the sloping roof was large enough to shade the dozen people who were gathered under it, plus the kitchen facilities that were serving the midday meal.

"I'm looking for Aggie Darwin," I said, but just then, I saw my old friend on the far side of the tent. He raised his hand and stood to greet me.

"Great to see you, Darren," he said, hustling over with a serious look on his face. "So sorry for the short notice, but I am very happy that you've come."

"This is Alana," I said, introducing my companion. "We were together on the Amalfi Coast when you called. Thought you wouldn't mind if I brought her along."

"No, of course not," Aggie replied, shaking Alana's hand. When Aggie and I met up in Vienna the previous year, I told him about Alana, so he already knew that she was a police officer.

"Darren kept you from me in Vienna," he said. Alana nodded but wouldn't be bested in that.

"He said you were a rogue and that I shouldn't trust you," she replied, grinning back at him.

Aggie laughed then looked at me.

"She's far too nice for you, Darren."

Aggie's charm was his unorthodox behavior and iconic look. His beard was perpetually three days old, his graying hair was tied back in a braided ponytail. He had a sweaty kerchief tied loosely around his neck, and his loose-fitting clothes hung from his bony shoulders. He held a sweat-stained baseball cap in his left hand, one that had some university emblem on it that was obscured by the dust and dirt.

Just then, a slender woman in khaki pants and a white cotton shirt approached us. She settled in next to Aggie, close enough for their forearms to touch, and I assumed she was Tesa. Her long brown hair was held in a ponytail and fell down her back; the top two buttons on her shirt were left open, and the soft cotton collar fell casually to the side. I noticed a certain sadness in her green eyes, a subtlety that suggested a contradiction between her outward appearance and her inner feelings.

Aggie turned to look at her and reached out his hand, which she took.

"This is Tesa Richietta. She is...was, that is...Charlie Dielman's understudy here."

"Please sit down," Tesa suggested, indicating a bench beside an empty table. "You must be hungry. I'll get you some food," and she spun on her heel and headed toward the grill table before I could decline. We were quiet for a moment as she retreated, then Aggie turned to Alana and me.

"She's a master archeologist but, as you can see, still quite young," he commented, glancing back at Tesa. "Charlie was the senior member of the team and responsible for this project."

It seemed to me that Tesa was in her mid-to-late-twenties.

"She's a Ph.D. in physical anthropology," Aggie added with

some animation. "With special expertise in early Etruscan studies."

When he looked over his shoulder toward Tesa, Aggie's feelings for her were apparent. Alana must have seen this, too, as she gently tapped my thigh under the table and shot me a look while Aggie's attention was diverted.

"So," I began, "what's going on?"

Aggie slipped his fingers through the curved handle on his coffee cup, took a sip, and began to explain.

"Charlie Dielman was the senior archeologist here. He died two nights ago. Fell into the pit of the dig. Or was pushed."

"Whoa, slow down," I said with my hand up in a gesture. "Too many suppositions. Let's not get sidetracked by theories yet."

Soon, Tesa returned to the table with a couple trays of food —roasted chicken, grilled fennel, and breadcrumbs, a rendition of risotto that was short on the cheese that I would normally have expected in a finer Italian dining spot. No wine, but bottles of water.

"What Aggie tells you is right," she said. "Charlie was working late one night when the rest of us had gone back to our hotel rooms in Civitavecchia. We were celebrating a recent success, but he wanted to stay on and work a bit longer. He was the only one left at the site ... or so we thought."

"What 'recent success?'" Alana asked.

"We found a bit of gold," she replied, "just a fragment, but it had some scratches on one edge."

"What do you mean, scratches?" I asked.

"They could have been made naturally, contact between the gold nugget and a stone, or river rock," Tesa explained. "But two of the scratches were parallel."

"And what does that mean?" Alans pressed.

"Nature doesn't do things in an orderly way. Let me

explain," Tesa said, pressing her hands forward as if to stop the narrative and begin again.

"Nature loves randomness. Human invention loves order," she began.

"Yeah, not the humans I've met," said Aggie with some disdain, but followed by a laugh.

Tesa let him have his moment of doubt but pressed on.

"The lines of nature are random. Look at the branches of a tree, the meandering stream, the outline of a cloud. All answer to the laws of physics and nature, sure, but you don't see parallel lines and geometric shapes in nature."

"Except for the nautilus and some crystals," I threw in.

"Yeah, sure, nature is not devoid of these things, and nature loves order in her own way. But archeologists are trained to look for straight lines, geometric shapes, parallels, and so on. These things suggest human invention."

"So that matters how?" Alana asked.

"Whenever we see parallel lines, even the smallest hint of them on things like this nugget of gold, it makes us think that there was a human actor involved. Not just some random natural scratching."

"So, what's to celebrate?" I asked.

"You have to understand," Tesa continued, "in the life of an archeologist, finding anything that was made by humans is important, intriguing. And so, we were quite excited."

"Back to where you were," I asked, abandoning discussion of the find and returning to Charlie's demise, "you and the team went to Civitavecchia, is that right?"

Tesa nodded.

"And Charlie stayed here, after you were gone?"

Tesa nodded again.

"And he was alone at the dig, that's when he fell into the pit," I said as if it was a fact.

Tesa's head was tilted down as her eyes focused on her fingers wrapped around a water bottle. Her eyes raised, chin still pointed downward, and she looked at me. She nodded assent to my comment, but her demeanor strayed in another direction.

"You think he didn't fall?" Alana asked.

Tesa shrugged, and Aggie stared at her.

"I don't know. That's what the *polizia* are saying," Tesa responded. "Inspector Indolfo was here yesterday."

"Is that Rafaela Indolfo?" Alana asked.

"Yes," Tesa said. "Do you know her?"

"I do," Alana replied. "I'm a member of the Austrian police, the *Bundespolizei*. Rafaela and I worked a money-laundering case last year, a gang that worked along our international borders. She's very good. Do you mind if I call her?"

"No," Tesa said, "of course not."

I nodded in Alana's direction but returned to a discussion of the accident.

"Where was the team that night?"

"We all board together at Albergo dei Fiori," Tesa continued, adding for correction, "not altogether in the same room, but altogether in the same hotel. I didn't hear Charlie come in later in the evening, and so I went to bed."

"Is the hotel so small that you would have heard him come in?" Alana asked.

"No, not that small, but that's not it," Tesa explained. "Charlie's room and mine are adjoining. As long as I was awake, I would have heard his door open and close. I didn't. After a while, when I was tired, I gave up and went to sleep."

"The next morning ..." Aggie began but was cut off by Tesa.

"The next morning, when I went to wake him, I found that Charlie was not in his room."

Tesa sighed heavily and looked down at her water bottle.

"We gathered the team and returned to the site, where we found him at the bottom of the excavated pit."

"His body was twisted," Aggie explained, "legs turning right and torso turning left. His head was cocked at an unnatural angle, and there were black and blue marks and swelling on his neck."

"We could see even from the lip of the dig that he did not survive the fall," Tesa said.

"But a fall doesn't seem right," Aggie added.

"Why do you think that?" I asked. "How deep is the dig?"

"Not that deep," Aggie explained, "about ten feet."

"We're studying the living quarters of the early settlement," Tesa offered. "Most of the burial mounds ..." she said, pointing to the west, "have yielded artifacts that relate to the death and afterlife of the person. But we're not working there. We are digging into the habitation area itself, near the burial mounds, to uncover tools and implements of daily life. In the middens."

"Mittens?" Alana asked.

"Middens," Tesa corrected. "It's something like disposal sites, for debris. The throw-off of the life cycle."

Tesa allowed a moment for this to sink in, then proceeded.

"Middens are small collections of debris that accumulate as a tribe or family occupies an area. Unlike the burial mounds, where certain items are placed purposely alongside the deceased, middens comprise the unused detritus of living. It is there that we can find evidence of how the people lived."

"Why does that relate to the depth of the dig?" Alana asked.

"The excavation that we're focused on—the one that Charlie fell into—is below several feet of deposits that grew over the centuries," Tesa explained. "We were working our way down into the oldest remains, uncovering firepits and living quarters as we went, digging up shards of clay, ornamental shells, and metal objects that were probably used as decorative accessories.

"To find the right places to explore, we use many technologies. Once disturbed, an archeological site must be precisely recorded, or else everything found and removed reduces the chances that future scientists can decipher the meaning of the layers."

"What kind of technologies?" I asked.

"Well, satellite imaging is helpful," said Tesa. "It can reveal irregularities on the surface of the ground which might suggest earlier habitation. Magnetometry allows us to see what might be below the surface, same as ground-penetrating radar. We also use something called electrical resistance survey."

"Sounds pretty high technology," Alana noted.

"Yeah," Tesa continued, "but in the end, we've got to dig. We use those techniques and others to find the best place to concentrate our efforts, and then we line out the site."

"Literally?" I asked.

"Yeah, literally," Tesa said. "We use survey and construction techniques to line out the contours of the site we want to investigate, probe certain areas based on achieved data, and begin digging."

"With a shovel?" Alana asked.

"Sorta," Tesa replied. "There's a balance between 'getting into it,' as we say, and not disturbing the site. We want to dig to find the layers and time boundaries that will yield the most interesting material, but we also don't want our pick and shovel to fuck up the artifacts below."

"How do you control for that?" I asked.

"There are both vertical digs and horizontal digs ..."

I raised my hand to slow her down.

"What's the difference?" I asked.

"Vertical digs are used to probe the area to be studied,"

Tesa replied. "*Sondage* are like test pits ..." but again, I had to stop her. Tesa saw my confusion and explained.

"*Sondage* is the French term for test pit. We dig them to see if we're in the right area to begin with. Once we're comfortable that we have found a site worth excavating, we employ horizontal digs—they're also called area digs—to create a layered, or stratigraphic, profile of the periods of habitation on that site. In that way, we can dig down slowly, horizontally, and unearth each modern layer before disturbing an older layer, and so on down to the last evidentiary layer in the mound."

"Let's go back to what happened to Charlie," I suggested, waving my hand as if back in time. I accented the remark by taking another mouthful of chicken.

"He was fascinated by the 'reveals' in the test pit," Tesa said.

"Really fascinated, I would say," offered Aggie, which drew a condescending smile from Tesa.

"The test dig often tells us only that we're in the right field," Tesa added, "right acre. It is not intended to reveal a long history. But sometimes it does."

Then she paused and sipped from her water bottle.

"Think of digging in the sand at the beach, randomly ... well, not completely randomly," she continued. "After about two feet, you find a lost watch. After four feet, you find a wooden timepiece that is a bit rotten, but there is still enough that you can see how the machine kept time. And then, after six feet, you find a thin column of glass with sand in it. It's not quite an hourglass—it lacks the shape—but you can't shake the thought that this thing was a progenitor of the timepieces that were buried above it in the sand."

We sat in silence, glued to Tesa's explanation. Alana paused with her water bottle midway to her mouth. I put down my fork, eyes focused on Tesa. Aggie grinned, accustomed as he was to this woman's way of bringing ancient stories to life.

"The thin tube, that column of glass, is a master invention. The material that made up the tube itself is so thin and so fragile that you're afraid it will dissolve in your hand."

Another pause.

"Which," Tesa added with finality, "it does." Sitting back in her folding wooden chair, she smiled.

"The tube of glass just breaks apart and falls through your fingers," she says. "It is a find that only you have seen and which appeared and disappeared too quickly for you to capture on film. For the remainder of your life, you will have that visual memory but no object to prove what you saw."

"Okay," Alana says, putting her coffee cup down. "You've cast the spell. What does this have to do with Charlie?"

"Nothing, and everything," explains Tesa. "Sometimes archeological finds are fleeting. In a broader sense, we have to accept that digging through the past is a destructive activity."

"Meaning...?" I asked.

"Meaning that as we scrape, brush, and shovel our way through the layers, we are destroying the setting forever. If we're careful, we preserve what we see and what we find so that future scientists can relive our experience vicariously. Careless diggers destroy what's beneath their feet without recording it, and the past is lost for all time.

"We made a test dig, a vertical dig," Tesa continued, "here, which found more in a one-meter-wide hole than we expected, and Charlie couldn't let it go. We were weeks, maybe months away from getting a horizontal dig down to the layers that he saw in that hole, and he couldn't wait to find out more."

"About what?" I asked. I felt like I was jumping ahead to the last chapter of a mystery novel, but I had to know more.

Tesa paused, sighed lightly, and looked directly at me.

"Oh, sure, there were Etruscan finds there," she began, "but we also found that gold nugget."

"Gold," Tesa repeated. "Well, not just gold. Something more than gold."

That was hard to believe, and my expression probably conveyed my doubt.

"Electrum," was all Tesa said. "That's what Charlie said at the time."

After the silence that followed, Aggie jumped in.

"Electrum is an alloy of gold and silver."

He sounded like an expert, but knowing Aggie, I could tell that he was just sporting some recently acquired knowledge.

"Electrum was the metal used to strike the first coins," he said, but Tesa took the conversation back from him.

"The first coins in the world," she explained.

Her announcement left me speechless. So, I waited for more.

"There are debates about whether coins in human history were struck in the East earlier, but most scientists—Western and Eastern—agree that the electrum coins," Tesa continued, "called *staters* from Lydia, were the first-ever coins struck in the world."

"So, you—Charlie, that is—found these *staters* in the hole?" I asked.

"No, not *staters*. At least, I don't think so, considering how rare they are. Possibly variations on that coinage, smaller bits of the coin called *trites*," was all Tesa would offer. It sounded a bit like a dodge but was probably the usual scientific reluctance to jump to early conclusions.

"The gold nugget appeared to be electrum. That's what Charlie was so excited about," she added.

"Help me," Alana asked. "Explain electrum."

"Electrum is a naturally occurring alloy," she began, "of gold and silver."

"Alloy?" I asked. I thought I knew the answer but wanted to be clear since this might be an essential point.

"Alloys can be made of any combination," Tesa explained but then paused. "Well, not any. But most metals. In this case, electrum is one of the few naturally occurring alloys."

"Gold and silver," Alana said for emphasis. "Naturally occurring? That sounds pretty amazing."

"It's not common," Aggie offered, "but it does occur."

"Particularly in the ancient area known as Anatolia, or more anciently, Lydia," Tesa added. "There was a river there, the Pactolus, from which the people could mine electrum."

"Gold and silver," I said.

"Well, yes, but really electrum," Tesa explained. "Gold and silver weren't really available individually, but electrum was. An alloy of the two."

"Alright," I said, "I need to take a step back. Why do we care about this?"

"Electrum coins were used by the people from Lydia ..." she began.

"Lydia is Anatolia," Alana said, "old Turkey."

"Yes, quite," Tesa nodded.

"Why would they be here, in Tuscany?" I asked.

"And that, my friend, is precisely what got Charlie so excited," Aggie said with a flourish.

"He couldn't let it go," Tesa added. "He thought we were really onto something and told me he couldn't just quit," Tesa explained. "I told him we could return in the morning. He just smiled and patted me on the back. 'Time for you to put the shovel down for the day,' he said. That was his term for quitting after a long day. I smiled at him, told him not to stay very long, and to join us at the bar for drinks when he got back. He said he would. And we left."

After a painful pause, Tesa asked if we would like to see the dig. She sounded like she needed to get back to the business of work and quit talking about Charlie Dielman.

"Sure," Alana said, more quickly and more compassionately than I would have been able to do.

# THE DIG

As we exited the tented enclosure, we walked side-by-side toward the dig where the team had already resumed work. In our quiet passage, I wanted to ask more questions.

"Okay," I said, "you found a gold nugget with some scratches on it."

"Yes," Tesa replied.

Aggie turned to face her and get her reaction. His face registered that he already had his own opinion, perhaps he already knew the answer to my question.

"And," Alana jumped in, "if he found a Lydian coin ..."

"We can't actually say that he did," Aggie interjected as Tesa looked at him.

"If it was a Lydian coin, how much more important is that than just finding gold?" Alana asked, but Tesa avoided the question.

"He came to the tent," Tesa said, "that tent," indicating the place we had just come from, "very excited. He said he thought he had a *trite*, a coin that is a third-*stater*, but that it was very worn, and the image might be mistaken for a ripple in the metal. Everyone looked up from their meal ..."

"Who's everyone?" asked Alana, always the cop.

"Everyone. Diggers, helpers, everyone at the dig was still there. It was late afternoon, but we had just finished the day's activities, and no one had left yet," Tesa replied.

"Was there anyone missing?" Alana asked in a follow-up.

"No." This time it was Aggie, but when Tesa failed to chime in, I accepted Aggie's answer as solid.

"But he was very excited," she continued. "He spun around and ran right back to the pit. I went after him because, as his understudy, I wanted to know what he found. But by the time I caught up to him, he was at the pit—actually in the pit—scraping away at the sidewall of the dig. 'Can you tell me more?' I asked him. He nodded and waved his hand in a distracted way. He didn't verbalize an answer to my question, but he had this childlike smile on his face. Then he went back to scraping."

"How important is this *stater* thing?" I asked, repeating Alana's question.

"Huge!" Aggie said, but I could tell that his impression was based only on a superficial knowledge of the archeology that Tesa was studying.

"Well," she said with a smile, "I would have to agree. Huge! You see, *staters* were struck by the Lydians, from Anatolia, on the eastern edge of the Mediterranean. Around 700 BCE"

"And if they're found here, in Tuscany," Aggie chimed in, "it means that the Lydians were here."

"Well," Tesa intervened, patting Aggie on his arm. "We know the Lydians were here. Whether they brought their monetary system with them is another matter."

"And why is that distinction so important?" I asked.

"The Lydians settled in this area but might have done so as

migrants or seafarers. Maybe even refugees. But if they brought their coinage, we might conclude that they planned to set up a remote Lydian civilization here."

"Here," Alana interjected, "where the Etruscans were?"

"Yes," Tesa said, but then corrected, "but the Etruscan lineage was only beginning at that time."

My quizzical look drew Tesa's attention.

"Who came first?" she asked rhetorically. "The Etruscans or the Lydians? And ..." she paused for effect, "were the Lydians, in fact, the real Etruscans?"

I was getting a bit lost and wasn't sure how the findings at a dig would explain the cause of Charlie's death. I wanted a pause and planned to get deeper into the details, but I wanted to see more of what was around us first.

"Can we see the dig itself?" I asked.

Tesa nodded and invited us to follow her to the area under study.

I saw several deep holes, the so-called vertical digs that Tesa had described, but otherwise, the area was peeled open like a construction site. Horizontal layers were laid upon lower horizontal layers in a step-like fashion, each layer revealing a more ancient past. Workers were carefully stepping across and upon the layers, down and around each plateau. Other workers were already crouched in the lower levels with scrapers, brushes, and hand-held air puffers, all used to gently uncover material and artifacts from the dirt.

The entire area was a hive of activity that didn't pause with our approach. The team members who swarmed around the site were all dressed in khaki shorts, short-sleeve shirts, and floppy hats—men and women—and most had sweat-stained handkerchiefs tied around their necks. Rugged, ankle-high work boots completed the ensemble.

"This is the primary excavation," Tesa said, sweeping her

hand across the broad stretches of the horizontal dig before us. "But these," she added, pointing to deeper pits at several places, "are the vertical pits that we use to assess the area before laying out the site."

I walked over to one of the pits and peered below. It was wide enough to admit light and not as deep as I expected. Maybe six to eight feet. Seeing nothing of note—at least to my eyes—I moved on, followed closely by Alana. Another vertical pit yielded little more than I saw the last time, so I moved on again. Upon departing each hole, I noticed that Tesa peered below and, at times, called a worker over to point out something that she spied in the depths.

I realized that, with my untrained eye, I wouldn't see things that would otherwise be obvious to someone like Tesa.

"Where did you find Charlie's body?" I asked. Tesa led us to another vertical pit and pointed down into it.

This one was a bit wider than the others, the sloping sides indicating that additional work had been done to it, perhaps in response to Charlie's added interest. There were a few boards at the upper lip held in place by a vertical support beam, a type of scaffold that would allow a person to lean in or lay on the platform at the top edge of the pit and still peer into the hole itself before descending into it.

"He was right there," Tesa said, her voice quavering for the first time. "Right there at the bottom."

The pit was about eight feet deep, not much of a drop, but I could see how someone falling into it would have enough momentum to break some bones, especially someone of Charlie's age.

"Was he climbing down into the pit?" Alana asked.

"Don't know," said Aggie. "We found him twisted oddly at the bottom."

"Any pictures?" Alana continued, always the investigative policewoman.

"Yes, we have some," offered Tesa. "I'll show them to you later. Inspector Indolfo will also have some."

"Did Charlie often work alone?" I asked.

"Yes, and no," Tesa replied. "He was in charge of the site. He worked with us, but he would often pursue his own leads when he wanted to."

"Was he here, at this pit, by himself?" I followed.

"On that day, yes," Tesa explained. "But Charlie has worked on the edge of digs for fifty years," Tesa explained, "and he's well familiar with the scaffolding that surrounds the lip of the hole. Falling doesn't seem possible, but ..." and then she paused.

"But what?" Alana asked.

Tesa had to consider this first, weighing how to respond. Then she seemed to retreat.

"There is no reason for foul play, so it must have been an accident," she said.

Now it was Aggie's turn to weigh his words.

"Accidents happen," he said, slipping his hand through the crook of Tesa's arm in a comforting squeeze. "But there's something not quite right about this."

"How do you mean?" I asked.

Aggie looked at Tesa as if he was soliciting her permission to continue. She nodded.

"The dig had just turned up some significant finds," he began, but Tesa's edginess made it apparent that she wanted to intervene.

"In addition to the coins?" Alana asked.

"Yes," Tesa replied. "Before we found. We are studying the earliest times of the Etruscan culture. We are finding things that we didn't expect to find."

"Like what?" Alana asked.

"The necropolis is near here," Tesa explained, pointing with a finger toward the burial mounds that made this area so rich for archeological research. "But we are focusing on the habitation areas, the home sites and fire pits of a village that would have existed long ago. Of course, they buried their dead in the mounds over there," again with a pointing finger, "the *tumuli*, but we are focused on what they did when still living."

"Including ...?" I postured.

"Implements of trade. What they were. Whether the specific items related to local commerce or distant commerce," she added.

"So," Alana jumped in, "were the finds consistent with local or distant?"

"Both. It seems that the early Etruscans made a living with tooled goods locally, but also shipped many overseas."

"Where?" I asked.

"As I noted earlier, the Lydians were here," she continued, "we know that. But when did they come here, why, and how?"

"And are they related to the Etruscans?" I asked.

"I'm an archeologist, a physical anthropologist," Tesa said, "and I'm concerned with what we find. We—I—leave conjecture and theories to the cultural anthropologists. But there's a lot at stake. A connection between the Lydians and the Etruscans would lend credence to some of the theories being expostulated by the Turkish government ..."

"Why them?" Alana chimed in.

"The Lydian Kingdom was in ancient Anatolia, which itself is the ancient name for the land mostly occupied by Turkey now."

"Why does that matter?" I asked.

"Lots and lots of cultural pride," Aggie added.

"But..." Alana began, "there must be more than pride."

"Recovery," was all Tesa said at first. "But for that, you should talk to someone like Yusuf Demir."

"Who's that?" I asked.

"A very smart, very connected, cultural anthropologist."

"By very 'connected,'" Alana said, "what do you mean?"

"He works for the Turkish government."

Alana was snapping pictures of the hole where Charlie was found, then rested her phone on her hip while she did a visual scan of the area below.

"Okay," I said, taking my partner's hint that we were done there. "We'd like to check into a hotel, hopefully, one where you're staying, and continue this later."

"It's the Albergo dei Fiori in Civitavecchia," Aggie said. "It's due south on route E80, about a half-hour. We'll meet you there."

# CIVITAVECCHIA

WE DROVE SOUTH AND REACHED CIVITAVECCHIA IN ABOUT thirty minutes, just as Aggie had indicated, and checked into the Albergo dei Fiori hotel. When we told the desk clerk that we would be staying only two nights, he looked surprised at the size of our vacation luggage. I decided that exchanging a smile would allay any questions rather than have the Italians' common curiosity kick in, then he gave us the key to our room on the second floor.

"It faces the front," he said in accented English. "Sorry, but we are mostly full now, and so I can't give you a room facing the garden in back of the hotel."

"*D'accordo*," I offered, "agreed."

"We're with Dr. Diel..., I mean Dr. Richietta's team," I added, "so I thought the hotel might be full."

"Ah," came the clerk's knowing reply, and his welcome turned suddenly warmer. "I'll send up some bottled water. Everyone on the team has that delivered each day."

I had already read a bit about this town, supplemented by the descriptions in guidebooks read aloud by Alana while we were in transit. "Ancient city" was the translation of its name, a label that adhered after the settlement was already several centuries old. Dating to the early 2nd century CE, the original town was built on even older Etruscan ruins, called *Centum Cellae,* for a thousand years while it passed onto and through various lords by papal decree.

Today, it served as a major shipping port as its coastline made clear to even the casual observer. The locals, *Civitavecchiese,* were a pleasant people but earnest about their business. We saw several open-air markets while driving toward the hotel and wondered whether this was a feature of Saturdays only. We also noticed several cruise ships docked in the harbor, white gleaming hulks of modernity that seemed out of place in the ancient city. From here, we were less than a two-hour drive from Rome and figured the cruise lines were using Civitavecchia as a staging place for road trips to the Eternal City.

I assumed that if there any Etruscan ruins of interest in the town, Tesa would tell us. The industrial feel of the city didn't lend itself to that sort of thing.

After dropping our bags, Alana headed straight for the shower. I managed to catch up to her before the water was turned off, so we stood there as hot water rained down on our heads and washed the dirt from traveling off our bodies. Toweling off, we got dressed just as a knock came at the door. It was the desk clerk bearing two bottles of water. I thanked him, looking forward to having the fresh water do for our insides what the shower did for our outsides.

Italian hotels don't have the little markets at the front desk like in America, a place to buy snacks, water, and wine. But they do have access to the restaurant kitchens at most hours of the day. I asked the clerk about this, and he nodded quickly and held up a single finger for me to *"aspetta, per favore,"* "please wait."

By the time Alana was out of the shower and toweled off, the clerk had returned with a bottle of red wine. Fortunately, she had already wrapped the only-barely modest bath towel around her, and the young man at the door smiled in undisguised admiration. I had not placed a request for the wine, but he correctly guessed that after the water, that was what we would most want. I smiled and thanked him.

"*Giorgio,*" he said, unsolicited, pointing to himself.

"*Si, Giorgio,*" I replied. "*Io sono Darren,*" and pointing the wine bottle at my fetching partner in the skimpy towel, I added "*lei è Alana.*"

"*Mi piacere,*" he replied, but with his gaze on Alana, the customary phrase "my pleasure" in Italian seemed to carry more meaning than just the simple greeting.

Turning to the corkscrew on the nightstand, I considered how this non-descript little hotel didn't match the Villa Poesia or the Amalfi Coast, but the bottle of wine in my right hand would make the transition easier for us.

My phone rang, and Aggie's voice came through the line. He suggested that we meet them at Bar Nettuno around the corner. It was just a few minutes past five o'clock, far too early for dinner, but it seemed like a good idea to get out and see more of Civitavecchia.

Alana was dressed, looking refreshed from the shower, satisfied smile and all. Her loose-fitting white linen shirt hung just past the waistline of her form-fitting jeans, with a rainbow-colored web belt looped around her hips, the end dangling just beyond the buckle. A string at the neckline of the shirt tried unsuccessfully to hide an expanse of her tanned skin; her damp hair cascaded down her back in a fittingly casual look that made me think of a vacation photo shoot. I knew she wore her long brown tresses tied up in a bun when in uniform, but my heart skipped a beat when I saw her in this relaxed way.

She accepted the glass of wine I offered and sipped it, still looking directly into my eyes. After a quick kiss on my lips, she turned toward the table, gulped down the rest of the wine in the glass, then poured another helping.

"Aggie suggested that we meet them at a bar around the corner," I said. "A place called Bar Nettuno."

"Oh," Alana said, "okay." Then she looked at the new pour of wine and, with a shrug of her shoulders, downed that too.

"Okay. I'm ready," she said and took my hand to head out the door.

We stepped across the threshold of the Albergo dei Fiori onto the Strada di Vulci, turned left as the clerk had instructed, and were soon at the bar Aggie had mentioned. Our friends were seated, and they already had drinks on the table when we sat down. I could tell from the aroma that Tesa was drinking a Negroni, a cocktail of gin, vermouth, and Campari. Garnished with a slender orange peel, the drink is sometimes cut with sparkling water, but from the scent and color of this one, I concluded that Bar Nettuno didn't subscribe to that watered-down recipe.

We were in the region of Lazio, which encompassed the land sandwiched between Orvieto in the north and Naples in the south—but the region was comprised specifically of Rome and its surrounding areas. More important to me at that moment were the wines of Lazio. Their ancestry went back to the Roman Empire, and I quickly recalled the prominent vinous gifts of the region, including the white Frascati and the red Montiano. Still, I knew I'd find something from the noble Cesanese grape here.

When the waiter came to the table bearing a plate of cheese, salami, and olives, I asked for a bottle of the local Cesanese and received a pleased look of approval from him.

"Thanks for the tour of your worksite," Alana said to Tesa after the waiter had departed the table.

"You're welcome. Thanks for coming at Aggie's request."

"Have you been long on this project?" I asked.

"Yes," she replied. "This is the only one I have worked on, temp-ing here during summers and then taking over for my mom a few years back."

I lowered my gaze, not wanting to seem too nosy. Alana was not so reticent.

"Your mom was an archeologist, too? Where is she now?"

Tesa paused before tackling an answer.

"She died a few years back. She became sick. We didn't recognize it at first, and she hid the symptoms from us the best she could. But over a two-week period, she became weaker, and her skin was turning pale, almost translucent, the doctors said."

Here, Tesa paused in her recollection.

"She died in bed, back at the hotel, the same Albergo dei Fiori. Her breathing was slow and pained, and she had a far-away look as if she had already left us. I tended to her for the last two days until she succumbed."

"Where was your father?" I asked.

"He was at home in New York," she responded. "He's a professor of literature at NYU. When my mother took sick, he offered to come right away, but I told him I'd take care of her. As her condition worsened, I called for him, but he didn't get here until it was too late."

Tesa went silent, and tears welled up in her eyes. Aggie turned toward her and put his hand on her arm.

"He got here the day after," Aggie explained, taking Tesa's place in the narrative. "He loved her very much. These times apart were hard on them, but Tesa's mother and father were also pursuing the inspiration that motivated them. He a teacher, she a researcher. They accepted the separations with some trouble, but this one was heartbreaking."

"That was four years ago," Tesa continued, picking up the story. I was just finishing college and had my Ph.D. studies to focus on. After making the arrangements to bury my mother ..."

"Where was that?" I asked.

"Mom loved the archeology here, especially the Etruscan people. Dad agreed, and we buried her in Italy. I returned to the States afterward to continue my education at the University of Maryland in their anthropology department."

The waiter returned with a bottle of the Cesanese red wine and brought a basket of bread to serve with the tray of nibbles that he delivered before. I poured some of the wine for Alana and then for me and raised my glass.

"To your mother," I said.

"Thank you," Tesa replied. "And here's to Charlie."

I wanted to shift the discussion away from Tesa's mother and her demise, so I volunteered for a short lecture on archeology and how it is done.

"Well, as you know," Tesa began, obviously relieved to move on to something else, "There are several types of sites that we would focus on."

"Well, no," I said with a light laugh, "I don't know, but please tell me."

"There are habitation sites, kill sites, ceremonial sites, burial sites, trading and quarry sites, art sites, sometimes defensive sites. Ceremonial sites and burial sites are often collocated, and the burial sites often incorporate some form of art, so these may be investigated as ceremonial sites too. Kill sites usually refer to areas where game is lured for the kill, such as when early man would cut or burn a clearing in a forest and then bait it with small prey. When the larger animals came to collect these smaller animals, the men would emerge from the trees and slaughter them."

"Weren't there people who herded large animals over cliffs?" Alana asked.

"Yes," Tesa replied. "These are kill sites too. The hunters would scare the herd into a stampede and then guide it toward a cliff. Once the momentum of the herd got going in that direction, the animals at the front couldn't escape and were rushed off the cliff, either dying in the fall or becoming disabled and ready for slaughter. The hunters would gut the animals and collect the meat and the offal. Boneyards like this are perfect kill sites for scientists to investigate.

"But sometimes ceremonial sites are kill sites too," she added.

It took only a moment to decipher her meaning. The "kill" would involve the animal—or human—sacrificed in the ceremony.

"Etruscan sites around this region are predominantly burial sites, like the Monterozzi Necropolis where we are, the Banditaccia Necropolis near Cerveteri, and other places like it. The burial mounds and *tumuli*..."

"Wait," I said. "I heard you say that before. What is a *tumuli*?"

"A *tumulus* is a burial mound; *tumuli* is the plural. They are often constructed of rows of stone arranged in a circle to form the perimeter of the mound. Row after row is added, angling slowly inward, then an earthen dome completes it. The burial room inside is often dug below ground so, to enter the *tumulus,* you descend a ramp or few steps into a simple, circular room with an earthen floor. The walls, sometimes, include some incredible artwork, paintings left by the survivors of the clan to honor their dead relatives. It is from these paintings and the personal goods buried in the *tumuli* with the deceased that we learn so much about ancient societies."

"The pits I saw you working at your site were wide open," Alana said. "It didn't seem to me that they had been burial mounds."

"No, exactly right," Tesa responded. "We have been focused on the habitation sites that sit on the periphery of the burial area. People lived there, Etruscans and—before them— the Villanovan people. We're interested in what artifacts a habitation site will yield, what it will tell us about the daily life of the people from that period."

"Exactly what period is that?" I asked.

Tesa raised her Negroni and drained it, waving to the waiter for another round. Aggie had finished his beer, a Peroni, and took advantage of the waiter's attention to order another one. Alana and I were still working on the bottle of Cesanese.

"You like the wine?" I asked Alana.

"Yes. It's soft, not aggressive," she responded. Considering that her favorite drink was a wet martini, I figured all wine would seem soft to her, but maybe her palate was more calibrated than I realized. Tesa smiled and returned to her lecture.

"The Villanovans already occupied the region, but we're pretty sure they arose as a consanguineous culture from the earliest part of the 1$^{st}$ millennium BCE, probably around 900 BCE. Our earliest records of the Etruscans in this area date from between 700 and 600 BCE."

"So, who are you studying?" Alana asked.

"Both of them," Tesa responded, "but mostly the Etruscans. The two tribes inter-married, and the Villanovans are mostly lost to the literature from that period. They didn't die off, and the Etruscans didn't wage a war of extinction against the Villanovans. We think they mingled and, in so doing, mingled their genetic makeup. Culturally, the Etruscans arose from the period as the dominant culture and the rest, as they say, is history."

"Yeah," Aggie offered, "Etruscan culture is much more revered and analyzed as the outgrowth of that merger. Any serious researcher of European history has to bow to the importance of the Etruscans from that earliest period."

"So, where are they now?" I asked. "The Etruscans, I mean."

"All around us," Tesa said with a note of mirth. "The Etruscans didn't go anywhere. They're still here. Most chronologies of the era indicate that the Etruscan League—the association of a dozen Etruscan cities in this region—ultimately succumbed to Roman rule. But they didn't disappear either; they just continued to exist in the folds of the Roman Kingdom, which became the Roman Republic, which then became the Roman Empire before it fell into decay."

"Okay, Tesa's the archeologist," Aggie broke in, "but I'm more into the history. And I can tell you that the Etruscans were more to Rome than just a bunch of subjugated villages."

"How so?" asked Alana.

"The theory is that, without Etruria, there would never have been a Rome," Aggie replied. "In fact, one way to put it is that Etruria evolved into Rome, and therefore seeded the era that has long been called the Roman realm. Did you know that two of the early Roman kings were Etruscan?"

"No, I didn't," I admitted, sipping from my wine but enjoying my friend's narrative immensely. Aggie was on a roll.

"Lucius Tarquinius Priscus—an Etruscan—was followed on the Roman throne by Lucius Tarquinius Superbus. Around 600 BCE"

"That's just at the beginning of the rise of Rome," noted Alana.

"Exactly," said Aggie, "right at the beginning of the Roman Kingdom."

"Tarquinius?" I invited. "Sounds like Tarquinia, where you're digging?"

Tesa nodded.

"Who is he," Alana asked, "or should I say who was he?"

"Here's what we know," Aggie began, but Tesa tapped him on the arm to slow him down. I knew Aggie was particularly energized by Old World history, and apparently, Tesa knew, too, that he must be corralled once in a while. But she let him continue.

"Lucius Tarquinius Priscus was the king of Rome from 616 to 579 BCE. He came from Etruria, and we have every reason to believe that he was Etruscan, but he went to Rome to find his fortune. Despite his origins, we doubt that he was that nice to the Etruscan tribes he left behind. He conquered several of the Etruscan city-states and then controlled them. He was murdered for his crown, and his grandson, Lucius Tarquinius Superbus, ascended to the throne in 535 BCE. He ruled until he was overthrown in 509 BCE."

Alana and I returned to our wine, me refilling the glasses during Aggie's narration.

"So," I said to Tesa, "bring us back to the dig."

"My mother's focus has been on Etruscan origins. She was a cultural anthropologist," she explained. "Actually, a philologist."

"Explain," I said simply.

"A philologist studies language. A cultural anthropologist with a concentration in philology, such as my mother was, would try to make connections between peoples and cultures using linguistic analysis."

"How does that relate to this incident?" I asked.

"My mother studied the connections between the

Etruscans and the Lydians from Anatolia. So did Charlie, who, as I said, was more of a physical anthropologist. My mother—her name was Olivia d'Alantonio—sorted through the linguistic traits of the two cultures and tried to find roots, morphemes, and other rudimentary artifacts of language that would match. She didn't."

"And ...?" Alana asked.

"So, she decided that the Etruscans had nothing, or at least little, to connect them to the Anatolians of modern-day Turkey."

"Why is that important?" I queried.

"Charlie was not so sure," Tesa continued. "As a physical anthropologist, he followed the artifacts as evidence and thought that the remains of the habitation sites here, in what was Etruria in ancient times, might reveal connections to the Lydians of Turkey."

"Did they have disagreements over this?" Alana asked.

"No," and then Tesa laughed. "They agreed on so much. They were very close."

"So," Alana chimed in. "Your mom tried to find the linguistic links ..."

"And Charlie worked on the physical artifacts and finds," concluded Tesa. She drained her second Negroni but didn't signal for another one. Aggie sipped at his beer, not quite finished yet, but eyeing Tesa's empty glass.

"And your mom, you said," continued Alana, "didn't find any clear links to the Lydians."

Tesa nodded.

"Right," she added. "But Charlie thinks he might have."

"How so?" I asked.

Tesa paused but then said, "I think that's why he wouldn't leave the dig that night. And their origins could mean a lot to the overall history of Europe, of the world. If the origins of the

Etruscans can be traced ... it's almost like the 'begats' in the Bible?"

"The what?" Alana asked.

"The 'begats,'" Tesa repeated. "You know, Abraham begat Isaac, Isaac begat Jacob, and Jacob begat Judas. It's the genealogy of the Christian Bible."

"I'm sorry," I begged with hands up. "I'm lost."

Aggie laughed and suggested that we pay the bill and move on to dinner at a place called di Rosa. Having finished the last of our wine, Alana and I were quick to agree.

# SARDIS, CAPITOL OF LYDIA

## 610 BCE

ARDYS SAT ON A GLEAMING THRONE, LEANING ON HIS RIGHT *fist and looking down sadly on the subjects gathered before him. He was a compassionate ruler, a thoughtful man, but he faced threats to his kingdom that his father, Gyges, had not had. These weren't threats from outside their realm; these threats were from inside.*

*Ardys had put down minor uprisings before, just as any ruler would. But now, as he contemplated the fate of his people, he had to wonder why the gods had thrown down the series of troubles that afflicted his kingdom. There had been droughts, followed naturally by failed harvests. Famine followed the failed harvests, as did the slowing flow of water in the Pactolus and other rivers that served his people. There had even been an earthquake, a punishment not frequently meted out by the powers in the heavens but massively destructive to his people.*

*It seemed like the gods had turned against his people, the Lydians, leaving their farms fallow and their people starving. The yearly crops of barley, emmer wheat, and legumes had not appeared this summer, and the farms produced little ... too little* to feed even the farmers themselves, let alone the city dwellers who filled the neighborhoods and districts of his kingdom.

It was a sunny afternoon, one too bright for the dark news that he was considering. Ardys summoned his advisors and his sons, Lydus, Sadyattes, and Tyrrhenus, to decide on the best actions for his people. Famine had threatened before, but it had never lasted this long. The previous harvest was weak but sustained the people, the current harvest was completely unsatisfactory, and the omens as interpreted by his priests told him that the next year's harvest would be devastatingly poor.

Without some long-term answer, his people would starve—if they lived long enough to withstand the predators at their borders who could see the weakened state and who imagined Lydia to be an easy conquest.

No one spoke before the king, and the king's long silence struck fear into the hearts of the gathered court.

"Antonidas," Ardys said, turning to the short, gray-haired man to his left. "What do you say about the harvest this year."

Antonidas had long been one of Ardys' advisors since the king's earliest time on the throne. He stood up with a stiff backbone and an erect pose, a necessary posture when delivering news to the king, but his chin sagged, and he fell silent as he considered the news he would have to deliver. Good news was welcome; bad news was threatening. But lying to the king was worst of all.

"I see the crops come in, and they are strong," then he hesitated, "but they are also few."

Ardys swung his attention away from Antonidas and toward the right of his throne.

"And Xenus," he began, measuring his words and guarding them against exposing the disappointment and doubt that he felt. "What say you? You know the people. You know what they want."

*Xenus, another trusted advisor, was reluctant to follow the words of Antonidas, reluctant to add to the somber report.*

*"What they need," Xenus told his king. "What they need," he repeated, but he didn't finish the sentence immediately.*

*Xenus's failure to immediately address the subject or answer the king's question made everyone present look away. Xenus himself let his eyes cast downward before resuming.*

*"Some are dying," he added in a slow rendition that proved his sorrow at the report. "And more will die."*

*The Lydian kingdom was rich in natural resources and had enjoyed a bountiful harvest of crops for many generations. But now, although the precious metals and ores found in the ground were still plentiful, the food was not. The Pactolus River, which gave them the precious, yellow metal used as their source of trade would not feed the people. The imbalance between the river's deposits of electrum and their crop of edible foods troubled Ardys. "You can't eat gold," he mumbled quietly to himself.*

*He stood from his throne and took the two steps down onto the stone floor where his advisors waited in silence. Looking each of them in the eye and then passing on to the next, Ardys worked his way around the circle until he stood once more in front of his throne.*

*"The great King Midas dipped his staff in the Pactolus River and gave us the gleaming golden metal that we have used for many years. It is part of our trade; part of our heritage."*

*Then he paused for a long moment, an extended pause that left the court in an eerie silence. Tears seemed to come to his eyes.*

*"Would that I had a staff that I could dip into the earth and make the food grow the way that Midas made the gold come to our river."*

*Ardys looked down and considered his next action. Pulling on the shoulder of his* chlamys, *the knee-length covering draped like a tunic about his body, he returned to the throne. No one moved, not his advisors, his sons, nor the two women on the edge of the gathering. Ardys leaned back and sat down on the throne with a tired expression on his face. He rubbed his chin with his right hand while he stroked the cool granite arm of the throne with his left. He seemed to be looking for inspiration in the mindless movement but remained stone-faced and contemplative for several minutes.*

*"What of the terror in the earth?" he asked suddenly, referring to the recent rumblings that ripped jagged cracks in the surrounding countryside and toppled buildings. No one replied until Xenus stepped forward.*

*"It has ended, sire," he reported.*

*"For how long?" asked Ardys.*

*Xenus didn't want to hazard a guess, so he bowed and held his tongue. The king was a fair man who looked out for his people, but he would punish any advisor who misread the signals from the gods.*

*"For how long?" Ardys repeated in a low whisper. It was more of a self-reflective mumble this time, not directed at anyone in particular.*

*"Our river runs with gold, but our farms run dry," he continued. "The gods are tormenting us, turning against us."*

*The king was not blind to certain facts of society in those times. When the gods turned against a people, the people often had no choice but to turn against their ruler. He knew that this might be in the offing.*

*Pointing his finger at his three sons, he crooked it and signaled for them to approach the throne.*

*"I will have you in private," he said. "We must set a plan."*

———

*Ardys reigned from his throne in a palatial building in the center of Sardis, the capital of his kingdom. Inland on the Pactolus, the river that flowed through Manisa, emptied into the Gediz River and, from there, into the Aegean Sea at Phocaea. The region had enjoyed agricultural bounty and limitless natural resources for time unknown, and the electrum that the Lydians took from the Pactolus not only financed their economy but formed the source of their monetary exchange.*

*Stamped into* staters *and carrying the image of a lion on one side, many of these coins were divided in size into fragments of thirds—called* trites—*and quarters. These roughly rounded electrum disks became the first coin known in the world. Ardys was fond of reminding his people that King Midas had given the electrum to them. It was an ancient story of the king to whom everything was given. Midas was granted special favor by the gods, a power that would turn everything he touched into gold. A blessing beyond imagination.*

*But Midas could not control this power. Everything he touched—even his food—turned to gold. And it was when he reached out to caress his daughter that he turned her into a cold gilt statue that Midas knew he would have to find a way to rid himself of the power and the curse.*

*He went down to the River Pactolus and dipped his staff into the waters that flowed by. Under a bright blue sky and wispy white clouds, the power that had given Midas such immense riches flowed through his staff into the water of the river below his feet. Lifting his staff, he wondered if the act had worked. He prayed to the gods to take back the force, then turned and touched the staff to a little animal by his feet. The animal jerked at the point of the staff, then scurried away.*

*It had remained as it was, a furry little animal that had no meaning to Midas—except that his curse had been taken from him. He tried again, pointing the staff at a stand of flowers next* to the Pactolus, and they remained as nature had created them. A servant who stood by the king shrunk in horror as Midas pointed his staff at the man, but the touch rendered nothing. The servant was preserved in all his nervous state, though he smiled and then laughed, that he had been saved.

King Midas smiled at himself and at his staff. When he looked back at the river that had received the blessing of gold, he could see many mounds of gleaming particles under the undulating waves of water as it rushed by.

Ardys told this story often when times were good and when his full-bellied people could enjoy the bounty that the folklore promised them. He remarked on the same to his sons, now gathered before him, but with a more immediate problem to solve.

"My father, Gyges, ruled our people during times of great bounty and security," he began, bowing his head in a deferential way to the man who preceded him on the throne.

"When he ruled, our people had food and peace, and they were happy."

His sons couldn't miss the disappointment in his voice.

"With my father's leadership, the people of the Lydian kingdom did not know war, famine, or hunger."

At that, he turned around, facing his sons and lifting his chin to stare directly into their eyes.

"But, under my reign, we are losing everything."

His sons wanted to disagree, to give hopeful predictions, but they knew that these words would matter little to their father.

"It is the gods," Tyrrhenus offered but was silenced by his father's raised hand.

"The same gods who granted Gyges such benevolent times?" he asked rhetorically.

Tyrrhenus dropped his chin and returned to silence.

Ardys wandered back and forth in front of the large stone portal that looked down upon the city of Sardis. Once a thriving capitol, its gleaming buildings and lively marketplace belied the slowly creeping destitution of the society that inhabited it.

The king circled back to his sons and confronted them.

"So, I have decided that you will go far away and bring our people with you to discover new lands, new farms, and new hope."

It was such a grand plan that it took the three men by surprise. What could their father intend—shipping the entire Lydian population away from their homeland?

"Father, sire, what is it that you mean?" asked Sadyattes. "Do you wish to leave our place, to leave Lydia?"

"Yes, and no," said Ardys. He began pacing again as if this action helped him see the scope of his plan.

"I want Tyrrhenus to plan a journey. You," he said, pointing to Sadyattes, "will remain here to lead the people of Lydia."

"And you, father?" asked Sadyattes.

"I will continue as the ruler of our land; you will assume the power of leadership."

"What of me, sire?" asked a suddenly concerned Lydus. His place in the birth order—and his name—indicated his stature, but he also knew that Ardys had groomed his two brothers for prominence.

"You, Lydus, will also remain here," Ardys replied. "You will be responsible for remaking our farming communities."

It seemed like a small assignment after hearing that his brother Sadyattes would rule the kingdom. To allay that concern, Ardys spoke up.

"Ruling the people is impossible without feeding them. You, Lydus, are going to fill their bellies, and then, only then, will they be subject to rule."

Tyrrhenus stood patiently by while his father made arrangements for the resuscitation of his homeland, the kingdom of his birth. He didn't know what was in store for him yet and wondered when Ardys would return to explain his role. He didn't have to wait long.

Ardys turned to Tyrrhenus.

"You, my son Tyrrhenus, will lead half of our people to a better land."

"Half?" Tyrrhenus and Sadyattes blurted out simultaneously. It seemed to be an impossible task to split a kingdom in two and yet have both societies survive.

"Yes, half," Ardys confirmed.

The sons looked at each other in dismay and confusion. Lydus immediately began calculating his chances of having to feed only half as many people.

"Sire," began Tyrrhenus, "I don't understand what you are planning. Am I to go away from Lydia and bring half of our people with me?"

"Yes," was the reply. "But not at first," Ardys explained. "You will take one hundred men and women first, find the place to settle, and then come back to announce your plans. It is at that time that you will set ship to sea and bring the entire half of our population to your new land."

The plan seemed crazy and nearly impossible, but the sons knew not to question the king, even if he was their own father. Throughout the conversation, Sadyattes remained silent, thankful that he was asked to remain in Sardis and rule the people of his birth.

"Where will we go?" Tyrrhenus asked. "Should we go to Heracleion, the city at the mouth of the River Nile? We've been there and know the people."

"No," said Ardys with a dismissive wave of his hand. "Not Heracleion. Yes, we know the people, but they would not welcome so many of our people. It would be threatening."

"Would we go to Sikania, the vast island in the middle of the sea?" he asked about the ancient island of Sicily. "The island is sparsely populated. We could make a stand, farm the land, and maybe establish a new colony for you, sire."

Ardys thought for a moment and had to consider that, but he had already made up his mind on another place.

"Yes, Sikania would be fine, but you know that the island has now three tribes warring for control. The Elymi, the Sikani, and the Siculi all fight over the same space," Ardys explained. "If you were to land on the eastern part of the island, you would have to wrestle with the Siculi who have a firm grip there, not one they want to share with us. Neither would the Greeks who already have a claim to some of the island."

"Where, then?"

"We have been to the land farther north, on the great peninsula that cuts through the middle of the sea," he said with confident finality.

"Yes, we have," Tyrrhenus said. "Up along the western coast, north of the island of Sikania. There are many fine bays and ports to put our ships into. But there are people there too."

"Ah, yes, but those people—what do they call themselves?" Ardys asked, checking his fading memory.

"Villas, or Villanovans, to some people," said Sadyattes, eager to promote this plan yet stay out of it himself.

"Yes, the Villanovan people," responded Ardys. But they are few, and they are widely settled. There is plenty of land in the middle of that great peninsula that no one has taken yet."

Turning to Tyrrhenus, he added, "And you will take it. And you will take our people there."

So, the plan was settled.

# DI ROSA RISTORANTE

WE RECONVENED AT DI ROSA RISTORANTE AS THE SUN WAS setting over the rust-colored stone buildings surrounding this piazza. The dozen or so tables that crowded the intimate space in the interior were lit by the dim light of sconces on the walls, muted more by the faded colors of the sweeping murals on the walls that seemed to drink in and soften the bare light that suffused the space.

We chose the outdoor space, wanting to take advantage of the soft evening air, and we were quick about it since only one table for four remained to be had. The tiny party lights that snaked randomly among the tables of all the cafés surrounding the cobblestone piazza shown more brightly as the rays of the sun faded behind the buildings, casting a delightful glow on the crowded tables filling the open space. Faint sounds of violin and mandolin were barely perceptible from somewhere I couldn't place, and the musical presence created a backdrop to the evening air, almost like an audible fresco on a medieval painting.

*"Buona sera,"* said the waiter as he swept to our table

bearing a basket of bread, bowls of olives and rosemary-scented carrot sticks, and a bottle of Pellegrino water. Just as quickly, he turned and sped away, snatching an empty bowl or plate from each table that he passed on his way back to the kitchen door of the restaurant.

We considered the menu and prepared for the waiter's return. He came back bearing a tray of little offerings before we ordered. *Bigne,* a rose-shaped fist-sized bread unique to Lazio, was served in a bowl. This we tore into pieces by hand to be dipped into the herb-scented olive oil on the table. The waiter also brought a plate of *bruschetta,* thin toasts slathered with a mixture of chopped tomatoes, roasted red onions, and lightly crunchy sea salt. As the aromas of the dishes began to tease out the saliva in my cheeks, he added a plate of *provatura fritta,* a type of fried cheese that is rolled in egg and breadcrumbs, then deep-fried to golden perfection.

In Italy, restaurants don't fear that too much food at the outset will stunt your appetite, unlike in the U.S., where the waiters are discouraged from delivering too many morsels *a la table* until they got a food order driven by your hunger. In Italy, the tradition was to treat you like a member of the family and to put you at ease, assuming that you would still not give up the chance to order a proper meal of several courses.

I was hungry and needed something substantial, so I chose the *fettucine alla papalina,* the region's version of *spaghetti carbonara,* with tagliatelle tossed with beaten eggs, Parmigiano, peas, ham, and black pepper. Alana took the lighter approach to this first course, ordering *minestra alla viterbese,* a vegetarian version of soup thickened with semolina. Aggie went whole hog, literally, asking for sliced grilled *cinghiale,* a meat of wild boar more famous in Tuscany, but it was on the menu here at di Rosa. Tesa was content with sampling the platter of tidbits offered already, but she added *crostini di provatura e alici* to the order, small slices of bread brushed with oil and topped with chopped anchovies then baked.

This would be the first course, and we knew that we would have to refocus on the menu for a more substantial dinner when we were ready.

Once the order was placed, we resumed our conversation from the afternoon.

Take anyone who enjoyed solving mysteries and have them spend a few days or weeks in central Italy, and they were immediately drawn to the enigmatic Etruscans, a civilization said to have given rise to early Roman culture. That they appeared around 800 BCE in central Italy was accepted by most scientists, but how they arrived—and why and how their culture grew—was routinely debated.

I had no immediate reason to connect the elusive Etruscans with the death of Dr. Dielman. Their civilization faded over two thousand years ago, and although the romantic notions of Etruria and Etruscans still sparked interest, it didn't seem that it would also spark violence. But Dielman died—suspiciously or not—at an Etruscan dig. So, it seemed like a good place to start.

Of course, Tesa was well educated in Etruscan archeology, and Aggie—ya' gotta love him—continued to insert himself into the conversation. But when I began to ask more probing questions about the tribe's history, Tesa demurred, seeming to be more interested in the physical artifacts than the cultural history.

"You should talk to Yusuf Demir," she said, repeating her recommendation from earlier.

"You mentioned him this afternoon. Tell me more about him."

"Yusuf is generally regarded as a leading expert on the origins of the Etruscans," she replied.

"And you're not?" I had to ask. For someone like Tesa, who

spent her days—and her life—literally in the pits of the Etruscan heritage, it seemed as if she would care about the culture that gave rise to the things she dug up.

"I am somewhat of an expert," she said with a humble reticence that immediately drew a doubting look from Aggie. "I find things, and I know how to classify them. But interpreting the impact of these findings and, from that, extrapolating a cultural meaning … well, that's someone else's job."

"Like Olivia's," Aggie intervened, referring to Tesa's mother and drawing a quick, sharp look from her.

"My mother was a philologist," Tesa intervened. "but you know that. She studied culture through language." At that, Tesa cast her gaze downward.

"She was one of a kind. Someone who knew more about the evolution of language and culture than anyone in Europe."

"But," I interrupted, not ready to get into the story of Tesa's mother. I wanted to draw the conversation back to Demir. "But this Yusuf Demir knows about Etruscan history. The origins. Where would I find him?"

"He's Turkish," Aggie said but was interrupted again by Tesa.

"Yusuf works for the Turkish government. He has written extensively about the early Etruscans," she began. "That's where it gets interesting," Tesa said with a smile. You'll have to talk to him."

"Again, where can I find him?"

"It turns out that he's vacationing in Cerveteri just now," Tesa said.

I turned over her phrase "just now" in my head. She had a curious accent to it, a highlight in her voice, and I wondered whether Demir's presence at this moment in time in a nearby town– one with its own Etruscan origins—made her wonder too about his sudden presence in the vicinity of the dig.

We talked a bit longer about this guy, and I found out more that would be useful. Demir was a historian from Turkey whose specialty was the ancient civilizations of the northern and eastern Mediterranean basin. I was also warned that he was a very private man whose true intentions could be well disguised behind a veneer of certitude and graceful conversation. His "true intentions" often ran to support for the Turkish government's demand for more international recognition.

Demir had been used as a scholarly resource in the country's argument for an active role in various world organizations, including NATO, and he was cited in many accounts testifying that early Mediterranean civilizations owed their origins to the Turkish people. Rome, Egypt, and Greece were sometimes mentioned in his writings, proposing that their origins were tied to ancient Turkey, although that seemed too grand a claim.

"What's your impression of Demir," I said, my mind going back to the mention of his being nearby "just now."

"Tesa speaks highly of him," Aggie said, turning to look at Tesa for approval, "at least of his education and knowledge of ancient history."

"You're leaving something out," I said. "What do you mean 'at least?'"

"Well, she fears him." Again, Aggie looked at Tesa, but this time a dark cloud passed over the archeologist's face.

"I don't fear him," she explained, "but I don't trust him either."

I looked at Alana, who was atypically quiet, but I could tell she was processing all of this.

"Why?" Alana asked, getting to the question before I could.

I put down the *bigne* so I could pay closer attention to Tesa. She paused, chewing on a *bruschetta*. I knew Aggie well from our time at the Tall Cedars commune after the war but was still learning to read Tesa.

"Demir works for the Turkish government," she repeated, to which I nodded acknowledgment. "He works at the Ministry of Culture and Tourism. The Turkish government has a law called the Protection of Cultural and Natural Property which he has been instrumental in observing."

"It was passed in 1983," Aggie injected, "and Demir was one of the sponsors of the legislation."

"Why does that matter here?" Alana asked.

The appetizers had arrived, and we alternated conversation with morsels of food.

"That law speaks directly to Turkish cultural history," Tesa began, "and promotes the repatriation of culture—specifically, cultural artifacts—to the Turkish people."

"Does Demir want to repatriate artifacts from Tuscany?" I asked.

"More specifically," Aggie added, "does Demir and his government think that artifacts found in Tuscany—if they can be proven to be remnants of the Lydian culture—are actually Turkish cultural matter?"

"Etruscans," I said, "Does that mean the Turkish government thinks the Etruscans are Turkish or, let's say, Anatolian, and therefore their heritage is actually Turkey's?"

"It gets even more interesting than that," Tesa said, but then she shifted her attention back to her plate. Aggie was ready to jump in.

"Remember my story about the two of the early Roman kings?" he asked provocatively.

I nodded.

"If Turkey can show that the Etruscans were actually Turkish..." Aggie continued, but Alana cut him off.

"By way of Anatolia and Lydia," she clarified.

"Yeah," Aggie went on. "Precisely. If Turkey can show that the Etruscans were actually Turkish, then under the 1983 law, the Turkish government would call for the repatriation of Etruscan cultural artifacts ... even claim the heritage of the great Roman kings!"

"Well, claiming the rights to artifacts is one thing," I said, "getting the artifacts repatriated is a heavy lift."

"Not under NATO," offered Tesa. "Turkey's membership in NATO gives them greater influence and power to carry out their aim."

"If they can prove that the Lydians seeded the Etruscan civilization," Aggie suggested.

"It can't be that easy," Alana said, "or that complete. Archeological finds are made all over the world, and their movement from place to place usually suggests migration patterns and mingling of cultures and regions."

This drew an approving smile and a nod from Tesa.

The waiter returned and stood patiently waiting for our dinner order. I ordered *abbachio alla cacciatora,* lamb prepared with garlic, rosemary, white wine, and anchovies. Alana went for *baccalà,* floured salt cod that is fried and topped with tomato sauce, pine nuts, and raisins. Aggie ordered *garofolato,* pot roast stewed with onions, tomatoes, and white wine, while Tesa followed Alana's light lead and ordered *mazzancolle fritti,* fried shrimp topped with crushed garlic, parsley, white wine, and lemon.

Tesa shifted the conversation a bit while we waited for the food to arrive.

"My mother spent most of her professional life applying linguistic tools to try to identify the origins of ancient people, particularly the Etruscans."

"And what did she find?" I asked.

"She had masses of data," and with this, Tesa laughed at the image. "My mother papered the wall of her study with traces of linguistic roots and branches, all stemming from

Etruria, but all ending with question marks at the far ends of the branches."

"So," Alana persisted, "your mother didn't find a root for the Etruscan people, their language?"

"Yes, and no," Tesa said. "She didn't find where the language and, therefore, the people came from, but she found certain areas, areas of the world thought to be the origin of the Etruscan people, where they could not have come from."

"Could not have?" I asked for clarification.

"Yes," Tesa continued. "That's what she said."

"Could not have ... where? Come from where?" I pressed.

"They could not have come from Turkey or that part of the Mediterranean."

My mind wandered back to my military service and work in intelligence, where we sought not just truth from the people we interrogated but the presence of untruths in their narratives. It seemed to be not unlike the approach used by Tesa's mother.

"How sure was she?" Alana asked.

"Are you asking how good was she?" Tesa asked.

"Yes," Alana asked, but smiled. "I'm sure she was excellent. But..."

"She was excellent," Tesa added. "One of a kind. But I'm not just trying to take my mother's side. Yes, she found much to consider and analyze. No, she didn't find strong linguistic roots to the Turkish language, ancient or modern. So, no, she didn't conclude that the Etruscans hailed from there."

"Alright, let's see now," I said as our food was being delivered. "Your mother, Olivia, didn't find language connections between the Etruscans and the Turkish people."

"She didn't find any," Tesa interjected, "but that doesn't mean there aren't any."

"That's exactly what Charlie used to say," Aggie offered.

I looked at him for clarification.

"Charlie would laugh and say that Olivia's findings were Olivia's findings, but that he still believed in the connection," Aggie said.

"They would disagree on some things," Tesa said with a smile, "but they got along so well. Charlie and my mom would have long debates, usually carried out under the lantern-light of the mess tent, and they would go on for so long that the team would give up and leave the camp for the night."

"So, Charlie thought there was a tie between the cultures," Alana said as a question.

"Yes, he did," Tesa responded. "But he loved ... excuse me, respected my mom so much that he couldn't just dismiss her conclusions. After she died, he continued his research, not to win the debate but almost to prove her research."

"How do you mean?" Alana asked.

"Charlie felt that my mom's findings were valid, but he also believed that once they were added to his on the physical anthropology side, they would be more concrete."

"What if he found evidence to prove that the Lydians were connected to the Etruscans?" I asked. "Would that disprove your mother's work?"

"Not according to Charlie," Tesa said. "He said it would prove the depth and excellence of her study by combining the results to strengthen the case."

"That's why he was so excited about the dig the other day," added Aggie.

"Because if he thought he was on the brink of finding something ..." I began, "something that he, Charlie, thought might be a remnant of Lydian culture would be important."

"Yes, and no," added Tesa. "That the Lydians were here is settled science, even in my mom's own research. It's deeper than that."

I paused to process that.

"Why?"

"The Lydians were here," Tesa repeated. "Let's start with that. But did they only migrate here, mingle with the population, and produce generations of half-Lydian, half-Villanovan people?"

I shrugged.

"Or did they rule this land?" Tesa asked poignantly.

"Explain," Alana asked.

"Are you familiar with the numismatic terms 'face value' and 'metal value' for coins and the difference between the two?" Tesa asked.

I shook my head no, as did Alana.

"We have found physical traces of Etruscan culture, things like pottery, remnants of textiles, some personal ornaments. These were most likely made here. Charlie had done a lot of research into coinage, though, including the world's earliest coins ..."

"The Lydian coins," Alana said with conviction.

"Right," replied Tesa. "With coins, face value refers to the value of something determined by a controlling power, a government, or whatever. Such coins usually have a stamp on the surface. It's what they say something is worth, and it implies that there is some stamp of proof. A royal seal, or what have you," Tesa explained. "Metal value is the worth of the hunk of metal itself, be it gold, silver, or electrum."

"Electrum," Alana said. "You said that was the compound used to make *staters*."

"Yes, and all the lesser coins," Tesa replied. "Metal value is controlled by market forces. If gold or silver—or electrum—trades at a certain rate, that is its value, and metal value may change across regions depending on its availability and desirability."

"And why does face value matter?" I asked.

"If a government or some other controlling entity establishes a face value to a coin, that's what it's worth," Tesa explained. "Period."

"You mean across regions?" Alana asked.

"Yes, in a way. But face value can only survive across regions, for example, if Region A, who establishes the value, is respected in Region B, where the coin then shows up."

"By 'respected,'" Aggie chimed in, "she means by government edict or control. A coin can only hold its currency, so to speak, within the realm of the government that declares its 'face' value."

We paused to consider this, and I tried to formulate a question.

"If electrum *staters* left Lydia and ended up in Tarquinia, they would only be worth what the hunk of metal is worth here. Their metal value," I stated, although it came out more like a question.

"Exactly," confirmed Tesa. "The *staters* could be traded as is or melted down and would be worth the same. Unless ..."

"Unless," Alana jumped in, "the controlling power of Tarquinia at the time—the government—said a *stater* was worth 'this much,' don't tamper with it."

"Who would do that?" I asked.

"Only Lydians," Tesa said, "and only if they were the government of Tarquinia at the time."

"But you said they only mingled with the local people," I protested.

"I said 'if' they only mingled. Maybe finding *staters*, and not just hunks of melted-down electrum, means that the Lydians were the government in power then."

"This is getting interesting," Alana added.

"I think we need to talk about this more," I said, stabbing a forkful of Aggie's *cinghiale*.

"For that," Tesa said, "I think you need to talk to Corwin."

"Who's that?

"Daniel Thomas Corwin," she replied. "He's an Australian coin collector, a numismatist, who specializes in ancient European coins. He has a shop in Rome called Croesus Gold."

"Crosses?" Alana repeated.

"No. Croesus. He was a king of Lydia. Very rich, or so the story goes. There's a common expression 'as rich as Croesus,' meaning ... well, what it sounds like."

"And so, this Corwin guy," I said, "he named his shop after Croesus."

Tesa nodded.

"And he knows about coins?" Alana asked.

"More than anyone, probably. I suggest you talk to him," Aggie offered.

"So, I have Demir to talk to about the Etruscans. He's in Cerveteri," I summarized. "And Corwin. He's in Rome."

"It would be good," Tesa said.

I nodded before turning back to my food, but I was beginning to wonder how all this tied together.

Alana's phone rang, and she lifted it from the table.

"*Guten abend,*" she answered automatically in German.

"Alana, my dear, *buona sera!*" came the voice on the other end.

"Ah, yes, Rafaela!" she responded with a laugh then, covering the phone, told us that it was Rafaela Indolfo, the Roman police investigator whom she knew.

"You know I'm in Civitavecchia, no?" she said into the phone.

"Of course, I do," came the reply, still plainly audible from the phone even though Alana didn't have the speaker on. "Of course. I know what goes on in my country."

"Well, it's so nice to hear from you! Can we get together? Maybe tomorrow?"

"At the Monterozzi Necropolis, no?"

Alana laughed again.

"Okay, my friend. Yes, at Monterozzi. Someday I'll ask you how you keep track of everything that happens in Italy."

"Secrets, my friend," came the reply. "Secrets."

"We'll be there at seven," Alana said.

"I'll be there at ten," teased Rafaela, not wishing to agree to such an early appointment.

———

By the time Alana and I made it back to the hotel, we were worn out. A long day that began in the indescribable beauty of the Amalfi Coast, from our palatial digs at the Villa Poesia, by train to Rome and by rental car to the dig site, and then to a long, belly-filling dinner at di Rosa Ristorante amplified by several bottles of wine.

We were both ready to dive into bed and get a good night's sleep—until an unexpected call came on my phone.

"Darren, sorry to bother you, ol' buddy," Aggie began. "But I have something we need to talk about."

I wearily agreed, telling him to meet me in the lobby and asking if Alana should be present.

"No," he replied. "Let her sleep. But I think you want to hear this."

I pulled my pants back on, buttoned a shirt loosely around my chest, and trudged the two flights of stone steps down to the hotel lobby. Aggie was there, pacing back and forth.

"What have you got?" I asked quickly, my thoughts drifting back to Alana curled up between the sheets of the bed I wished I was in.

"Well, it's not what I've got, specifically," he replied. "But what I know."

I looked at him for a moment, waiting for the suspense to break.

"There's a guy who works at the dig named Hamza Yavuz."

"And?" I asked.

"He hasn't been seen since the night that Charlie was pushed into the pit."

"Or fell," I added for clarity.

"Yeah, well, this Yavuz guy disappeared."

"I hadn't heard this. Sounds like something you or Tesa might have raised before."

"He goes back and forth from the dig to Rome," Aggie said, "and it's only been a couple days. We figured he was on an errand and would return."

"Did he?"

"He's back, but he didn't return," Aggie added, "at least not of his own accord."

Again, I waited for Aggie to break the silence.

"And..." I prodded.

"Yavuz was found at the ferry station in Pescara this afternoon. He was acting strange, kinda nervous I heard, so the *polizia del porto* questioned him. He tried to talk his way out of it and kept eyeing the ferry that was preparing to launch to Croatia. When he realized that he wouldn't make it aboard in time, he changed his tactic."

"How do you mean?"

"The *polizia* said he fell silent for a moment as if he was considering his options. Then he spoke up with a seemingly well-planned narrative. Said he was an archeologist, working on an Etruscan dig in Tarquinia. He showed them papers to prove that he had been paid for that work and a pay stub with Charlie's signature on it."

"Then what?" I asked.

"The *polizia* seemed to lose interest and accepted his story. But before letting him go, they searched him. And they found a *trite* in his pocket."

"A what?"

"A *trite*. The coin. A third of a *stater*."

"The Lydian coin."

"Yeah," Aggie continued.

"So, a *stater* ... you said a *trite*. And he worked here at Tarquinia."

Aggie nodded his head.

"Do you think that's what Charlie found and was so excited about?"

"Probably."

"And you think this Yavuz guy took it and ran. Made it across Italy to Pescara and was bound for Croatia."

"Croatia at first, since that's where the ferry goes. But who knows where after that," Aggie speculated.

"The cops bought his first story about working at the dig, but they didn't like finding something like a gold coin in his pocket. Figured it was fishy."

"Then?" I asked.

"They returned him to Civitavecchia in search of Charlie Dielman to confirm Yavuz's story. Of course, they didn't find Charlie but could deduce that Tesa was the new boss. We were upstairs in our room when the *polizia* called her and explained everything."

"Where is he now? And the *trite*?"

"They've got him locked up in the city jail till we sort this out in the morning. The cops are also holding the *trite*."

"How can you tell it's a *trite* if you haven't seen it?"

"They described it to Tesa over the phone. It's smooth gold, with a lion's head and some lettering next to the impression, then two punch marks on the back. I could hear the conversation from the speaker on her phone, so I could follow along. Tesa's face went white when she heard it."

"Sounds like we might have a clue," I said.

"Sounds like we might have a suspect," Aggie responded.

# MONTEROZZI NECROPOLIS

DAWN CAME EARLIER THAN I HAD WANTED IT TO, considering the long day before. The sun shone through the gossamer curtains covering the window facing east, a soft tone at first but one that brightened by the minute. I kept my eyelids shut, but the light continued to illuminate the room and forced my eyes awake.

Alana was still asleep, a soft murmur escaping her, lips curled slightly at the corners of her mouth. I wondered what made her so happy in slumber but preferred to think that her dreams were of me or us.

I had a habit of planning my day as I woke, and this was no exception. Eyes open, I considered what lay ahead and how best to plan it.

It was now Sunday—one day left before Alana would have to train back to Vienna and leave me to fend for myself here in Tarquinia. First, we would go to the dig, meet Tesa and Aggie, then be joined by Rafaela Indolfo as we tried to untangle the events surrounding Charlie Dielman's untimely death. That would take up most of the morning, but I hoped to spend some time later looking for Yusuf Demir, whom everyone credited with being an expert in Etruscan history and culture, not to mention the long-lost stories of the Lydian people from Anatolia.

I wasn't sure how or when I would find him but remembered being told that he was "just now" in Cerveteri, not a very long ride from our present position in Tarquinia. I would ask Alana if she wanted to join me but didn't know whether that would be of interest. If she declined, I decided that I would schedule the search for Demir in the afternoon, leaving the evening for the two of us to spend together before she returned to work in the morning.

After that, I could plan to visit this Daniel Thomas Corwin in Rome. His reputation as a coin expert, not to mention his affinity for Lydian treasure, would be a treat of unexpected pleasure.

I lay still in the bed, covered only by the light cotton sheet to ward against the morning breeze drifting through the open window, but somehow, I managed to wake Alana. She didn't move at first, just opened her eyes, but then she rolled toward me and curled up in the fold of my arm. The smile inspired by her dream remained on her lips, and I enjoyed her look of happiness and pleasure.

"What are you doing awake?" she asked.

"Just awake," I replied but pulled her closer to me. "Did you sleep well?"

"Uh-huh," she breathed. She buried her chin in my chest, her lightly curled fingers resting on my chest, and her hair splayed across my chin.

"We could get coffee and bread here, in the room," I suggested.

"Yes, we could, but then we'd never get out of bed," Alana said this with a satisfied sigh.

Taking that as a signal, I pulled the light sheet back and moved to get out of bed but was restrained by Alana.

"I didn't say you could go yet!" she complained. Her impish smile made me realize that breakfast would have to wait.

———

After showering, I shaved and pulled a brush through my hair. Not much effort was put into my appearance, and I smiled as Alana followed suit. Of course, her luxurious head of long brown hair and tanned skin didn't need fussing or makeup.

"It's about time," Aggie said across the breakfast room as we entered through the curved portal. "Tesa has been at the dig for over an hour. I told her I'd wait for you. Although I've been enjoying multiple cups of espresso, I didn't expect to have to wait so long. I suppose Darren is going to blame you, Alana."

"Yes," I admitted, "but not because of the time she needs to present herself for the day."

Aggie quickly realized that I wasn't talking about Alana's shower time, and he smiled.

We collected some fresh bread and fruit and were served piping hot cups of coffee by the young woman tending the room. Double espresso for me, cappuccino for Alana.

"We're meeting at the dig this morning, right?" I asked.

"That's correct," Aggie replied, "to meet Inspector Indolfo, Alana's friend on the Italian police. But soon after that, we're going to visit Yavuz in the jail here."

Aggie swigged down the dregs of his coffee cup and prepared to stand.

"I'll let you get some food into you, but I promised Tesa I'd push you toward the dig. For me, it's time to go." With that, he left the table and headed out the front door toward his rental car.

"He sounds passionate about this dig," Alana said, sipping her cappuccino.

"Or passionate about the digger," I said with a grin. "No worries," I added. "We'll catch up to him."

———

We drove to the dig and parked the rented car in the same spot as the day before. Archeological sites don't have much traffic nor many visitors, so it wasn't hard to reorient ourselves to the site and find the group tent to ask around about Tesa's whereabouts.

"Over in that direction," said one of her team members, pointing in the general direction of the hole we inspected yesterday.

Alana and I walked toward the pit indicated by the pointed finger and saw four or five people standing around the edge of the dig. Aggie was there, standing next to Tesa, her sunhat pulled firmly down on her head. There were two other team members recognizable by their worn pants and dusty boots. And one other person, a woman, older than Tesa, with long, grey-streaked hair bundled up and tied at the back of her head.

"Hey," Aggie said, turning in our direction. "About time."

"Yeah, yeah," I said, waving away his comment with a smile.

"This is Rafaela Indolfo," Tesa added, but Alana and the woman were all ready to embrace.

"How are you, Raffie?" Alana said with obvious glee.

"Wonderful, my friend. It's been so long!"

Alana grinned at the warm greeting, and the two women hugged.

"We were just explaining to Rafaela what happened here," Aggie offered.

"That's good," I added, "since we don't really know what happened."

"This is my friend, Darren Priest," Aggie said, introducing me to Rafaela. "He's from U.S. intelligence services ..."

"Not anymore," I corrected quickly, trying to cut Aggie off before I would have to explain more.

"Yeah," Aggie amended his introduction, "but that's his background. We know each other from the Afghanistan conflict."

"It's my pleasure to meet you," Rafaela said, offering her hand.

"Thank you. My pleasure, too."

"We were just going over what we know, how it might have happened, and what we should be concerned about," Aggie continued.

I noticed that Tesa was quiet during these minutes and seemed to be slightly disconnected from the conversation. Mindful that her mentor, Charlie Dielman, had just died in the pit, her pensive mood was not unexpected.

"Charlie apparently either fell, or was pushed, into the pit," Aggie continued.

"Yes, I have seen the photos," Rafaela commented. "His death was caused by a broken neck, but a fall of this nature could have caused that whether it was intentional or accidental."

For once, Aggie stood by silently but reached out and squeezed Tesa's hand.

"True," he then added, "but he has been digging like this for fifty years. I'm sure he knows his way around archeological digs. Besides," Aggie said, pressing his fingers into Tesa's palm, "we think there was a motive."

"And what was that?" Rafaela inquired.

"Gold," Aggie replied, but at this, Tesa interjected.

"Not necessarily gold, but we think it might have been electrum. Gold-like coins, called *staters* or maybe *trites.*"

Rafaela winced and shook her head, waiting for an explanation.

"*Staters* are—were—the coins of the Lydian Kingdom," Tesa continued. "They were first struck between 650 and 620 BCE and are believed by many coin collectors and experts to have been the first coins ever to appear in the world."

"If there were these *staters*, as you called them," Rafaela said, "were they very valuable?"

"Yes, in a certain way," Tesa responded. "Lydian *staters* have been found, mostly *trites* ..."

"Wait," Rafaela interrupted, putting her hand up. "*Trites?*"

"*Trites* are a third of a *stater,*" Tesa explained. "Like *hektes* and *hemihektes*, other smaller denominations of the *stater*. But they are the only true Lydian coins found and circulating on the market."

"Why would the discovery of *trites* matter in this case?"

"There's the matter of face value and market value," Aggie began. He was eager to continue, but Tesa raised her hand to slow him down.

"It's complicated," she said, "but, in short, market value is the value of the metal in bulk. In this case, electrum. Face value conveys the value as set by a governing power."

Rafaela scrunched up her face, still out of step with the conversation.

"Finding melted lumps, or bars of electrum, might allow us to trace their origin to the ancient Lydian kingdom," Tesa offered. "But finding surviving coins minted by that kingdom might indicate that they, the Lydians, ruled this land and maintained their system of coinage here as the medium of exchange. Over the years, people have found many *trites*, *hektes,* and *hemihektes* ..."

"Whoa," I said, holding up my hand. "Explain."

"*Staters* are the full coin. Incredibly rare. I've never seen one," Tesa expounded. "*Trites* are one-third of a *stater*, *hektes* are one-sixth of a *stater*, and *hemihektes* are one-twelfth of a *stater*. Again, these fractional coins are circulating through the numismatic market; but *staters* are very, very hard to find."

"And if they're found?" asked Alana.

"It would probably mean more to us. But that's not the case here."

"The Etruscans ruled this land before the Romans took over," Rafaela inserted, "first the Roman kingdom, then the Roman Republic, then the Roman Empire. How ... no, why do the Lydians fit into this?"

Tesa knew the answer but was slow to respond.

"One interpretation might be that if lumps of melted electrum are found here, it would confirm that the Lydians migrating from Anatolia settled here," Tesa explained. "That's simple and straightforward. Many peoples, tribes, whatnot, migrated around the world and populated new regions."

"And?" Rafaela asked with some prodding.

"But if a sizeable cache of stamped Lydian *staters* or *trites* shows up—remember the point about face value representing the value attached by a ruling government? That would be proof that the Lydians didn't just migrate here and mingle with an indigenous Etruscan population. It might be proof that the Lydians were the rulers of this region, the forerunners of the Etruscans."

I was following the conversation closely, having already heard some of this in bits and pieces. Still, I was focused on the impact that Tesa's words would have on Rafaela, the only other native Italian in our circle at that moment.

"It could be that the Lydians came to this area," Tesa

continued, "interbred with the native Villanovans, and their progeny is what we call the Etruscans."

"Who later became the Romans," Rafaela added, mixing a note of wonder with skepticism.

Tesa only nodded but shrugged her shoulders as if to say that this was only a theory.

"What do people, I mean the scientists, say?" Rafaela asked.

"There are adherents to various theories," Tesa responded and held up her hand again to allay Aggie's intervention.

"My mother didn't believe there was a connection between the Lydians and the Etruscans," Tesa continued. "Based on her analysis as a philologist. Charlie wasn't so sure. He is a ... he was a physical anthropologist and thought he could prove or disprove the connection based on the physical evidence left behind in digs like this."

"And if he found *staters* or at least *trites*?" Rafaela asked.

"It would support the connection."

"Did he?" pressed Rafaela.

"We think so," replied Tesa. "But that's where we get to Hamza. Hamza Yavuz."

"Who's that?"

"He was a digger here, well thought of, and has been on the site for almost five years," she explained. "He has been unaccounted for since Charlie's death but was recently picked up at the port in Pescara, ready to board a ferry across the Adriatic."

Rafaela looked intently at Tesa but waited for more information.

"He had a *trite* in his pocket," Aggie blurted out. "He's being detained in the jail in Civitavecchia right now, awaiting questioning. In the *Casa di Reclusione* on Via Tarquinia."

"We think it *might* be a *trite*," said Tesa, emphasizing the doubt she felt without inspecting the find. "We haven't seen it yet."

"A third-*stater*?" Rafaela asked for clarification.

"Right."

"Well, I think we need to visit this Hamza ... what is his name?"

"Hamza Yavuz," Aggie offered.

# PHOCAEA, AEGEAN SEA

## 610 BCE

TYRRHENUS WAS ALREADY AT THE EDGE OF THE WATER BEFORE the shipbuilders, dock workers, and slaves arrived. The sun rose behind his back as he faced the broad expanse of the Aegean Sea to the west. He was a great commander of men and a well-respected leader, and he always arrived early to inspect the work from the previous day before beginning the new day's activities.

On this day, with three ships built and two more to create before the trip was turned to, he wanted to check the wood timbers and rope bindings that were held in store for the construction. Between the piles of these materials, he walked toward the hulls of the ships already built, vessels that floated in the shallow waters off the edge of the port in Phocaea, the embarkation point that the Lydians had used for many years to explore the Great Sea and the lands to the west.

Control of Phocaea—later named Foça—was a natural seaport craved by Greeks, Lydians, and other tribes in the eastern part of the Mediterranean Sea. Positioned on a broad, rounded peninsula that jutted out into the Aegean, Phocaea's harbor was a nearly complete C-shaped inlet that protected the docks from the breaking waves of the large sea to its west, allowing ship-building and launching of craft in calm waters. The hilly cliffs that encircled the harbor on the land side were not too high to prevent transit from land to sea but high enough to offer some protection from the outside world.

The Lydians had to make frequent treaties with the Greeks to use the port, and Phocaea had become a common shipbuilding and export site since the time of Ardys's father's father, Gyges. From there, they would launch their seafaring merchants to the islands scattered throughout the sea near Greece, to the coastal cities of northern Africa, and as far away as Sicily—known then as Sikania—and the long narrow peninsula of the Italics that jutted down from the European landmass northward. With so many cities and villages dotting all these islands and coastlines, Gyges and his descendants in the kingdom of Lydia gradually built up a vigorous and thriving market for their goods.

With so many different cultures interested in their crops and products, barter systems could too easily break down, so the Lydians acknowledged the advantage of developing a more constant and reliable medium of exchange.

The kings who inherited the Lydian throne from Gyges developed coinage, hammered impressions on round disks of electrum, an alloy of gold and silver found in abundance in the River Pactolus, which they could present to the distant peoples and collect as payment. The stater, as it was called, and its various denominations like the trite, the hekte, and the hemi-hekte became a formalized system throughout the region. Non-Lydians who received the electrum coins often melted them down and traded them for their worth in bulk, but some stores of the coins were set aside in treasuries for future dealings with the Lydians when they came to market their products and wares.

Nowhere had the other tribes in Greece, Africa, or Sikania adopted the electrum stater as their own currency; they based their exchange on the barter system still and preferred to maintain that system for their internal dealings.

Tyrrhenus knew this because he was his father's favorite ambassador for Lydia, the son most often sent abroad on commercial ventures. He knew that he could make deals with some of the villages on the islands strewn across the Greek settlements on the Aegean Sea and those along the journey to the Italic shore. At each stop, he would leave some of the staters there in exchange. And he knew that the local people would set aside some bags of the coins as usual, but otherwise turn the medium to their own uses as bulk metal, sometimes simply turning it into trinkets and personal adornments for their women.

For the present excursion, Tyrrhenus made grander designs necessary to organize and contemplate the removal of vast numbers of Lydians from their homeland to settle elsewhere in the region. For that purpose, the Lydian ships built to bear his teams of explorers, those sent to find a new land, would need to bring with them the stores of goods to trade and to survive on. They would also bring a small treasury of staters for trade along the way and to establish a post for themselves once they found a suitable place for settlement on the Italic coast.

With the sun rising at his back, the morning's activity picked up; small groups of workers began to arrive and make their way down to the assemblage of boat parts on the waterline. Men and women in the Lydian system worked together, although the men outnumbered the women on the crews. Tyrrhenus remained focused on the rippling of the small tidal waves and the soothing sounds of the water as it lapped up onto the stony shore. The sounds of work and hustle slowly increased as construction was resumed on the two unfinished boats. In just a few days, these would be ready too, and Tyrrhenus would inspect them before approving the vessels for shipping.

Although the Lydians were mostly land people, they had inherited the trades and seafaring skills of various tribes who preceded them. From ancient peoples as well as the Greeks and Assyrians who still populated the area around Phocaea, the Lydians had improved their skills at boatbuilding and expanded the range of their sailing adventures. The desire was there— Ardys had pursued a vigorous trade routine during his reign— and the talent was developed as Tyrrhenus broadened his father's plans. But it would not have been possible without intense development of seafaring knowledge and skills among the Lydians.

This expedition had broad purposes but limited scope. Tyrrhenus was told by Ardys to assemble one hundred of the best men—and a consort of dozens of women—to make the voyage. Limited in this way to manpower, he had had to trust the quality and endurance of the men; but he still pondered the broad purpose as he stood listening to the sounds of construction all around him.

"How will I know where my father wants us to settle?" he wondered. "The sea is great, and the land beyond is even greater. If I choose the wrong place and return for our people before the gods can bless the choice, will more die than those who stay behind with my brother?"

Tyrrhenus assumed that he would establish a settlement close to the water. Where else would a seafaring people be comfortable? And even if they were to truly move half of their people to this new place, there would have to be regular contact with the homeland, so sea travel would remain a fixture for them. He knew of earlier trade with the Italics; he preferred them to the people of Ifriqiya on the coast of the great continent to the south, and he preferred them to the Maleth on the tiny island to the south of Sikania. And as Ardys had recommended, he intended to steer clear of Heracleion in the Egyptian kingdom.

The great island of Sikania itself remained a possibility, but the Greeks had gained a strong foothold on the eastern end of the island and would not welcome the Lydians. Through the process of elimination, Tyrrhenus was convincing himself that he should seek landfall in the same area they had ventured to in earlier commercial voyages, landing on the western coast of the great Italic peninsula, halfway up and away from Sikania to avoid conflict with the Greeks and close to the Villanovan people that they had come to know in that region.

"Sire," he heard, a call that woke him from his thoughts. Tyrrhenus turned to see Xenus, his father's advisor who had been assigned to accompany the new expedition and offer the sort of advice that normally was reserved for a king. Tyrrhenus had smiled at Xenus's assignment to him. He couldn't decide whether it was a promotion from Ardys for a lifetime of support to the king or punishment for delivering unhappy reports of the state of the Lydian people while in court.

"Yes, Xenus. What is it?"

"The three ships are ready, and I have asked the foreman about the other two. He says they will be ready in two morning's time." Xenus paused to let Tyrrhenus consider this. "So, we can set our plans to sail on the second dawn."

"Let that be the third dawn," Tyrrhenus said. "We'll leave some time for finishing work and then a long evening of relaxation with wine and women before setting out."

"As you say it, sire."

Xenus was not a shipbuilder but a seer and, on some days, a prophet. Tyrrhenus respected him but realized Xenus's lack of experience with boats and seas, so he thought it best to account *for more time and not rush the departure. Besides, Tyrrhenus also knew that when he left Phocaea, it would likely be the last time he would see his homeland. Others may return with word of their success and to plan more travel for the Lydian people, but once a settlement was established in Italia, he would have to remain to rule the land.*

# CASA DI RECLUSIONE

THE MORNING'S ACTIVITY AT THE SITE WAS COMPLETED, and Rafaela's questions were mostly answered. What remained was to interrogate Hamza Yavuz at the jail in Civitavecchia, the *Casa di Reclusione*. Rafaela drove her own car, saying she would have to return to Rome immediately afterward. Aggie drove himself and Tesa in an old Jeep; Alana and I followed along in our rental car.

Rafaela led the caravan down E80 and onto SS1 toward the city, which became the Via Tarquinia. She hadn't been to that particular jail before, but the trip from the archeological dig to the center of Civitavecchia was easy to follow on her car's navigator.

All three cars pulled to a stop in front of the building, and we climbed out. The seemingly orchestrated arrival of a squad of cars made me think of an assault force that I had long ago managed in my life in counterterrorism. The thought of it brought a smile to my face, then I stood and leaned back to take in the immensity of the *Casa di Reclusione*. I was told that Yavuz was in jail, a word that, to my American psyche, conjured a small structure with a handful of cells and a small force of guards. But this *Casa* was an enormous building with multiple wings radiating from the center building, with the size and shape of a true penitentiary.

We came in through the public entrance, and Rafaela presented her credentials to the uniformed officer at the desk. He was curt, professional, and polite, but when he saw her badge, he stood and saluted her. Rafaela turned to Alana in a gesture that must be well known to European police forces. Without a word to convey her meaning, Rafaela made it obvious that Alana should present her credentials also. During the time we spent at Villa Poesia on the Amalfi Coast, I had pushed into my subconscious her connection to police work, so I hope to be forgiven for thinking that she wouldn't carry her badge with her. But, without further prompting, Alana reached into her bag and quickly located her Austrian *Bundespolizei* badge. It reminded me of the saying I had heard too often— "There are some things you can't unvolunteer for." For me, it meant never being able to stray too far from my intelligence service; for Alana, it meant never being able to completely shed her police and investigative persona.

The desk officer nodded respectfully at both of them as Rafaela asked about seeing a prisoner named Hamza Yavuz. Before responding to her request, the officer scrutinized each of us whom he assumed were not police or officers of the state.

"*E loro?*" he asked.

"I would like to speak with Signor Yavuz, and it is about a possible murder," Rafaela explained. "These individuals were workers and possible witnesses, and they are needed to identify the prisoner."

"*Sì, capito,*" he replied with a nod of his head. "This way, please."

He called another officer to watch the desk while he

escorted us down a long hallway in the cinder block structure. Checking paperwork that he carried in his hand, he glanced at two doors then passed on until he satisfied himself that he had found the cell containing Yavuz.

"*Ecco*," he said, pointing to the door that he was about to unlock. "Here."

He signaled to another guard situated at the entrance to the wing, waving his hand to suggest that the door be opened. With the thunk of an electronic switch, I heard a bolt drawing back. The officer who had escorted us turned the handle and pushed the door open.

The walls of the room inside were sheer white, bright enough to hurt the eyes, but the sullen man sitting on the edge of the cot didn't seem to notice. I guessed that his time here, even if only a couple days, had adjusted his eyesight and his expectations. However dimmed they might be.

Hamza Yavuz had the ruddy complexion common to Turkish men, but his was undoubtedly enhanced by the long years of physical work done under the Tuscan sun. He looked to be about fifty years old, though his jet-black hair showed no sign of grey. His stay in the jail was too short to account for the short beard covering his chin and cheeks, so I assumed that his unshaven look was a permanent feature. His dark eyes showed no emotion at our arrival, and he looked up at us with disinterest.

He didn't rise from the cot at first but fixed his eyes on Tesa. It seemed that his gaze was a mixture of contempt and fear. After a few seconds, he swept his eyes past Aggie, whom he must also have known, to the other three of us whom he had never met.

Yavuz was still clothed in the baggy clothes of a digger. His short-sleeve shirt hung loosely from his shoulders and was smudged with dirt. His cargo shorts were long enough to cover his knees and hung roughly to the middle of his calves. The legs of the shorts were wrinkled as might be expected of someone who had been kneeling and sitting in the dirt. And they had a misshapen look as if they had been worn for many days.

After the officer admitted us to the cell, he withdrew from the room and closed the door behind us. I wondered whether he would remain outside the door in case we needed him, but the departing clicks of heels on the stone floor quickly dispelled that notion.

"Hamza," Tesa began haltingly. "What are you doing here? What have you done?"

It seemed from her voice that she had already convicted Yavuz of something, either stealing the Lydian *trite* or killing Charlie, or perhaps something unspecified.

He didn't answer right away but looked at her with the same mixture of anger and suspicion.

"Signor Yavuz," began Rafaela, "I am Inspector Rafaela Indolfo of the Italian state police. I am here to speak with you of the death of Dr. Charles Dielman."

Yavuz's eyes grew a bit wide but retreated almost instantly. I watched closely to try to understand what he was thinking and what was on his mind. I sensed that something was occupying his thoughts, but I couldn't tell what right away.

"Signor Yavuz," Rafaela began again. "You are aware that Dr. Dielman is dead, no?"

Yavuz remained silent for a short moment but then looked up at his questioner.

"No, I did not know that. I am sorry, but I did not know that."

Why was he sorry? And what was he hiding?

"You did not know that he was dead," Rafaela continued, "but you worked at the site with him, and then you disappeared. You were found in Pescara the next day with a coin, a find from the archeological dig, isn't that right?"

Yavuz was silent.

"Hamza," interjected Tesa, "why are you here? Did you take that coin, the *trite*, from Dr. Dielman? Where were you going?"

But Rafaela put up her hand to regain control of the interrogation.

"You worked at the dig," she began, "and you worked with Dr. Dielman. We know he was excited about a find in the dig. He died from a fall, and then you disappeared—with a coin that could only have come from the excavation."

She paused for effect. I watched Yavuz's eyes to see how he reacted to Rafaela stating that Charlie died from a fall.

"Seems quite suspicious, doesn't it?" Rafaela asked.

Yavuz looked down at his hands, fingers interlaced in an almost prayer-like position in his lap, but he said nothing.

Tesa marched a couple steps forward, then to the left and right, finally retreating to the circle of us standing near the door. It seemed to me that she had something to say or had just realized something. Watching as she pressed her thumb and forefinger to the bridge of her nose convinced me of this.

"My mother died at that dig ..." she said.

"No, she didn't," Yavuz said quickly. "She died in bed."

"That's not the point," Tesa blurted with barely restrained energy. "She died working at that dig. And now Charlie."

Yavuz looked down again, and I could see the whites of his knuckles show as he squeezed his hands together to suppress the desire to comment.

Rafaela once again raised her hand, sensing that the line of questioning had gone off track.

"Why were you in Pescara, Signor Yavuz?"

"I live in Split, Croatia. I was going home to see my wife and two children."

"Were you going to tell us?" asked Tesa, but Rafaela held up her hand.

"You were going to Split. To see your family," Rafaela continued. "That's good. Did you think to inform Dr. Dielman or Dr. Richietta?" she said, pointing to Tesa.

"No, I didn't," he replied. I had hoped to hear Yavuz say, "I couldn't tell Dielman because he was dead," but he didn't. Such an awkward admission would have belied his earlier denials.

"Where did you get the coin?" Rafaela asked.

"The gold coin?" came the reply from Yavuz. It was clearly an attempt to feign innocence. "I found it. I admit I found it in the dig. And I took it."

"And did you have to push Dr. Dielman into the pit to steal the coin from him?" asked Rafaela.

"No!"

The reply was quick and intense, but I felt that it included a slight hint of planning, rehearsal, or foreknowledge.

"I took the coin," Yavuz continued, "but I know nothing about Dr. Dielman's death."

"What were you going to do with the coin?" asked Tesa. "The *trite?*"

"*Trite?*" Yavuz asked. His intonation sounded a bit contrived, as if he was not supposed to know what a *trite* was.

"The coin!" Tesa persisted.

Yavuz looked down at his hands.

"It looked shiny and nice. I thought my little daughter would like it."

I recall hearing from Tesa that Yavuz had worked at the dig for about five years while both Charlie and her mother, Olivia, were still at the project. If he was there that long, he would be familiar with the Etruscan heritage, their culture, and the stories told of how they came to be. It's unlikely that he didn't know what a Lydian *trite* was or understand the importance of such a find. However, I had to think it was possible that he wanted this "shiny and nice" piece as a pretty bauble for his little girl, despite my misgivings.

Rafaela retrieved a notebook from the police satchel hanging from her shoulder. She flipped through several pages and then paused.

"Hamza Yavuz," she read. "Born 1969. Fifty-one years old. Works for Mehmet Arslan, son of the Speaker of the Grand National Assembly of Turkey; nephew of the leader of the Stolen Works Department of the Turkish Ministry of Culture and Tourism."

She paused and looked at Yavuz.

"Why do you work at an archeological dig, Signor Yavuz?"

"I'm interested in archeology," was all he would say.

"Why not the digs in Turkey?"

"The Turkish people have traveled far. We have an interest in things that our predecessors did many years ago," he said by opening up. "Maybe even here."

"Do you think the Turkish people settled here? Long ago?"

Yavuz looked at her but then bent his head down and held his tongue.

"About Dr. Dielman," Rafaela continued. "You worked with him. Was it for a long time?"

"Yes. About five years there," he said.

Rafaela looked down at her notebook again.

"Says here that your family lives in Šibenik, Croatia. Not Split."

"It's nearby. Not far," Yavuz responded quickly. "If I say Šibenik, people don't know where I mean. So, I say Split."

Rafaela consulted her notes again.

"Says here that you have two children."

Yavuz remained silent.

Looking up from her notes and directing her gaze at Yavuz, Rafaela continued.

"Both boys."

Yavuz's gaze swept left and right, a common maneuver that we knew in intelligence indicated uncertainty and a bit of fear. He had said he took the coin as a gift for his daughter.

"I didn't kill Dr. Dielman," he said suddenly. The protest seemed genuine enough, but it also communicated to me that he was ready to confess to the theft of the coin to avoid complicity in Charlie's death.

"If you didn't," Rafaela began, "and I am not saying that you did, why did you run? It was not to present a pretty gold coin to a daughter who doesn't exist."

Yavuz coughed and covered his mouth with his fist.

I looked at Tesa to gauge her impressions of the man. Her skin color had turned a bit pink, suggesting a rise of blood into her cheeks. Her eyes were open wide and moist, suggesting an emotional response. And her hands, hanging by her sides, were clenched into fists.

Yavuz remained silent, staring down at the floor of the cell, not responding to Rafaela's question.

"You said my mother died in bed," Tesa said through pursed lips. "What did you mean by that?"

Rafaela looked at Tesa as the archeologist steered the conversation to events four years ago. The inspector had a quizzical look on her face that begged understanding. A look that showed she knew something was afoot but was not directly connected to the question at hand. She let Tesa's query proceed.

"Why did you say that?" Tesa continued.

Yavuz looked at her but didn't respond.

"Why did you single that out?" she said. "Why bring up that she died in bed?"

"You're accusing me of killing Dr. Dielman at the dig," he responded, "and you said that your mother died at the site. She didn't. I want Inspector Indolfo to know the truth. Your mother did not die at the dig—she died in bed. And I did not kill Dr. Dielman."

Rafaela studied Tesa for a moment, trying to unravel the meaning of her questions, then relented.

"Signor Yavuz," she said, "You will remain here at the *Casa di Reclusione* until we can determine the reasons why you went to Pescara and why you had the *trite* in your possession."

Then she turned on her heel before Yavuz could respond and rapped on the door to the cell for assistance in exiting the room.

## LA CASA CORVINA

We finished our business with Hamza Yavuz around one o'clock, perfect timing for a meal. Tesa recommended La Casa Corvina, which was halfway between the jail and our hotel, so we drove separately in our cars and reconvened there.

"Signora Richietta!" It was Dante, the owner of the restaurant, who recognized Tesa as we entered the door. "And, of course, Aggie," he continued, embracing them both with a hug and a kiss on each cheek. "You have a small party today," Dante added with pleasure, seeing the rest of us come through the door.

"*Come stai?*" Tesa responded. "How are you?"

"*Va bene; tutto bene,*" he replied. "Would you be comfortable at the table in the corner, at the window?"

"*Perfetto,* Dante," Tesa said.

After we settled into the corner booth, Dante slipped away and returned quickly with three wooden boards with parchment stapled to the front. The day's list of dishes was tacked to the boards in hand-written notes.

"*Mi dispiace*," our host said, "I'm sorry, but we have only three for your table. You can share, *si?*"

"*Si*, Dante. No problem," said Aggie.

I noticed that there were no wines included on the list, but while we looked over the day's offerings, Dante returned with two liters of unlabeled red wine. Pointing to one, he indicated that it was a local wine from the Lazio region, from the Cesanese grape. When he pointed to the second flask, Dante shrugged his shoulders.

"Lazio's wines are not known much outside of our region, so the winemakers are moving toward other, international grapes. This one is made from a combination of grapes, mostly from other regions."

Although he seemed proud to present the wine for us—or else why would he have delivered it without asking what we wanted—he also was a bit on edge waiting for our impression. Best that he not know that I was a wine writer for *The Wine Review*.

Tesa, Rafaela, and Aggie pointed to the first bottle, and Dante satisfied their request by filling short glass tumblers at their side of the table. Alana and I went for the second choice—me mainly because I wanted to figure out what this anonymous wine might be. Dante answered by filling our tumblers with wine and then turned away to attend to other business.

"Not bad," Aggie said of the Cesanese. The ladies at the table nodded approval.

I might be the wine writer among us, but most women were born with better sensory equipment than men, an evolutionary result of their role as gatherers in ancient societies. I looked at Alana for a second before tasting the wine to see her reaction, but she smiled back and left her glass on the table, waiting for me.

Clearly, the wine tasted like a cabernet blend, probably

cabernet sauvignon, although I could pick up the peppery accent of a bit of Cesanese in the wine. Still, quite a beautiful wine, and one simple enough to enjoy at a midday meal.

"You like?" Dante said when he returned to the table with baskets of bread, shallow dishes for the olive oil and dipping, and a platter of grilled peppers, mushrooms, and onions.

"Yes, very much," I replied. All eyes were on me as the wine taster, which put me a little on guard. I preferred to keep a low profile and never persisted in my own impressions of wine. But I was silently overruled by the four others at the table.

"He's a wine taster," Aggie said, lifting his eyebrows a bit in playful kidding.

"Sì, è vero?" Dante replied. At first impressed, I could see a little cloud of doubt pass over his face as if he wondered whether his simple tastes and offerings were up to being reviewed by a professional.

"Yes," I said, but I raised my hand in retreat. "But I prefer to enjoy wines with meals, not analyze them. And I like this very much," I added, raising the glass to salute Dante in thanks.

The menu was varied and featured some iconic dishes of Italy as well as a handful that I didn't recognize. From this, I deduced that La Casa Corvina was a popular place for the people of Lazio who cherished these obscure dishes. There were typical pasta dishes with sauces like carbonara with its pancetta, onion, pecorino, and egg, and I saw the creamy, cheesy Alfredo right below it, followed by cacio e pepe, a pasta dish of pecorino, crushed black pepper, and caciocavallo cheese. Each made my mouth water, but first, I would have to check out the antipasti on the menu.

There was calascioni, a turnover-shaped baked panzerotti stuffed with cheese and peppers. That was enticing, but I was set on pasta and thought the other dish—plus a typical second course of fish or meat—would be too much. I glanced at the basket of bread and rolls, including the regional *filone*—a long, crusty bread similar to a French baguette—and the bowl of olives, roasted garlic, and sliced *provolone*, and decided that I would be satisfied with this while waiting for the pasta.

Alana chose a different path. She asked for *suppli al telefono,* rice croquettes stuffed with minced mushrooms and diced mozzarella, served with a *ragù* sauce.

"After that," she continued, handing the menu back to Dante, "I'll have the *baccalà in guazzetto*." It was floured salt cod that was pan-fried and accompanied by a tomato sauce with anchovies, pine nuts, and raisins.

"I'd like the *cacio e pepe* first," I said, trying to remember the second course list since Alana had given away the menu. "And, after that ..." I stalled, "I'll have ..." stalling again.

"I will bring you the best *coda alla vaccinara* you've ever had," Dante said, rescuing me from my indecision. "It is a very authentic Roman dish. It goes back to ancient times and was savored by legionnaires and Roman citizens alike."

"*Va bene*," I said. "Very good."

When Dante took the other orders and retreated from the table, I saw that Rafaela was smiling at me.

"*Coda alla vaccinara* is a true Roman dish," she said. "But I see you are very adventurous."

"He's a wine and food writer," Alana said. "I'm sure he's encountered lots of surprises at the dinner table."

She was right, and I was something of an omnivore, but I focused on Rafaela, hoping for an explanation. She picked up on my curiosity.

"*Coda alla vaccinara* is very traditional. You see, not all the parts of a cow can be served as steak. What makes it so traditional, and so ancient, is that the Roman people didn't want to waste parts of the cow that were left after filling the stomachs of the rich families. Some of the innards of the cow—the stomach, liver, and intestines, even the tail—would make fine food once they were stewed or fried in lard, then dressed up with onion, garlic, celery, and herbs. The resulting dish is then rendered into a stew with pine nuts and raisins added, then some white wine."

I was truly an omnivore, but I tried to maintain an honest smile while I considered how much of the entrails of a cow I would be eating. "Maybe the pasta will fill me up," I thought. But I couldn't insult Dante and not eat the *coda alla vaccinara*.

"When you said your mother died at this dig," Alana said, turning to Tesa, "why did Yavuz insist that she died in bed?"

I had helped myself to some bread and olives, as did Aggie and Rafaela, but I listened in as I chewed.

"She did, in fact, die in bed," Tesa responded. "But she was working at this dig with Charlie and me. When she took sick, she gradually declined and, at one point, she couldn't rise from her bed in the Albergo dei Fiori. I stayed with her, but two days later, she died."

"Why was this minor fact important to Yavuz?" I asked, joining Alana in this.

"I don't know, but ..." Tesa paused. "Why would it matter?"

"Maybe he was worried about being accused of pushing Charlie into the pit," added Aggie, "and any talk of someone else dying at the dig would sound threatening to him."

"No," I pondered aloud. "It was more than that. As if he was aware of her condition and somehow followed her decline. Leaving him with a distinct visual image of where she died. That visual image was what prompted his quick response."

"That sounds ominous," Rafaela added.

The first course arrived, and I smelled the rich scent of pepper and cheese rise from the dish placed before me.

"What did your mother die of?" Alana asked.

"The doctor here said it might have been an infection, judging from the symptoms. He ran her blood for various infectious agents found in this region, particularly related to the area around the dig. Nothing turned up."

"Then what?" asked Rafaela.

"Then what?" Tesa replied, wondering why there would still be a question. "The doctor listed cause of death as *idiopatica*—idiopathic—possibly bacterial infection from working in areas of ancient habitations."

Rafaela retrieved her notebook and laid it next to her plate.

"*Idiopatica* means 'of unknown cause.'" As she scribbled some notes, she continued. "That was all?"

"Yes," Tesa said, but a gray cast of doubt passed over her face.

"Where is your mother buried?" asked Alana.

"Here. In Tuscany. Actually, not far from Tarquinia."

Rafaela added more notes to her book, then turned toward Alana, catching her eye and getting an unsolicited reply from the Viennese investigator.

"I agree," Alana nodded without being asked a question. Rafaela then turned her attention to Tesa.

"Would you agree to further testing of your mother's remains?" she asked.

"You mean to have her exhumed?"

"*Si*," said Rafaela.

"Yes, I suppose. Why?"

"As police, we don't like *idiopatica* as a cause of death," Alana replied. "It leaves too many questions unanswered."

"Especially when there are more deaths to explain," said Rafaela. "With your permission, I will make the arrangements."

Tesa only nodded, then seemed to lose interest in her food.

During the meal, Rafaela seemed conspicuously occupied with thoughts of Olivia's demise and what she had heard from

Yavuz this morning. Walking out to the cars, I caught up with her.

"You have suspicions?"

She nodded.

"Because," I began, "it seems exhumation of a body dead four years ago doesn't seem neatly tied to the current circumstances."

"Perhaps," she replied, "but I don't believe in coincidences."

Funny, that. It's a phrase that I have used often.

# CERVETERI

THE BIRTH OF THE ETRUSCAN CULTURE COULDN'T HAVE been spontaneous, in a scientific sense. There was evidence of another tribe, the Villanovans, who inhabited the territory of central Italy before that time, but the archeological evidence did not support the theory that the Villanovans simply evolved into the Etruscans. The usual detritus of civilization left by the two peoples was distinct enough to confirm that they were separate cultures—at least before 600 BCE. And the enigmatic Etruscan language had thus far stymied cultural historians and prevented them from literally "reading" the record.

Yusuf Demir, whom everyone thought was an expert on the Etruscans, happened to be on an extended holiday in Cerveteri, another ancient Etruscan settlement. Leaving La Casa Corvina, Alana and I drove down there to find him. We still had the remainder of today, Sunday, before Alana had to catch a train to Vienna in the morning, so I wanted us to stay together, even if it was on business.

I couldn't shake some vague suspicions about him, although I had not yet met him. It was probably rooted in Demir's proximity to the Tarquinia dig around the time of Dielman's death. That Demir was also associated with the Turkish government, its program of restoring antiquities to the ancient land, his well-documented interest in Turkish origin stories, and Yavuz's theft of a Lydian *trite* made it seem all the more suspicious. "I don't believe in coincidences," I thought as I recalled my own words that had been repeated by Rafaela.

Cerveteri was a new adventure and, not knowing the layout, I ended up parking the rental car too far from the old city center. The walk down the twisting, hilly streets brought back sweet memories of other European hamlets, though, so Alana smiled and slipped her hand into mine as we worked our way down to the bustling center of the commercial area.

Cerveteri was a small town. In 600 BC, it was known as Cisra by the Etruscans and considered important enough that it was listed as a principal member of the Etruscan League, a treaty-bound assemblage of twelve Etruscan cities that promised to protect each member from attacks. Today, it was the site of some of the most important Etruscan archeological digs—possibly an innocent and plausible explanation for Demir's presence. I had heard he was in the city, but not where he was staying, so we had to do a little snooping. I asked about him in two of the little hotels on the main square, but the clerk in the first did not recognize the name and the clerk in the second responded to my query with suspicion. After some walking about, Alana and I found a table in a nearby café, and I pursued my question with the waiter.

"Do you know a Signor Demir? Yusuf Demir? A Turkish man?"

I had no reason to suspect that my waiter would know him or that he would admit to knowing him. But I had to start somewhere, and the hotel search had produced no results.

"*No, signore.* I don't know this man," came the reply.

I sipped my espresso while Alana enjoyed a sweet roll and a café-Americano, then I turned to the waiter to retrieve the check, *il conto*. Doing so, we rose from the comfort of the shaded café and walked along the narrow road that mapped the center of Cerveteri while we discussed other ways to find Demir.

"It might sound a bit of a reach," Alana suggested, "but why not ask the *polizia?*" As a cop in Vienna where we met, I wasn't surprised by her suggestion, but I still didn't know how it would work. I worried that approaching a policeman in this town and asking about a man I'd never met—a man whom I would have a problem even describing—might turn against me. But Alana was up to the task and already heading in the direction of the uniformed officer standing in the middle of the traffic square.

"*Mi scusi, signore,*" she began, and I wondered how far her Italian would take her. I knew she was fluent in English and German, but I had heard her use Italian only sparingly in Praiano while we vacationed at the Villa Poesia.

"*Stiamo cercando un uomo si chiama Yusuf Demir. È un professore di storia, da qui, e da Turchia. Lo conosce?*"

"*No, signorina,*" the officer replied, returning his gaze to the traffic swirling around the piazza and waving his hand at the cars.

"*Sono molto impressionato!*" I told Alana when she returned to me on the curb. "I am very impressed!"

I knew that Demir was in his seventies, and I was told that he wore a neatly trimmed beard and mustache, salt and pepper in appearance. His face probably resembled the polyglot of European humanity, so I took a chance and settled on a mental image of what he looked like. We approached another café, and I tried my luck there.

"I am looking for my uncle, my *zio*," I asked a man at the door of the café. "He is about this height, grey beard," I said, stroking my chin, "and very distinguished. *Molto gentile,*" I added in Italian.

The man at the door was paying more attention to Alana than me, but she smiled back at him and pointed to me—a double meaning that we were together and that he should respond to the question from the man who she was with.

The inquiry was greeted with a shoulder shrug, so we turned to leave. With that movement, I nearly walked into a man waiting behind me at the door. His broad smile suggested a private joke that I wasn't party to, and I couldn't put my finger on it.

"You're not my nephew," he said with a subtle laugh, then looking over my shoulder and nodding at Alana in greeting. He was about the height that I had imagined for Demir. With a short grey-black beard and mustache, his medium-length hair was combed back from his forehead and temples and bent in waves in a common European hairstyle for men, thick locks reaching his collar and falling slightly over it. His smile remained as I realized that I had been found out.

"But you are Mr. Darren Priest, yes?" he continued.

I nodded.

"And who are you?" he asked Alana, offering his hand to take hers.

"I am Alana Weber. A friend." I noted that she left off mention of being a police inspector from Austria.

Returning his attention to me, Demir said, "And since you have pretended to be my nephew, I think I have the right to ask about your intentions and why you are looking for me."

Although his face seemed friendly, his eyes blazed with an intensity and purpose that made me realize that I should not trifle with this man.

"Yes, I am Darren Priest, as you say. Although I don't know how you were aware of that."

Demir waved the semi-question away as if it was of no importance.

"I was asked by a friend to resolve some matters up in Tarquinia," I continued, "but those matters are probably of little interest to you. Instead ..."

"Oh," he interrupted to raise his hand before me. "The sudden death of an esteemed colleague in my field is of great interest to me," Demir said.

His knowledge of current events foretold how and why he had come to know my identity.

"Of course," I said to regain my place. "I didn't mean it that way, only that the events surrounding Dr. Dielman's death are probably not your concern. What I had hoped was to learn something from you about the history of the Etruscans."

I paused to see if I could get him off the thought of Dielman's demise and onto history and science. Demir's face was unreadable. His eyes were on me, and his smile remained fixed, although I detected some movement of the skin around his ears as if his thought process was churning while his face remained inscrutable.

"Where would you like to begin?" he said finally. "The Etruscans go back many centuries. There would be much to talk about."

"Yes, precisely, and it's that early history that I was thinking about."

"Why?" he asked, with little compromise evident in his voice.

I knew that my response would have to be plausible but also carry the innocent curiosity of a student.

"I am Italian-American myself," I began. "I have often read about the Etruscans, even visited some of their early sites like Fiesole. Since I am here in Italy on other business, I thought I could spend my free time learning more about them."

Pitching this as a quest for general knowledge while on holiday might strain credulity, but it was all I had.

"Does this have anything to do with Charlie Dielman's dig?" he asked. Demir was not dissuaded by my explanation.

"No. Well, yes." I was trapped and had to give him something or else Demir would break off contact.

"Dr. Dielman was well known to a friend of mine, Arnold Darwin ..." I thought that throwing in Aggie's name might sell my pitch as both true and virtuous. "In talking to Aggie—sorry, that's Arnold's nickname—he kept mentioning the doctor's research. As I said, I have heard so much about the Etruscans over the years that while trying to help investigate the man's death, I couldn't resist spending my free time finding out more about the people themselves. If Dielman's death was related to the Etruscan finds, it would help to know that."

There. It was out. If Demir was in Cerveteri and near Tarquinia to claim archeological finds for Turkey—or worse, if he was an instigator in the crime involving Dielman—he would now know that I was connecting the dots. On the other hand, if Demir was above suspicion, his insights could be crucial to solving the crime. I had to risk it.

Demir turned toward the man behind the desk at the entrance to the café, then pointed toward a table near the edge of the covered terrace.

"Let's sit and have a coffee. I can tell you a little," he said, "but to understand the Etruscans, you must know a lot."

We sat in silence for a moment while waiting for the server to bring our espresso. Demir engaged in small talk with Alana, mostly in Italian, but I occasionally heard him use a phrase or two that was not Italian. Alana laughed, sometimes offering the demure look of a little girl as if in response to some flattery. I knew her too well and was sure this was an act, or maybe just a conversational joust with the older man.

"*Oraya hiç gitmedim, ama belki bir ara,*" she said with a smile.

"Forgive me," Demir said to me, with a playful smile on his lips. "But I couldn't help chatting up your beautiful companion. I asked if she had ever been to Istanbul."

"I said no," Alana broke in to explain the conversation, "but perhaps another time."

I knew that Alana was remarkably well-traveled, and I had a suspicion that she had, in fact, been to Istanbul. Did she also speak Turkish?

The waiter delivered my double espresso, *un doppio*, served Alana an iced tea with a sprig of mint floating on the top, and brought a large cup of black, aromatic coffee for Demir. A little tray of cookies and chocolate was added to the order and placed in the middle of the table.

Aggie had told me that Demir had close ties to the Turkish government and might be connected to the attempt by a man he called Mehmet Arslan to tamper with the retrieval of artifacts from the dig worked by Dielman and Tesa. Arslan was the son of the Speaker of the Grand National Assembly of Turkey and nephew of the leader of the Stolen Works department of the Turkish Ministry of Culture and Tourism. His father and uncle hold powerful positions in Turkey's government, but according to Aggie, Arslan was a more impetuous version of them.

Whereas father and uncle were working within the bureaucracies of the country to repatriate Turkish treasures, Arslan was known to work outside the system—even outside the law—to retrieve such artifacts. He had been raised in a stew of cultural resentment that convinced him in his adult years that his mission was to recover Turkish treasures—even from pre-Turkish times—that could be traced to his culture's art and ingenuity. He grew up with stories of the greatness of his ancient civilization, how the people from Anatolia swept westward and seeded the societies of Syria, Greece, and Rome, and how the people of modern Turkey were the real source of the magnificent art and history of the Mediterranean and European cultures.

Arslan's certitude, and his willingness to resort to extralegal means to reclaim Turkish culture using the authority of the Stolen Works department as cover, had injected a reputation for lawlessness into his actions.

Was Demir his mentor, I wondered?

There was Turkey's law called Protection of Cultural and Natural Property, which Arslan used as a legal cause and which Demir would be very familiar with. The 1983 law was among many responses the country had to the cultural diaspora in ancient times, a spread of influence that could be proof of Anatolia/Turkey's cultural importance but also lead to the exportation and loss of many of its own significant artifacts.

Aggie had explained this to me, but more significantly, he commented that the spread of Anatolian society over the millennia, populating other regions with the blood of their civilization, meant that many religious, cultural, and artistic artifacts were thought to belong to the earliest Turkish people. Geopolitical experts might dispute that, noting that all tribes and societies spread over time and the results of their migration belonged in the places where they landed. But some people believed that the Turkish government had a responsibility to use that 1983 law to demand the return of many things that could reliably be traced to early Anatolian society.

Arslan was determined to fulfill that demand.

I didn't know where Arslan was, but Demir sat here before me, and Dielman was dead.

"So, where shall we begin?" he asked after a sip of his coffee.

"Maybe I should just ask, 'Who were the Etruscans?' I know that seems overly broad, but I'd like to know who you say they were."

Demir sipped his coffee and put the cup down softly. Biting into one of the almond-flavored *cantucci* cookies from the plate, he cast his eyes upward before replying.

"There is no dispute that they were a great culture, that they were dominant in the central part of the Italian peninsula in the first millennium BCE, and that they were ultimately replaced by—or some think transformed into—the Romans."

"Wait, let's start at the ending," I said, and Demir laughed. "Were the Etruscans defeated by Rome or subsumed within it?"

"Either of your two options assumes that the Etruscans and Romans were distinct societies," he responded. "What if the Etruscans simply became the Romans, that the Romans owe their origins to the Etruscan people?"

"If that is true, wouldn't we find linguistic and cultural bridges between the two?" Alana asked.

"Yes. It's natural to assume that, but not necessarily. The Roman civilization might have grown out of the Etruscan people. Who themselves, it is also said, grew out of the Villanovan culture."

I remained silent for a moment, letting that sink in.

I considered Demir's age, his years of study, and all that he had researched and learned. But he still seemed young in an odd way. Whether it was a life spent in the heavy work of physical anthropology or just good genes, Demir surely enjoyed more vitality and strength than many men half his age. Enough to push a man over a scaffolding? I couldn't help but wonder.

"Perhaps we need to continue this another time. Perhaps over dinner—and I hope Ms. Weber will join us." Turning to me, he added, "You buy." At that, he stood, gently laid a twenty Euro note on the table, and turned to depart.

As he reached the door, he looked back toward me and suggested that we meet at the Eioli Osteria that evening. I nodded.

# PHOCAEA

## 610 BCE

T YRRHENUS HAD MADE THIS TRIP BEFORE, SEVERAL TIMES. *They launched the boats in the morning, steered to the north of the islands just off the coast of Phocaea, then swept south into the Aegean Sea to maneuver through the scattering of islands still governed by the Greeks from Athens. He directed his ship and those who followed to steer south of the island of Aigilia—known in later times as Antikythera—and between it and the island of Heraklion. This arc of sailing would keep them even farther from interference by the Greeks and avoid unanticipated encounters.*

*Tyrrhenus had experimented with this route on his earlier journeys and appreciated the open waters. Although it would take two days of continuous sailing to round the southern tip of mainland Greece and wedge between Aigilia and Heraklion—he wanted to set a standard passage that he could encourage the Lydians to follow once he had established a settlement on the peninsula of Italia. To ensure no loss of pace, the king's son kept the rowers at their oars in case the wind failed them. Resting their calloused hands on the smooth* wood without having to pull the strokes seemed like a light holiday for them.

Fortunately, there was a kind wind at their backs, saving the men from hour upon hour of backbreaking rowing to escape the territorial waters of the Athenians.

"It has gone well," said Xenus as he approached Tyrrhenus standing on the bow of the lead ship.

"Yes, calm waters and a steady breeze," Tyrrhenus responded. He sounded satisfied and composed, although he kept his eyes on the water and didn't turn to face Xenus. The king's counselor and son had a strained relationship. Tyrrhenus wondered whether Xenus had achieved his trusted position with Ardys by flattery; Xenus wondered whether Tyrrhenus was the right son to put in charge of this massive assignment. But both realized the eminent power of the kingdom and recognized that Ardys wielded it absolutely. So, they cooperated.

The boats used by the Lydians during this period were among the most advanced for travel for that time. Mediterranean merchants and military forces had experimented with many designs over the centuries of vying for command of the great Middle Sea, and the Lydians culled that experience for answers to their own designs.

Each boat could carry twenty to thirty people, including rowers, so there were five vessels in this fleet. The hulls were constructed with a mortise and tendon design in which the horizontal planks laid edge by edge upon each other to become the hull were held in place with wedges of wood—the tenons—which themselves were nailed into place with wooden locking pegs. This design kept the planks of the hull aligned and avoided shifting while on heavy seas, but the seams between the planks had to be filled with pitch or some other caulking material to prevent leakage into the hold.

The rowers—eight on a side—worked on deck, so they were

exposed to sun and wind. But the shallow draft of these crafts kept the men high enough to avoid the spray of small waves. It was only when the seas were high that this deck-side rowing became a challenge of strength and endurance.

The deck was topped with a square-rigged sail which required that wind come from behind to propel the ship forward. Whenever there was any wind, even a light one such as on the days of this journey, the sails were kept aloft, replacing the need for rowing or at least reducing the need. The ships were steered from aft, with a helmsman plying the water with a specially shaped oar on one side of the boat. Bigger than the oars used to move the ship through the water, this paddle included a spade-like end that the helmsman could push back and forth to keep the vessel on course. It was not centered on the stern but instead was tied to the side of the boat, so it couldn't be moved side to side. The design required great expertise to steer the boat.

They had passed through the gauntlet of islands surrounding Greece's southern coast and spent the next two days sailing the Mediterranean Sea. As they turned to a northward tack, land appeared on the horizon.

"Is this our destination?" asked Xenus. He had not been on such an extended voyage before, preferring to remain at the king's side in Sardis. This was another reason why Tyrrhenus questioned his father's decision to send Xenus with him.

"No, it is the strait of Zancle, a busy shipping port on the tip of the island of Sikania, there," he said, pointing, "to our left. Across from it is Regia," he added, pointing to the tip of Italia to the right. "We will pass through the strait and then sail north up the coast of Italia before putting in to shore."

From ancient times, Zancle—later known as Messana, then Messina on Sicily's eastern tip—and Regia—now charted as Reggio Calabria on Italy's mainland squeezed the sea into a narrow straight. They were both busy trading ports, both between the island and the peninsula and among the many merchant ships that sailed the open seas from across the region. Homer's tale of Odysseus battling Scylla and Charybdis on his return voyage was based on the proximity of these two places, each featuring hazards for sailors and an unenviable passage through the dividing waters.

Tyrrhenus knew of the threats posed by the rocky shoals of these parts but was confident that his experience on earlier voyages would serve him well. But to ensure his odds of success, he ordered the fleet of ships to stow their oars and lower the sails, slowing their progress until the winds had died down. He preferred a perfect calm that would require movement only by his control of the oarsmen, without struggling to control the whims of the wind that could rise at any moment.

The sun was high above his head which was not perfect. Tyrrhenus would have preferred to enter the strait in the early hours of the day, giving him more time to navigate the treacherous waters between the two ports. But his decision to wait for calmer seas seemed to outweigh the time advantage. It would take several hours to get all five ships through the strait, and it might mean working after sunset, making spotting rocks and outcroppings more difficult. But flat water seemed to be more important.

His plan worked. The winds died down, and the sea calmed. As soon as he felt that all the factors had come together, Tyrrhenus called for the men to put the oars back in the water while leaving the sails stowed and to row in a strict cadence to get up to speed. The four remaining vessels followed suit and fell into a line behind Tyrrhenus.

Another two hours were needed to even get into the strait, and although he wanted the men to pull hard, Tyrrhenus knew that they would be at it for six to eight hours altogether. So, rather than rowing at race speed, he told the drum-beater to establish a steady, moderate pace to conserve the men's energy for the ordeal. Captains of the other vessels could see the pace of the oars in Tyrrhenus's boat, so they didn't need verbal instructions to understand the command.

Two hours later, white water could be seen not far off the portside of the boat, a hint Tyrrhenus recalled from earlier experience. The swirling waves warned him of danger, but he also knew that he had to maintain a bearing that brought the boats close so that he could avoid the swirling seas on the other side. Standing tall upon the bow, he watched the waters beat against the rocks and motioned with his hands to the helmsman aft, making small adjustments to the path to effectively beat the odds on both sides of the strait.

Another two hours of rowing and the lead ship emerged from the turbulent waters of the strait. Xenus had maintained a nervous state of expectation throughout the experience, while Tyrrhenus exuded confidence in his decisions. As soon as the vessel sailed past the rippling waters behind them and he knew the threat had passed, he signaled to the helmsman to steer slightly left and to the drum-beater to bring in the oars. He wanted to reward his men with a rest while steering out of the way of the next craft emerging from the strait.

In this way, his little exploratory fleet entered the sea above the island of Sikania and was in sight of the great peninsula called Italia.

# EIOLI OSTERIA, CERVETERI

Alana and I arrived at the Eioli Osteria at eight p.m., as agreed. It wasn't without some funny experiences. Not knowing the layout of Cerveteri and never having been to this little restaurant, we asked around to find its whereabouts.

"*Eccellente!*" said one man on the street, but he couldn't remember where it was. I decided that he had never been there or, else, had an experience that included substantial amounts of wine.

"*Sempre diritto,*" another man said, standing at a corner of a minor intersection. He pointed up into the busy section of the city, saying "always straight," but I knew that this *sempre diritto* expression was a common fallback for Italians who weren't quite sure where to send you.

"I know it well," said a woman whose English was better than my Italian, albeit with a strong accent. She rubbed her chin to collect her memory.

"I think it is about two blocks in that direction. See, there," she said, pointing to a doorman at the hotel on the corner. "He would know."

We crossed the busy street, waving *"ciao"* and *"grazie"* to her and approached the man at the door.

He stood as still as a Swiss guard at the entrance to the Vatican, pretending not to notice us, assuming no doubt that we were just some American tourists confused about their surroundings.

*"Mi scusi,"* I began, offering as much of a Tuscan accent as I could. *"Dov'é Eioli Osteria?"*

At the sound of an obviously obscure restaurant, the doorman brightened and turned a smiling face to us. To Alana, actually, but I took that as progress.

*"É li,"* he said. "It is there," pointing around the corner at a green awning above an intricately carved wooden entrance door, just one-half block from where we stood.

*"Grazie mille,"* said Alana, to which he tipped his hat and offered the warmest smile he could manage. I was content to simply wave my thanks since it was apparent he wasn't paying any attention to me.

We soon found out why the Eioli Osteria was not only obscure but one that would elicit such bright comments from the strangers we met. The menu was posted outside the main entrance, as is usual in this country. "Eioli Osteria" was printed above the parchment and *"Il buonissimo cibo degli Etruschi"* below, "the best food of the Etruscans."

I pulled on the curled wrought iron handle to swing the heavy door outward. Alana swept past me, and I followed her into a darkened anteroom. It was small, no more than ten feet square, and adorned with replicas of ancient paintings, the kind that was featured in the Etruscan *tumuli* and remnants of their common buildings in archeological digs. Heavy drapes framed each of the murals, pulled back as if they were opening onto a stage, and pegged at the wall with ornamental iron hooks.

We stood there alone for only a moment before the curtain

in front of us drew back. With the front door to our back, this heavy drape was what separated us from the dining room, and a thick-chested man in the closely cropped beard smiled and welcomed us inside.

The dining room was large but broken up into sections by tiers, three in all, in concentric circles. The lowest tier was at floor level and occupied the center of the space; the next tier was built nearly all the way around it, and the third tier was above that, separated from the intermediate section by a handrail. Flute music played softly from the back part of the room, accompanied by the sound of some stringed instrument that I could not identify.

"*Lui è Signor Priest, no?*" he said.

"*Si, io sono,*" I replied, but I couldn't figure out how he knew.

"Signor Demir, he called," the man responded in halting English. But realizing my confusion, he continued.

"Signor Demir, he said an American man, this tall," as he held his hand up to his forehead, "and a beautiful woman," pointing to Alana.

I wanted to protest that there would probably be more couples with a beautiful woman involved, but I quickly decided that suggesting that Alana wasn't singularly attractive might not be the best strategy.

"*D'accordo,*" I said, "agreed," and we followed him to our table.

Or maybe I should say couch. From the murals on the walls, the thick draperies, the music, and the lighting, it quickly became apparent that the attraction for Eioli Osteria was in part due to its Etruscan ambiance. In their day, dining was normally conducted while reclining on one-armed couches, resting to the side with feet up and the body horizontal. Food was then, and is now at Eioli, served on low tables set close to the couches that surrounded them, so the diner could simply reach out with his or her hand and snatch some of what the platters offered without having to lean too far or even sit up.

To accommodate the guests, the waiter arrived to slide the table out and allow us to find our seat, then pushed it back in toward us. Since we initially sat with legs down, the attendants had trouble establishing the setting, so one of them signaled to me that we should swing our legs up onto the couch. Alana and I slipped out of our shoes, then followed his instruction. He smiled and then pushed the table closer.

The couches on our level, the uppermost behind the handrail, were arranged three in each grouping, in a C-shape, with the open end facing the center floor. We were seated opposite the rail, on the vertical member of the C, with both side couches unoccupied.

Water and wine were immediately brought to the table, followed nearly at the exact moment by Dr. Demir himself.

"Ah," he said with an expansive swing of arms, "I see you found it."

Before sitting, he called out to the waiter.

"*Gio, buona sera!*"

"*Buona sera, Professore. Come stai?*"

"*Bene, grazie,*" he said, clasping hands with a waiter with whom he obviously had a long association.

"We leave ourselves at your mercy," he added with a smile.

"*Perfetto,*" replied Gio, who then whisked away toward the kitchen.

He had already brought brass goblets for wine and some wooden cups for the water. Since Demir had already decided we would eat "native," I had no idea what was in store, but when Gio returned, I at least got a glimpse of the degree to which Eioli tried to replicate an actual Etruscan experience. The food trays were carved of a dark hardwood, as were the large flat plates we would use to collect our morsels of food. The handles of the utensils were also of carved wood, with the scoop of the spoon and the tines of the fork of shiny metal. Knives were not even offered since the food was already cut into mouthfuls. Some of the roasted fowl on the platter was well cooked and could be pulled off the bone with our fingers.

Alana sampled some of the wine and then smiled at Demir.

"I should have known that a man who spends so much time immersed in Etruscan culture would seek out a place like this," she said.

"It's a treasure," he responded. "Truly one of the few places in all of Tuscany that tries hard to be true to the ancient cuisine and atmosphere."

The meal was delicious, proceeding from long-baked root vegetables that had aromas of honey and rosemary, a dark, crusty bread from the wood-burning oven I could see beyond the dining area, and an egg dish that had been sweetened with raisins. There was braised beef and morsels of marinated lamb, wild boar that had a specific flavor of chestnut and oak charring that came from roasting over an open fire. A variety of cheeses, both hard and soft, was accompanied by bread pancakes to serve it on, and the scent of herbs, mint, honey, and pepper emanated from the collection of food on the table.

And Gio made sure that the wine never stopped coming.

"Well," Demir began, "you said you wanted to learn about the Etruscans. What better way than to begin with their food."

Alana and I were so absorbed by the myriad flavors that I had trouble turning my attention to the lesson at hand. I hid behind my desire to learn about the ancient people while trying to figure out if Demir's presence in the region was somehow connected to the Tarquinia dig.

And to Charlie's death.

"You are Turkish, of course," I began. "How did you develop your fascination with the Etruscan people?"

"You are American, of course," he replied with a smile. "How did you develop your fascination with the Etruscan people?"

Okay, touché, I suppose. But I decided I needed to answer in order to get him to reply.

"Got it. Well, they are a people who have fascinated history students for many centuries. Where they came from, did they emerge as an indigenous culture in Tuscany, what is their relationship to the Romans, and so on? So, as I said this afternoon, as an Italian American, I'm just curious."

I stared at Demir with a carefully modulated intensity, hoping that my short answer might inspire a reply from him.

"As you said, the Etruscans are a fascinating people," he replied finally. "They arose, they reigned, and then they disappeared."

Alana looked at me, but I stared back at Demir with a furrowed brow. It wasn't that I distrusted his rendition, but the three-part history was simultaneously way too simple and way too understated. I could only smile.

"This afternoon," he said after a sip of wine, "you said let's begin at the ending. Right?"

I nodded.

"So, the ending. Funny to start that way, but it's also easier, considering the ending—so to speak—is closer in time to now, and there are more records from the third century BCE—the Etruscans' ending—than the ninth century BCE—their beginning.

"The Etruscans began to recede from the record with the rise of the Roman Kingdom. Between 1000 BCE and about 800 BCE, some indigenous Latin tribes had founded settlements in what is now Rome. They built their communal and military structures on what would later become the Palatine Hill."

I knew the Palatine Hill as the ruins of the upper-class neighborhood of ancient Rome, so I concluded from his description that even the earliest people recognized it as a special location among the seven hills of Rome.

"The Roman Kingdom was established in 753 BCE and lasted until 509 BCE when the kingdom was replaced by the Roman Republic," he continued. "But what is of interest to us, here, now, is that two of the last Roman kings were Etruscan ..."

"Yes," I interjected, "Lucius Tarquinius Priscus and Lucius Tarquinius Superbus."

Demir tipped his wine goblet and offered a smile of approval.

"And was Superbus the son or grandson of Priscus?" he asked to test me.

I could only shrug my shoulders.

"Not sure, either," Demir said with a grin, but then he continued. "Anyway, these two Etruscans reigned from around 616 BCE—with an interruption between them—till 509 BCE. Do you note the date?"

At first, I didn't make the connection but then remembered that Demir described the Roman Kingdom ending in 509 BCE, yielding to the Roman Republic.

"Based on what we know," he added, "Superbus—an Etruscan like his forebear—was the last king of Rome during the Kingdom era. A war with the Rutini tribes, a sordid conspiracy against a leader's wife, and in-fighting among Superbus's army ultimately ended with him being expelled from the kingdom. There's far too much detail to cover during our meal; you'll have to study up on Superbus's life and exile on your own.

"Suffice to say that the Etruscan kings held sway in the

early Roman period up until the foundation of the Republic in 509, a governmental arrangement that took over from the Kingdom. From that, we can put a likely firm date at the middle point of the Etruscan period."

"Middle point?" Alana asked.

"Again, working backward as your friend here suggested, we know that the Etruscans were still in evidence in 509 but losing power and influence. They came from somewhere, and their cultural influence languished for a while after the start of the Republic. But their decline had begun."

He paused for effect.

"But where did they come from? It's easier to reach conclusions about historical events for which we have the most data. As we move the clock back centuries, from the end of the Etruscan reign and formation of the Roman Republic to the beginning of the emergence of the Etruscans, we have to look for signs.

"When was a reliable system of writing developed?" he asked me.

"A few thousand years ago?" I ventured.

"A bit more than that," Demir corrected.

"The Sumerian forms originated around 3000 BCE," Alana offered.

"Yes, nearly perfect," Demir commented. "About 3500 BCE, but writing in different forms arose independently in other places of the world. Although writing systems existed in what was then Italia before their appearance, evidence of an Etruscan record of writing arose around 700 BCE, coincident with their appearance in the early-Latin or Roman period. But that means we have little or no written record of their society in the time prior to the Etruscans' engagement with the proto-Roman people. And, worse, scholars have had trouble translating the Etruscan language."

"Isn't there something like the Rosetta Stone, a linguistic key?" I asked.

"No," Alana offered. "Tesa's mother would have known, and she specifically said such a codex had not been found."

Demir smiled.

"So, it is with a written record," he said, "that people like Tesa Richietta's mother would have been able to solve the mystery of the Etruscans' origin. But," and he paused again for dramatic effect, "without a written record, the solution must be unearthed by people like Tesa and her mentor, Dr. Charlie Dielman."

I had to smile at the choice of words, saying the solution would have to be unearthed by a physical anthropologist.

"We think that the Etruscans were not just the kings of Rome," Demir said, "but possibly also the ancestors of the Romans themselves."

"So, wait..." I begged for patience. I held up my hand despite having a morsel of wild pig clenched between my fingers. "You're suggesting that the Etruscans, well, to use the Biblical term, 'begat' the Romans?"

"Yes, I am. In fact, I think that might be fairly certain. Now, let's wind the clock farther back. Let's assume the Etruscans did evolve into the Romans. That makes them the original Romans, entitled to the historical credit for their people founding one of the world's greatest empires."

I nodded but wondered where he might be going.

"But who were the Etruscans?" he continued. "We still need to solve that."

Demir helped himself to more food, a hunk of the crusty bread on the platter, and another cup of wine.

"There were a people called the Villanovans, shown in the record to have occupied this part of Italy before the Etruscans appeared. We're not sure where they came from, but most of us agree that the Villanovans were indigenous to the region, at least farther back than we have been able to trace. But then the Etruscans arrived. From where?"

I helped myself to some fruit and figs from the platter but leaned back on my elbow to hear more from Demir.

"Tesa's mother and Charlie Dielman were trying to prove that," said Alana.

"Quite so," responded Demir.

"The specific question of origins was put to them," she continued. "The question of whether the Etruscans came from Lydia."

"Exactly. And what did they decide?"

"Dr. Dielman was still looking at the physical record," Alana said, "including connections and means of exchange, like coins. Olivia didn't believe there was a connection..." Alana said, but Demir waved his hand in the air.

"I don't want to dispute her record, but it is not a conclusion," he said.

"How so? How are a scientist's findings not a conclusion?" I asked.

"It's a theory, perhaps, but not a conclusion. Besides, I said I didn't want to dispute it, but I don't think it is conclusive."

Demir exhibited a bit of certainty that seemed to be prejudiced by his own preferred outcome. I nodded vaguely but let the comment hang in the air.

Then I realized that I had let the conversation veer away from the Etruscan people to one involving the archeological dig, Dielman, and Olivia. That may have allowed Demir to ascertain my hidden purpose—I hoped not.

Another pitcher of wine was delivered, along with more fruit and cheese. For a few moments, we remained quiet, considering what we had discussed and deciding where to go next. I wanted to know if Demir was involved with the findings at the dig, Hamza Yavuz's theft of the coin, or even Dielman's death. But I felt like we were too close to the threshold to risk bringing that up without turning Demir off.

On the other hand, it was worth a try.

"Oliva didn't believe there was a connection between the Etruscans and the Lydians," I said and held up my hand to abate Demir's objection. "Dr. Dielman thinks—thought—that a connection might be established on physical evidence."

Demir nodded.

"The discovery of some interactional tools like coins might establish a link," I offered.

"Interactional tools," Demir said with a smile. "Very studious of you. Perhaps I have underestimated your knowledge of the field of archeology, Mr. Priest."

"No, not really. But let me proceed. Perhaps the discovery of coins that appear to be linked to Lydia—found in Tuscany—might be sufficient to conclude a connection between the two peoples."

"Perhaps," he allowed but refrained from adding any detail.

So, I jumped in.

"Are you aware that a man named Hamza Yavuz was found with a *trite* in his pocket at the ferry port in Pescara?"

Demir was either completely unaware or did an impressive job of hiding it.

"Yavuz, you said?" he began. "Don't know him. And a *trite*? Why at Pescara? These are all things that I do not know."

"Yavuz is a digger who has worked at Tarquinia for about five years," Alana explained. "He disappeared about the time Dr. Dielman died in the pit and was apprehended at the port in Pescara with this *trite* in his pocket."

"Okay," Demir leaned forward. "I'm with you so far. But what does all this mean?"

His disavowals to the contrary, I had trouble accepting that Demir was innocent of any knowledge of this.

"If Yavuz took the *trite* from the dig where Dr. Dielman died," I offered, "and then escaped to the other coast of Italy—preparing to take a ferry to Croatia—it would suggest that he had something to do with the accident that resulted in Dielman's death."

"Or it suggests that he was a common thief," said Demir with a confident look. "A common thief who saw a shiny object and thought it was something that his child might like to have."

I was stunned by the clear parallel between what Demir said and what Yavuz claimed as an alibi. Could the two men have conspired to write this scenario? But I knew the jeopardy of yielding to hunches too early in an investigation. Despite my distrust of coincidences, I decided that it was wise to dismiss this one to simply a logical conclusion by Demir.

We continued with small talk while we finished the meal, and I asked Demir when he thought he would return to Turkey.

"Why do you think I live in Turkey?" he asked.

He should have expected that I knew something about him, or else why would I have sought him out? Oh, that's right, my ploy was that I was an amateur student of Etruscan history, which I had probably ruined by seeking so much information on *trites* and archeological digs.

"Well, your name is Turkish," offered Alana, trying to salvage my gaffe. "And you said you were only visiting Cerveteri."

"Yes," he said, looking up at her from his wine goblet under lowered eyelids, "but not from where."

I decided to risk a bit more.

"Do you work for the Turkish government, Dr. Demir?"

He didn't answer right away but gave me the same thoughtful glance he had given Alana after the last question.

"Yes, I work at the Ministry of Culture and Tourism. Why?"

"You don't know Hamza Yavuz, you said," I replied.

"No. I don't. Should I worry about this line of questioning?"

"No, sir," I said. "Yavuz works for a guy at your Ministry. Someone named Mehmet Arslan."

"Oh, yeah," Demir said with a slight guffaw. "Troublesome little brute."

"Sorry?" Alana said with a laugh.

"Arslan doesn't work at the Ministry. He's the nephew of the leader of the department. But," he continued with obvious disdain, "I stand by my assessment. He's a troublesome little brute."

"In what way?" I asked.

"Arslan is an unforgiving, extreme convert to the cause that we have been pursuing for many years."

"And that is?" asked Alana.

"To sustain our heritage, support the investment and documentation of it, and to pursue repatriation of Turkish art, technology, and artifacts if they can be shown to have originated with our people. Arslan is just a punk with a connection at the Ministry. He resorts to clandestine methods and, frankly, some illegal activities in support of the same agenda that we have embraced peaceably and legally.

"Wait," he continued. "You said this Yavuz guy works for Arslan?"

"Yes," I replied.

"Well, then, I would steer clear of him. And you said he was found with a *trite*?"

Suddenly, it seemed Demir was impressively informed

about the matters that he seemed only moments ago to be unbriefed on.

"Yes," Alana responded, showing her own doubt.

"Hmmm," was all Demir would offer.

I had to admit, he seemed genuine on one level and thoughtful in the professional way of an expert. But I wondered how close he could be to both Yavuz and Arslan and yet be far enough away to be innocent.

## LOBBY BAR, ALBERGO DEI FIORI

IT WAS DARK BY THE TIME WE DROVE BACK INTO Civitavecchia and the hotel. Alana and I had talked intensely throughout the drive, picking apart what Demir had said and trying to decipher his involvement or knowledge of what was going on.

We arrived at Albergo dei Fiori around ten o'clock and went to the lobby bar. Ten was an early hour for Italians, and we had adopted their schedule. Just as we expected, Tesa, Aggie, and a few of the team were gathered there sharing cocktails before going to bed.

"Hey, there you are," saluted Aggie with a glass in his hand. I remembered from our earlier life at the Tall Cedars commune that he wasn't one for wine or a cocktail. He held aloft a frosted glass of beer.

"Did you find Demir?"

"Yep, sure did. Had dinner tonight."

"Have you ever been to Eioli Osteria?" Alana asked the room. A couple of favorable comments arose, but Aggie and Tesa said no.

"It's pretty amazing," she continued. "True Etruscan. Food, ambiance, wall paintings, music. Everything!"

"Sounds great," Aggie said while throwing a glance Tesa's way. "Maybe we should look into it?"

"What did you think?" Tesa asked. "Of Demir, I mean, not the restaurant."

"He's very interesting ..." I began.

"And slightly mischievous," Alana added.

Tesa smiled.

"Okay, let's start with mischievous," Tesa replied, "Sounds more fun."

"He's a flirt," Alana said, "but an old flirt. What is he, in his seventies?"

"Yes, I think so."

"But he's also kind of attractive," Alana admitted. "Nicely trimmed salt-and-pepper beard. Thick wavy hair, strong jaw ..."

"Hey," I interrupted, "were you paying any attention to what he was saying?"

"Of course. I think so," Alana added with a little chuckle and a smile at Tesa.

"Okay, here's where we get to the 'interesting' part," Aggie said, leaning forward.

"You know him, right, Tesa?" I asked.

"Somewhat. I've met him, and I've read about his work. He's with the Turkish government. With their Ministry of Culture. I've also read some of his articles about the Etruscans. Part of my work."

"So," Aggie interjected, "you talked about Etruscans. But also the Lydians and their money, the *stater*?"

"Yeah," I nodded, "we did. He also took us on a tour of Turkish history and how the Lydians might have seeded the Etruscan culture ..."

"He actually used the word 'begat,'" Alana said with a smile.

"Right. Begat," I continued. "Anyway, he talked about how the Lydians might have ... begat ... the Etruscans, who probably mixed with the Villanovans, from whom the Romans arose."

"Sounds like a genealogy chart," Aggie opined.

"Yeah, it does," I replied. "His theory is that, tracing backward, the Roman empire owed its roots to the Etruscans around 500 BCE, who emerged from the merger of the Lydians and the Villanovans between 700 and 600 BCE."

"And he speculated that the Lydians who, obviously, came from Anatolia-slash-Turkey," Alana continued, "mixed with but ultimately dominated the Villanovans here, in central Italy. Tuscany. To form the ancestral line that we now call Etruscans."

"Wait," I said, looking at Alana. "When did he say all that?"

"Near the end of the meal, in chit-chat. While you were looking at the toga-clad waitress at the other couch."

Ouch.

"Anyway, Demir's premise is that the Lydians begat the Etruscans who begat the Romans," I said.

"Making the Lydians or, shall we say, the Turkish people, the ancient progenitors of the Roman Empire," said Aggie.'

We sat quietly for a moment, each of us pondering the reach of the 1983 Turkish law about repatriation of art and culture that could reliably be tied to Turkish/Anatolian/Lydian ancestry.

"What about Hamza Yavuz?" Aggie asked. "Does he know him?"

"No," I replied, "but he knows Mehmet Arslan."

"He called him a 'troublesome little brute,'" Alana responded with a laugh.

"And we told him that Yavuz works for Arslan, which he seemed—or pretended—not to know," I added. "But Demir did suggest that if Yavuz works for Arslan, we should steer clear of him."

"Did you tell him that Yavuz had stolen the *stater* and was on his way to Croatia?" Aggie asked.

"*Trite*, not *stater*," Tesa corrected. "There are *trites*, one-third *stater*, in circulation. *Staters* are essentially impossible to find."

Alana stared at Tesa for two beats, and I could tell that her investigator's brain was spinning furiously.

"What would be the difference?" she asked Tesa.

"What difference?"

"The difference between Charlie finding a *trite* versus a *stater*?"

"If Charlie found a *trite,* it would be considered just another find in an old site. Evidence of some commercial connection between the local tribes and the Lydians."

"And if it was a *stater*?"

"I can't overstate the importance of the coin being a *stater*," she replied. "It's a larger coin, as is obvious, than the *trite*. But more importantly, *staters* had more market value than *trites*. Remember the difference between market value and face value? With so much electrum in the *stater*, it would be melted down by the locals as having more value in bulk on the open market than a stamped coin. *Trites* might have been preserved for barter, but *staters* were more likely to have been taken to the forge to be reduced to lumps of tradeable metal."

"Again," Alana pressed, "what if Yavuz's coin is a *stater*?"

"It would mean that the people of this region would have preserved this unit of coinage under the authority of the local rulers," said Tesa. "It wouldn't be melted down because it would represent the exchange protocol for the sovereignty—

and canceling the face value of the coin by melting it down would be an affront to the ruler, the king. But it isn't a *stater*. It's a *trite*. So, just another artifact from a dig."

"But you haven't seen the coin," I asked.

"No, but the description we got fits the *trite*, not the *stater*. One image on the coin; a lion's head. Punch marks on the reverse. We asked the police if we could have it, but they were holding it as evidence."

"Maybe we should get a look at it tomorrow," Aggie suggested, to which Tesa nodded.

# WEST COAST OF ITALIA

## 610 BCE

AFTER EMERGING FROM THE TURBULENT WATERS OF THE strait, Tyrrhenus's fleet slowed to a more leisurely pace. They still had their sites on the coast of Italia, but the strenuous work the oarsmen put in passing between Zancle and Regia had taken its toll, and the leader wanted to reward his crew with some rest.

Tyrrhenus stood upon the raised berth at the bow of his lead boat and surveyed the fleet that followed close behind. Each had battled the waters of the strait and survived the challenge, and the five vessels drew close together to regroup and plan the next part of the voyage.

"You want us to continue to the north," Lutus said, more of an announcement than a question. Although Tyrrhenus was the leader of the fleet and the captain of this particular ship, Lutus was the helmsman and second in command.

"Yes, I do," Tyrrhenus replied. "But we should tarry here for some time. Let the men have something to eat and regain their strength."

Lutus nodded at that, directed the rowers to stow the oars and resettle themselves for food and wine. Waving to the ships *that were slowly congregating behind this lead vessel, Lutus communicated the same "rest time" command to the others. He saw the oars being stowed and the men rearranging themselves on the decks of the other boats, confirmation that his command had been understood.*

*Tyrrhenus was well respected by this group of a hundred or so people, both men and women. He had been careful to select the men from those he knew and had worked with, confident that he could count on their effort and endurance. He let the men choose the women to bring along, either their wives or their lovers. The king's son knew that this would be appreciated by the people on his excursion and heighten the chances of their success.*

*"Where will we put in to port?" Xenus asked Tyrrhenus. "Will it be Ostia?"*

*Tyrrhenus was still considering the sail up the coastline of the peninsula and where would be best for his new plan. Xenus was impetuous, a characteristic that made the king's son consider the wise man unwise. Patience and deep thought were virtues, thought Tyrrhenus. Bringing Xenus into his father's court had not seemed like a wise idea, but he had to live with it.*

*Now, thanks to Ardys's commandments, he also had to live with Xenus in the new land.*

*"We trade with the people of Ostia," he began, turning toward Xenus and addressing him in an undisguised condescending way of teaching the gray-haired man. "But they guard their own villages. Probably," Tyrrhenus paused for emphasis, "they wouldn't appreciate having merchants from around the Great Sea taking their land."*

*Xenus stepped back from the criticism but stared boldly back at the leader of the expedition.*

*"I have not been on one of your merchant voyages, that is true," he said with power in his voice, "but your father brought*

me into his court because he respected my judgment. With respect, I intend to fulfill that role—and your father's confidence —on this business also."

Tyrrhenus had not had much use for the advisor at home and doubted his usefulness on this trip, but he was mildly surprised by Xenus's pushback. He smiled in an offhand appreciation for the man's courage, then turned his attention back to the waters that stood between his fleet and the land to the north.

"There is a place just north of Ostia," Tyrrhenus said to Xenus. "It is a small collection of villages called Alsium. They are called Pelasgians, and it seems they are from Greece. I have encountered many Greek peoples around the Great Sea, but they have mostly settled on the eastern edge of Italia, and some to Sikania. Those who went to Alsium are the only ones who moved so far from their islands and settled on this western side of Italia."

"Are we going there?" asked Lutus.

"Yes, we are. These Pelasgians may be Greek by origin, but they are far from their homeland. Like us. They might not argue with us about seeking land."

While they considered the landing spot, the sun had begun to sink toward the horizon to the west. Lutus suggested that they start to move on or else put the oars away and linger in the seas until the morning.

"Put five men on each side," said Tyrrhenus. "They have only to pull the oars easily. And only to maintain position. Let another five replace them after a few hours. Just slow progress rather than anchoring here. I don't want to tarry in the sea and become the victim of monsters or pirates."

"We will take a heading toward Alsium," he continued, "plow slowly toward it, and let the remainder of the crew rest. And we'll resume full rowing when the sun shows itself once again."

"Yes, sire," responded Lutus, and he sent the order down to the men. By then, the other four boats had pulled alongside Tyrrhenus's craft, so Lutus communicated the plan to them also.

————

Sea monsters and pirates aside, the way to avoid sea sickness was to keep the craft moving. Even a slow forward motion helped to keep the stomachs of the passengers calm, and Tyrrhenus knew that he would rather have some slow advance than wake in the morning with some of his passengers vomiting over the sides of the vessel.

At morning's first light, Tyrrhenus stirred from his sleep nest, pulled back the fur covering that he slept under, and stood to survey the sea around him. He looked left and right, then spotted Xenus standing aloft on the bow of the boat. Rather than be disturbed that the advisor would occupy his own spot, Tyrrhenus smiled in seeing that Xenus had risen before him.

"I might make a seaman of him yet," he mused.

Tyrrhenus stepped lightly across the deck to avoid waking the others. It was too early to resume the voyage, and the men needed their rest—even the ones nestled in the embrace of their wives.

"Xenus," he said, approaching the man. "How goes your morning?"

"It is good, sire."

Tyrrhenus noted that this was the first time that Xenus had addressed him as sire, heretofore reserving that salutation for the king.

He stepped up beside Xenus to survey their surroundings, and he could hear the soft rumble of sailors rising and moving about the deck. Their food was simple on these journeys, none cooked, and even the salted fish and pork was eaten cold. The men who had sailed with Tyrrhenus before knew this and were thankful just to have something in their stomachs. Those without the experience—like Xenus and the wives aboard—were a bit more untrusting of the victuals served by Instius, a man who doubled as a part-time oarsman and part-time food-storer.

The last rotation of oarsmen was given their leave, and they settled into the narrow space between the rows of oars to be the first to be served. So as not to lose momentum, another set of men were seated in their place and began to pull on the oars to keep the boats moving forward, even if at a leisurely pace.

"How is your morning, sire?" asked Lutus, approaching Tyrrhenus.

"It is good. And yours? Did you sleep?"

"Yes, sire, but it is not my job to sleep. I want to assure you that I woke with each interval and made sure the rowers traded places."

Tyrrhenus smiled back at him, and Xenus began to admire the relationship between these two men.

"It is also your job to survive, Lutus. Get something to eat, and once we set off for Alsium, I want you to go below and sleep."

"Yes, sire. Thank you, sire."

These boats' belowdecks were shallow, and the men and passengers mostly slept and ate on deck. The hold was reserved for cargo and had a head clearance too low to make much room for people. However, it was also quieter there, and Tyrrhenus knew that Lutus needed a period of undisturbed sleep if he was to recover in time to manage the rest of the journey.

Before he retired to the hold, the helmsman turned the responsibility for the ship's direction over to Instius, whose duties as food bearer were completed. Then he slipped through the broad opening in the center of the deck and into the moist darkness below.

The other four boats followed the observed movements of Tyrrhenus's ship and did not need any verbal commands. The ship's captain on each had traveled many seas before and knew Tyrrhenus's methods of sail. They merely had to remain close and watch the activities on board his ship to follow suit.

"How long before we reach Alsium?" asked Xenus. Then, realizing that his question might indicate impatience, he amended it.

"Excuse me, sire. I only meant to be curious. And to learn from you."

Tyrrhenus smiled and reminded himself of his earlier thought about turning Xenus into a true sailor.

"Yes, I understand, Xenus. We will row today and take advantage of friendly winds," he noted, with a sweeping gesture to the sky to indicate the heavenly bounty of winds. "By tomorrow, late, we should be passing Ostia."

"Thank you."

"We will sail close to the land, keeping it in sight all the way because the seas are more manageable there, rather than out on the waters. That means, though, that the Ostians will see us sail by. Rather than raise suspicions by evading their port, we will put in there first. Make some trades before disembarking for the northern site of Alsium."

"Did we bring items to trade?" Xenus asked.

"Yes. Do you remember the cloth, leather, and women's ornaments that we packed before we left Phocaea?"

"Yes, I do. I wondered why we would be bringing them."

"These are our traditional trading things that we bring to the Ostians," Tyrrhenus said. "They will not be suspicious."

"And we brought coins, many staters, trites, and hektes," Xenus said, looking for an explanation.

"Yes, but those are not for the Ostians. From them, we will take grain, herbs, and pigs. It is my plan that we will prevent their suspicions by trading with them but take aboard exactly the things that we will need immediately upon arrival in Alsium."

Xenus smiled and looked at Tyrrhenus with admiration.

"Such planning. You made a note of each step before we left our home and made arrangements for every step of the way."

Tyrrhenus smiled and enjoyed the man's dawning understanding of how to manage a great migration.

"We will leave Ostia two days later, staying long enough to allay their suspicion, and set sail only when the winds favor a northward journey. We will be able to explain going that direction because of the winds, letting the Ostians think that we will circle around and return south when the winds favor that. But, instead, we will stay the course and arrive at Alsium in one day."

Xenus smiled again and nodded. He was learning much about sailing, surviving on the water, and avoiding threats from the sea and land. And he was also learning much about Tyrrhenus and why his father had chosen this particular son to lead the Lydian people to their new land.

## CASA DI RECLUSIONE

In the morning, Alana got a call from Rafaela, telling her that she would join us at the jail where Hamza Yavuz was being kept in Civitavecchia.

"How did you know we were going there?" she asked Rafaela.

"My dear friend," and I could hear Rafaela's smile coming through the earpiece of the phone. "Don't you know by now that I know everything that goes on?"

Alana laughed, but she turned to me with a wide-eyed expression of wonderment.

"Also, we're having Olivia d'Alantonio's remains exhumed today," Rafaela said.

"I have to leave around noon," Alana mentioned. "Unfortunately, I have to return to Vienna to work. But I'll be at the jail to see you first."

"*Perfetto!*" exclaimed the Roman inspector.

That done, we finished packing up Alana's things since I had already agreed to drive her straight to the Roma Termini railway station after seeing Yavuz. She had a wistful look in her eye as I dragged the suitcase off the bed.

"It's been a wonderful vacation, Darren. Villa Poesia was the finest place I've ever lodged. I could have stayed at the house on the cliff every hour of every day—it was so beautiful. And when I stepped out onto the terrazza with my coffee in the morning, the view of the Mediterranean thousands of feet below took my breath away."

I smiled at that and had my own struggle with the parting.

"When can we return?" she asked.

"Friday," I said with a smile. "I've already called Julietta at the villa."

"You did?"

"Yep. I thought we might be finished here in a few days, and I asked if the Villa Poesia was available for the weekend."

Alana's eyes went wide.

"And...?"

"It is. When you get to the train station, why don't you inquire about a return trip on Friday?"

She threw her arms around my neck and let out a satisfied sigh of pleasure. She worked very hard at her job, and I knew that some of her "clients" were dangerous and difficult to manage. Finding some way to reward her for her work—not to mention finding a way for us to spend more time together—seemed like a win-win.

We went down to the lobby and met up with Tesa and Aggie. They were in the breakfast room, enjoying the light of the rising sun coming through broad windows, and I could smell the roasted coffee beans as the espresso hissed and streamed from the nozzle at the sideboard.

"*Buon giorno*," said Alana. "Did you sleep well?"

"Yes," Tesa said, but a bit laconically.

"Are you okay?" I asked.

"Yes, sure. I am."

Aggie told us that they had been talking about her mother, Olivia, and how the thought of exhumation brought back difficult memories.

"Are you sure you want to have this done?" I asked. I was okay with Rafaela's hunch and didn't want to interfere in the local legal system, but this obviously bothered Tesa quite a bit.

"Yes, I am. I guess. It's just ..." and she let the comment fall away without completing it.

"She wants to know," Aggie filled in for her, "but the death was hard enough. We talked long into the night about whether she wanted to know that something evil had been lurking behind her mother when this thing happened."

I was not a cop, having spent much of my professional life in military intelligence and a variety of clandestine activities. Alana was closer to the police-public connection and had interviewed many victims of the crimes she investigated. She also displayed her womanly compassion as she reached across the table to lay her hand on Tesa's forearm.

"You don't have to do it," she said, "of course. But Rafaela is very good and very smart. Perhaps, if she thinks something does not seem quite right, we should follow her lead. If the tests show nothing, you can have another period of mourning, and we will be there with you. But if the tests identify a clue as to the origins of her death—not just the *idiopathic* conclusion—you will know more."

Tesa nodded and sipped her cappuccino slowly.

Alana and I still had not had any food or coffee, so we helped ourselves to the rolls and fruit on the sideboard, then told the woman in the apron that we'd like coffee, me a double espresso and Alana a cappuccino.

"You know," Alana began as we sat down, "that I have to catch a train home this afternoon."

Tesa nodded.

"I'm staying," I added, "in fact, I have an appointment with ... uh, what is his name?" I checked my memory and pulled out my notebook.

"Ah, here. Daniel Thomas Corwin, right? In Rome, the coin collector."

"Yeah," Aggie replied. "At Croesus Gold."

"Okay, got it. Can you tell me more about him and about this Croesus guy?"

"Corwin is Australian, a well-known coin collector," Tesa said. "Especially with ancient European coins. I don't know him well, but I understand he's a bit of a cut-throat, too."

"In what way?"

"Well, the market for ancient coins has quite a range," she continued. "Focusing on ancient European coins reduces the scale of his field a bit, but since coins have been struck for two and a half millennia, even those still circulating from BCE times provide ample opportunity for haggling and trading."

"From BCE," Alana interjected. "So does Corwin look mainly for those that were minted ... or struck, I guess I should say ... before Christ?"

"Yes," Tesa replied, "but we say BCE. BC and AD are religiously oriented time-stamping, using the life of Jesus as the dividing line. BC is obvious—"before Christ"—but even AD has a clearly religion-centered meaning, *Anno Domini,* the year of our Lord. Scientists have adopted BCE and CE as references, although they still split at the same time, the Christian notion of Year 0. It's *Before the Common Era* and *Common Era.*"

"So," I said, "back to Corwin. His collection is all, or mostly, BCE?"

"Mostly," Tesa offered. "And as I said, there are many European coins to include. Although it is commonly accepted that the Lydian coins are the oldest. The first coins struck in the world."

"Even older than any from the Asia civilizations of antiquity?"

"Yes. There is some debate in numismatic circles but, not to slight the impressive technological accomplishments of the Asian people, it still looks like the Lydian coins were the first."

"When did they begin?" Alana asked.

"Begin? As in when was the first coin?" Tesa said, and Alana nodded.

"That's hard to say, and it's not my field of study. You would get more from Corwin, but it's probably somewhere from the mid-7$^{th}$ century BCE to the end of that century."

"So, from 650 to 600 BCE?" I asked for clarification.

"Yes. Again, you should ask Corwin."

"That helps to explain his fascination with Croesus," added Alana.

"Yes, in a way. But some of his peers think that his ruthless approach to the business and his avid interest in riches means he is trying to achieve the status of Croesus. You know, 'as rich as Croesus.'"

"I guess I'll find out more about him this afternoon," I said.

We finished our breakfast and headed to our cars. Again, I reminded the others that we would take two vehicles since I was driving Alana to the Rome train station. Aggie said he and Tesa would return to the dig after seeing Yavuz.

———

It was a short drive across Civitavecchia to the *Casa di Reclusione*. Rafaela was standing beside her car when we approached and waved.

"I thought it best to go in together," she said. "I don't want the desk officer to question your reasons for coming here. I can handle that."

Then, turning to Tesa, she made eye contact for an important discussion.

"Tesa, as you know, we're exhuming your mother's remains today. Do you want to be there?"

"No," came the reply, as Tesa looked meekly down at her feet.

"That's fine. I understand. We will have the tests conducted as soon as possible and then tell you what we've found, if anything."

Rafaela then turned without ceremony to the entrance of the building and strode through the front door as if she owned the place. Approaching the desk, I saw that there was a new officer on duty, which I should have expected. I appreciated that Rafaela had anticipated this as she approached the man.

"*Io sono Rafaela Indolfo, ispettore della Polizia di Stato, Roma,*" she said with a commanding presence.

"*Sì, la aspettavamo,*" was the reply. "We were expecting you."

"*Vuoi vedere Signor Yavuz?*"

"*Sì, e questa gente,*" she added, turning to point to us. "*Sono i suoi colleghi.*" "They are his co-workers."

"*Va bene,*" said the officer as he rose to guide us back into the building.

Yavuz was in the same cell, still dressed in his civilian clothes—the work t-shirt and cargo pants that he wore at the dig. He was lying on the cot when we entered but rose and sat on the edge of the bed. The desk officer exited the room and left us alone once again with the suspect. I supposed that wouldn't have been possible had Rafaela not been a State police officer, but I knew that jurisdictional turf battles in the

U.S. would have argued for keeping the officer responsible for the prisoner in the room with us.

"What is it?" Yavuz said with an undisguised insolence. Whatever timidity he had demonstrated on our previous visit was gone now, and he was in fight mode.

"We have a few more questions," Rafaela said, "and we want to get a look at the coin."

Yavuz made an odd and sudden movement, a minor sweep of his hand, that caught my attention. It was only a second, but the motion made me wonder why he reacted that way to Rafaela's comment. She paused briefly, and I think she caught the same movement. I looked at Alana, the other one with trained eyes, and I could see her studying Yavuz.

Rafaela took us back to the questioning.

"We know you took the coin, the *trite*. You admitted taking it. You said it was for your child. Why did you say it was for your daughter? As I said, you have only two sons."

It was such an obvious mistake, a gaffe in his alibi, that I tried to decide whether it had any basis in the investigation.

Rafaela considered her notes again.

"Your sons. They are ages twenty-one and twenty-two. Do they live at home with you and your wife?"

Yavuz remained silent.

"Signor Yavuz, please answer my question."

"No," he said reluctantly. "Well, yes, they do. They live with their mother."

Rafaela studied him and consulted her notebook. Yavuz began rubbing his hands together.

"You said on your papers entering Italy that you live in Šibenik, Croatia. But your passport registration says that you live in Polatli, near Ankara, in Turkey. Which is it, Signor Yavuz? Do you live with your wife and two sons in Polatli, or do you live in Šibenik?"

Tiny beads of sweat appeared in Yavuz's forehead, and his knuckles were becoming white from the rubbing.

"I live in Šibenik. With my wife and my daughter."

"Which wife is that, Signor Yavuz? I thought you lived with your wife and two sons in Polatli."

"My wife is in Polatli."

"You just said you live with your wife in Šibenik. Are both of these women married to you?"

"No. My wife, she is with my sons. I am married to her."

"Does your wife," Rafaela asked with emphasis on 'wife,' "in Šibenik, who has a daughter by you, know that you are already married to a woman in Turkey?"

Yavuz stared at the floor and didn't answer.

"Help me understand what this relates to," Tesa asked.

"Just a matter of truthfulness," Rafaela replied. "And how much we can believe what Signor Yavuz tells us."

"The coin that you say you stole from the archeological dig," the inquisitor continued. "We've asked to see it. Do you know what it is?"

Yavuz nodded, then said, "Yes, it's some kind of coin from the Etruscans."

"Or the Lydians, isn't that right?" asked Rafaela.

Yavuz shrugged.

"I don't know coins. I'm just a digger."

"A digger who works in an archeological dig in Tuscany but also draws a salary from the Turkish government. Isn't that true?"

The prisoner let out a sigh.

There was a knock on the door to the cell, and as it swung open, Rafaela kept her eyes fixed on Yavuz.

"We asked to see the coin that you were carrying so that Dr. Richietta could examine it."

A uniformed man entered the cell and handed a shiny coin over to Rafaela, who glanced at it but transferred it to Tesa.

"I'm not an expert in coinage," Tesa said, "but from what I know, this is certainly a Lydian coin. A *trite*, a third-*stater*."

She handed it to Alana, and we inspected it, with Aggie looking over my shoulder. I had never seen any of these coins but had done a little research online the last few days. It looked like any other gold coin to me, but it had markings similar to those I had seen on the internet.

"Yes, it's a *trite*," concluded Tesa after a little more inspection. As she said that, Yavuz once again swept his hand past his right leg in a motion similar to what I had seen earlier in this encounter.

Rafaela waved for the police officer to come over, and she said something *sotto voce* to him.

"Stand up," the officer told Yavuz, who followed his command with hesitation.

The officer told the prisoner to hold his arms out away from his sides and prepare to be searched. I'm sure he was searched when he was first brought to the jail, but he did still have his own clothes on.

During the pat-down, Rafaela signaled to the officer to pay closer attention to the lining of the cargo shorts, especially the folded hem at the bottom of the legs. He did so, squeezing the fabric between his thumb and forefinger and running his two digits all the way around the bottom of the pant legs. His hands suddenly stopped at a point on the outside of the right pant leg, squeezed again, and then looked up at Rafaela.

"*C'è qualcosa qui*," he said. I didn't need a translation to know that he found something.

Rafaela told the officer to find out what was there, just as Aggie came forward with a pocketknife. The officer was a bit taken aback seeing a weapon, even one with such a short blade, displayed here in the prison, but Aggie just handed it to him. He extracted the blade and stuck the point into the thick fabric of the cargo pants, just above the spot where he thought he had found something.

Squeezing his fingers once again and guiding them toward the slit that he had created, we saw another gold coin appear. Yavuz simply stared out into space with a resolute look.

The officer handed the coin to Rafaela, who immediately handed it to Tesa. It was easy to see even without putting the two coins side by side that this new one was larger, and the imprint was more detailed. Both coins had an image of a lion's head on one side facing the right side of the coin, with punch marks on the reverse. But the larger coin also had an image of a bull's head facing the lion.

"Oh, my God," said Tesa. "This is a *stater*."

Rafaela retrieved the coin, inspected it for a second, then handed it and the *trite* to the guard.

"*Tiene quest'uomo con l'accusa di omicidio*," she said to the guard. "Hold this man on murder charges." She turned promptly and headed for the door to the cell while we followed.

When we reached the front desk in the prison building, she told the desk clerk that she wanted to speak to the officer of the day. When a tall man with bushy black hair appeared at the doorway, Rafaela introduced herself, presented her credentials, and repeated that she wanted Yavuz held pending a murder charge. Furthermore, she wanted his room at the hotel, Albergo dei Fiori, sealed for search.

"*Non permettere a nessuno di entrare nella stanza*" she said with utmost urgency. "Allow no one to enter the hotel room!"

# ROUTE SS1 TO ROME

ALANA WAS AS TALKATIVE AS I COULD EVER REMEMBER her on the road to Rome. It made me smile; a sweet reminder of the incurably curious person who I had met in Vienna last year and the woman I had fallen in ... wait ... was I really about to say I'd fallen in love with her?

"This is incredible! Can you imagine this? We held a coin in our hands that was more than 2,600 years old! Possibly the first coin ever made in the world! I can't get over it! This is amazing!"

The exclamation marks leaped out in her voice as she spoke.

"Yeah, I have to admit, I'm not easily impressed," I said, "but holding that *stater* was a real thrill."

"What are we going to do next?" she asked.

The road rolled by in typical Italian fashion. SS1 to Rome was a highway that, much like other highways in Italy, seemed more like a long, straight raceway. The cars zoomed and passed at speeds that would frighten even a teenage hotrodder in America. The dashed yellow and white lines meant to demarcate the lanes flew by in a blur, serving more to test the nerve of the lane-changing drivers than to conduct the myriad cars through safely. I had become used to driving in the country, so I had no problem managing the frenetic pace. And I decided that it was good that Alana had something to occupy her mind, so she wouldn't notice the speed of our own car.

"I said, what are we going to do next?" she repeated.

"Well, we're going to Rome, and you're taking a train to Vienna. And to your daughter, Kia."

Alana smiled.

"Oh, yeah. Kia. I can't wait to hold her in my arms."

"Originally, you were joining me for a brief vacation at the Villa Poesia and would have returned to her rested and relaxed."

"Yeah, but then this stuff with Tarquinia came up. And the coins!" she exclaimed.

I laughed.

"Kia will still be there, anxious to see her mom. But instead of being rested and relaxed, I think you'll be all abuzz."

"I can't wait to tell her about the coin."

"Maybe it's better to leave that out of the conversation for now. Let's see what develops this week, get the results of the exhumation back, and then you can fill her in. After all, the coin's been around for thousands of years. The story can probably wait another few days."

Alana nodded in assent.

I considered whether to suggest that Alana bring her daughter with her on our return to Villa Poesia but hadn't crossed that bridge yet about us sleeping together in Kia's company. I decided it was best to put the thought away for now.

"Still, the coin. Really!" Alana said as the excitement returned to her cheeks.

I paused a moment and then turned my head slightly in her direction.

"What about the murder charge? You're a police investigator; have you nothing to say about that?"

"Absolutely, but we pursue murder charges fairly routinely, even in a peaceful city like Vienna. But I have never held a coin that is so old!"

———

The train station at Roma Termini was the busiest in the city, handling thousands of local travelers as well as an equal or greater number of tourists on any given day. "Termini" indicates that it was the end of the line for those tracks, so trains came into the station at the *binarii*, that is, the platforms, and departed in the opposite direction. That created an additional logistical complication since the tracks leading into the station had to accommodate train traffic in both directions. Italy had been the butt of jokes for a century about the untimeliness of its trains; in fact, all over the country, especially here in Rome, arrivals and departures were managed with clockwork precision to overcome all those complications.

We arrived at the station about thirty minutes before Alana's train was set to depart. Ordinarily, that would sound like enough time to sit for a coffee or two at the café in the station. But with trains coming and going and platforms being used and reused, her train was not in the station yet. It was probably being held to a slower pace to time its arrival for after the departure of some earlier train using the same platform. The result was usually that when a train's arrival was announced, there would be only a few minutes to get to the assigned car, and a dash by the dozens or hundreds of passengers would ensue and reach its climax all within about seven to eight minutes before the wheels turned once again in the opposite direction.

So, resting in a café with a cup of coffee was not in the offing. We stood just outside the security barrier at first, but when her train was getting closer to arrival, we were allowed to show her ticket and pass through the portals that allowed entrance to the *binarii* and proximity to the near-term train arrival.

"I hate leaving," she said, looking at me.

I could detect a sadness that I hadn't expected. A year ago, when we met, I was a suspect, and Alana was the police officer investigating me. At least until she decided that I was likely innocent. We were able to lower the official barrier between us, but still, our personal connection was only budding. Later trips to Vienna allowed me to spend more time with her and Kia, and we became very close.

Did I think the word "love" earlier?

But this trip sealed it for us. Alana was able to get a week off work and, more importantly, she was able to have Kia spend the time with her grandmother and grandfather in Hallstatt, Austria, about three hours from the city. At this point in our relationship, I had never visited their home, but I knew from speaking to friends that it was a young child's heaven. Nestled between the foothills of the Dachstein and the placid waters of the Hallstätter lake, it was a quaint and welcoming village.

So, we got to enjoy each other's company at Villa Poesia and explore the Amalfi Coast without worrying whether Kia was enjoying her time away from her mother.

"I hope she misses me," Alana mused as she waited for the train.

The departure sign indicated that her train would arrive on *Binario 12,* so we moved closer to that platform. The huffing of the massive engine as it pulled slowly into port was both

welcome—as a signal that it was time to begin her trip home—
and depressing as it meant that we would be pulled apart.

"It's only for a few days," I said. "Remember to check the
return trains when you get to Vienna."

Alana wrapped her arms around my neck, delivered a
longing kiss to my lips that ensured that I wouldn't forget her,
and spun around to board the train that had now arrived safely.
I watched her trek down a few cars to the First-Class cabin,
noting that she didn't look back. She didn't like to do that, she
told me many months ago, so I wasn't surprised, nor hurt.

# CROESUS GOLD

AFTER DROPPING ALANA OFF AT THE TRAIN STATION, I retrieved the car and checked the map and navigator to find how to get to Croesus Gold. Since the preliminary arrangement had been to keep the car for three days, I decided it wise to alert Hertz that I would need it longer. The agent at the rental office spoke only a modest amount of English, but my rudimentary knowledge of the Italian language was enough to get us through.

The neighborhoods of Rome were, on the one hand, neatly organized and separated. There was the Trastevere, the area around the Via Veneto, the line that connected the Palazzo Vecchio and the Forum, the tourist-and-local collection that embraced the Pantheon, and the broad assortment of streets that all bent toward the Fontana di Trevi. On the other hand, Rome's streets could be mind-bending and ultimately frustrating. While trying to get to Croesus Gold, I recalled from past visits how I had to drive backward down some one-way streets to get where I wanted to go, or to abandon a double-parked rental car to dash into a hotel, asking *"Dove sono?"*—Where am I?

I finally made it to the coin shop, having driven past it three times before deciphering the best and only way to park the car. Signs written in Italian were no problem for me; it was the unwritten and unposted customs that made me worry that the car might not remain where I left it.

I also knew that I should make tight circles around the streets and neighborhoods rather than risk getting too far from my target. Consecutive right turns were always easier than consecutive left turns, but either would have been preferable to alternately turning left then right or vice versa, until I lost my bearing and drifted too far from my intended destination.

On the third pass by Croesus Gold, a little Fiat 500 darted out from the curb and cut me off. It was fortunate, though, since it not only opened a space but made me slam on the brakes so as not to miss it. I saw that the space was only about as big as that little car, and my rental was several inches longer, but I dismissed any doubts and decided to pull in. I know a little about Roman drivers, and I knew that I had to keep the car astride the empty space until the traffic behind me had gone around. If I pulled forward in the typical American way of marshaling a parallel parking maneuver in reverse, some brave Roman would slip head-first into the space, and I would be left with nothing.

Once the other cars had cleared, I drove quickly alongside the car at the top of the empty space, threw the gearbox into reverse, and zoomed backward at a swerving angle before anyone could take advantage of my vulnerability.

Success! I got in just before another host of cars careened up behind me.

The entrance to Croesus Gold was more subtle than I had expected. Anyone who named his establishment after a historical figure might be expected to etch the iconic name above the door in large letters. In this case, probably gold letters. But "Croesus Gold" appeared in relatively unassuming white script that stretched across the satin black background of the sign.

I pushed on the large, curved brass handle to swing the door inward, and a subtle bell jingled above my head, alerting the owner in the back office that someone had come in. In the brief several seconds before his appearance, I glanced about the store and its glass counters. Some paintings hung from the walls, not the merchandise on offer at this shop but elegant adornments, nevertheless. Lights hung inside the glass cases that surrounded the room and were turned relatively low, relying on the soft whitish-yellow light of the incandescent bulbs to illuminate the coins displayed below them.

The carpeted floor quieted the footsteps that would have alerted me to the owner's approach. A young man soon swept through the parted drapes in the inner doorway and stepped forward with his hand extended. Smiling, he introduced himself as Daniel Thomas Corwin, proprietor. His soft Australian accent was soothing, and I took it to be a practiced persona to reinforce the presumed refinement of his chosen profession.

"Hello," I began. "I am Darren Priest. Thank you for agreeing to meet with me."

"Yes, certainly," he said. "Welcome to Croesus Gold. I believe you are here to learn more about ancient coins, no?"

"Yes, I am, but not to buy," I said almost apologetically.

"Pity," Corwin said with a wry smile, "but that's quite alright. I am happy to enlighten anyone with an interest. Who knows? If you're bitten by the same bug that got me, you may find yourself trading some of your own coins for some of mine one day."

I smiled back at his reference to trading.

"Please," Corwin said, waving his hand at a little bistro table and two chairs that occupied a prime location by the window at the front of his shop. "Let's sit and talk."

His motions, phrasing, and gestures would have made me think of someone in his sixties, anxious to talk about the subject that had occupied him in the many decades since his youth. But Corwin was clearly much younger; I estimated that he was mid-thirties, despite a demeanor based on a wealth of numismatic knowledge that he brought to the vast collection of coins that he held here.

"Where would you like to begin?" he asked.

I didn't want to give him too much of my own bio but knew that a sense of who I was and why I was in Italy would be required to focus on the matters of greatest interest to me.

"I am here at the request of a friend ..." I began.

"Dr. Richietta," he interjected with some confidence. His foreknowledge of my association with the dig at Tarquinia took me aback. Apparently, Inspector Rafaela Indolfo wasn't the only one with access to everyone's actions.

"Well, no, as a matter of fact. Although Tesa did send me to you for information. A friend—someone whom I am quite sure you do not know—a mutual friend of mine and Dr. Dielman asked me to come."

"Ah, yes," Corwin said with a show of sympathy. "I didn't know Dr. Dielman, but I am familiar with his work."

"What was that work?" I asked. "What do you know of it?"

"Well, he is ... I'm sorry, was ... an expert in ancient communication, and he used archeological evidence to support several theories about the migration patterns of tribes over the last several millennia."

"What does that have to do with coins?" I asked.

"I don't know, Mr. Priest," he added. "Why were you sent to me?"

"Darren, please," I began. "I understand from Dr. Richietta that he—Dielman, that is—had found some coins at the dig near Tarquinia ..."

"I didn't know he was looking for coins," Corwin said.

"Well, it's not apparent that he was, but Tesa said that units of exchange, monetary units, would figure in Dielman's research."

"In ancient communication?"

"Yes," I continued. "Communication can be verbal or written, and our languages arise from these two forms. But communication can also involve trade and exchange. Especially in matters of culture."

"And you think that Dielman was looking for coins that might indicate exchange patterns among the Etruscans in Tarquinia?"

"Well, yes," I said, "but also between the Etruscans and others outside of Etruria."

"Would these non-Etruscans, the people you are referring to as 'outside of Etruria,' understand and respect the medium of exchange?" he asked. "Coins, if I may say?"

"Possibly, and that's where you come in. If the Etruscans were communicating with tribes outside of that region, they would have had to be able to translate the other's language, and if they were trading with others outside of that region, they would have had to, let's say, translate their units of exchange. Their money."

"Just like languages that are understood by a single tribe but must be translated to communicate with another tribe, so too must the medium of exchange," he said.

I nodded.

"The dig we're talking about," Corwin began, rubbing the knuckles of his right hand on his chin, "I thought it dates to about 600 BCE. Is that what you heard?"

"I think," I replied, "although any dig has the potential to uncover older layers beneath it."

"But the era that Dielman had reached was about then, about 600 BCE?"

"Yes."

"And he found coins?" Corwin asked, although the tone of his voice made me wonder how much he already knew.

"Yes."

"May I see them?" Corwin's obvious passion for coins made it difficult for him to avoid such a question.

"Well, no," I responded. "There's a complication. Although Dr. Dielman's notebook includes reference to a small cache of coins, we have only seen two of them."

"And these?"

I paused to consider how to continue.

"They are with the police in Civitavecchia."

"How so?" Corwin asked, slumping back in his chair.

"It seems that a person made off with them, but he was apprehended."

"Don't tell me Demir is involved with this!"

Corwin's sudden implication of Yusuf Demir made me wonder even more. Should Demir be considered an accessory to this? An accomplice of Hamza Yavuz? For that matter, should Corwin's spontaneous accusation make me suspect him also?

"No, not that I know of. I met with Dr. Demir yesterday …"

"And?"

Corwin was obviously anxious to find out how much Demir was involved. And, again, this increased my suspicion of him.

"He and I talked about the Etruscans, their history, and their origins. There may be some clues there, but I was mostly following up leads to satisfy my own curiosity about the Etruscan people.

"Uh-huh," mumbled Corwin.

He stared out the window, and I couldn't shake the feeling that he could be involved in the theft of the Lydian coins. I had been warned that he was greedy for coins and had stooped to work the black market in the past to enlarge his collection. He seemed to know more about my movements, Tesa, Dielman, and Demir than I would have expected.

Looking back at me, Corwin continued.

"If Dielman's notes were correct," Corwin speculated, "and I don't suppose he would have fabricated them, he wouldn't have simply reburied the find."

"No, which suggests that someone else found the coins and removed them."

"You mean more than just the two you have mentioned?"

I nodded.

"What are the coins that you have? Or, should I say, that the police have?"

I stared directly at him to gauge his intent, but I really didn't want to talk about the type of coins. He would know more than I did about their value, and I didn't want to stoke more interest from Corwin at this particular moment. On the other hand, his knowledge of both *trites* and *staters* would undoubtedly help understand the background and import of the theft. So, I took a chance.

"A *trite*," I said, then paused. "And a *stater*."

Corwin's eyes grew wide, but he caught himself and relaxed quickly. It was apparent that finding a *stater* had surprised him, even activated the greed gland that I could sense throughout this conversation.

"A *stater*," he said, passing over the other coin. "Those are very rare. What was its condition?"

"I'm not a coin collector, but the impressions on the face were very clear, neatly incised lines, and the heads of the lion and bull were not worn down."

There was a glow in Corwin's face that unmasked his excitement.

"And there are possibly many more coins, hiding somewhere," he said more to himself than to me. "Do you have his notebook? I'd like to read the notes to see what he found."

"Inspector Rafaela Indolfo, from the *Polizia di Stato*, has it. Tesa found the notebook, but once its presence became known, Indolfo insisted on taking it as evidence."

"Did you see or read it before it went into the possession of the police?" he asked.

"Yes, and in answer to your next question, the notes were quite descriptive. Dielman said there were twenty-one coins, some of gold and some of silver, with markings on the front and back."

Corwin sat forward in his chair with undisguised excitement.

"What markings?"

"His notes referred to the head of a lion and a bull."

"You said there were both gold and silver coins," Corwin added for confirmation.

"Yes." I noted that he dismissed the reference to lion and bull in favor of the distinction between the metals.

"What is the significance of gold and silver found together?" I asked.

Corwin sat back to weigh his thoughts, smiled at me for a brief second, then rose and retreated to the main glass case in the room. Stooping down behind the counter, he retrieved a wine bottle, corkscrew, and two glasses and returned to our table.

"You'll have to excuse me, Mr. Priest ..."

"Darren, please."

"Right, Darren. You'll have to excuse me for forgetting my manners. I normally offer a glass of wine when I intend to engage a customer in a conversation, and I quite forgot myself this afternoon."

He said this as he expertly cut the foil from the top of the bottle and pulled the cork. Pouring some wine into each glass, he raised his a bit in a gesture of respect, and we both took a sip. I recognized the label on the bottle, a noble wine from Piedmont, a Barolo, and decided that the conversation must have taken a bright turn for my host to have presented such a wine at this moment.

"So," he said, returning to the discussion, "Dielman described both gold and silver coins, twenty-one in all, with markings of a lion and bull."

"Yes. Although, as I said, we have only two coins in custody and do not know where the other nineteen are. Why are the markings significant?"

"Oh, I haven't decided that it is significant yet, Darren."

"No? Then why open a bottle of Pio Cesare Barolo?"

Corwin looked down at the table and smiled. In his excitement, he had done too little to hide his thoughts. Then he sighed and began again.

"The lion and bull were considered symbols of the Lydian kingdom ..."

"Lydian?" I asked. I was already informed of the background and not surprised by this but wanted to hear him explain it.

"I'll get to that in a moment," he said, holding his hand up to forestall my questions. "It is said that before the time of Croesus—he was the last king of Lydia—the coins that had been used by the kings before him were stamped from electrum."

My eyebrows raised so Corwin could tell that I, once more, wanted some clarification.

"Electrum is a naturally occurring alloy of gold and silver."

"Naturally occurring?" I asked. "Where?" I knew this, too, but preferred to play dumb and let Corwin carry on.

"Various places, but we are interested at this point in the River Pactolus. It's in Turkey. Pactolus was its name in ancient times, now the river is called Sart Çayi."

"Okay," I said when it was time for me to hold up my hand in surrender. "You're throwing a lot at me."

Corwin poured a little more wine then leaned forward at the table.

"Electrum in the Pactolus contained both gold and silver in ratios of about ten to one. It was turned into coins by the kings of Lydia, but it wasn't until the time of Croesus, about 560 to 550 BCE, that the Lydians learned to separate the two metals."

"Okay, if Dielman found gold and silver coins, they were minted ..."

"Struck," Corwin corrected. "Minting refers to a later process."

"Right, struck," I consented. "If they were struck in separated metals, they had to come from the time of Croesus, about the mid-6th Century BCE."

"Precisely," he said in a small triumph of reasoning. "The obverse ..."

"Wait. Obverse?" I asked.

"Sorry. You've got the reverse—of a coin, the back, let's say," he suggested, "so the obverse is the ..."

"Front."

"Yes, but coin experts call it the obverse," he said. "Anyway, if the obverse had the lion and the bull, these were most certainly Lydian coins, called *staters* and *trites*, depending on their size. Until I see them, I can't tell whether they are from the time of Ardys—and from electrum—or from the time of Croesus and represent gold and silver individually. The gold coins in this new process were called *Croeseids* and are very valuable. They were, in fact, the world's first bimetallic coinage."

From what I knew and what Corwin was adding, the earliest coins made of electrum were from the time of Croesus's great grandfather, Ardys. Electrum had been abundant in the River Pactolus and was mined by Ardys, his son Sadyattes, and grandson Alyattes, but they were content to strike their coins from the original alloy. It wasn't until Croesus discovered the technology for separating the metals that allowed him to craft coins of gold and silver independently, an innovation that sealed his legacy forever as the Father of World Coinage.

I smiled at the dawning understanding of why a man like Corwin would want to name his shop Croesus Gold.

If the coins we retrieved from Yavuz were electrum, both the *stater* and the *trite,* they would be classed as very old, possibly from the time of Ardys or his immediate heirs. But Dielman's notebook referred to gold and silver coins, which would be younger, from the time of Croesus. Old may usually trump new in most collector's fantasies, but examples from the world's first bimetallic monetary system were a fantastic discovery in themselves.

We finished our wine, and I thanked Corwin for his patience and the lesson that I had gained, then stood to excuse myself.

"We should talk about the Lydians still," he said, sensing my intention to depart.

"Yes, I hope we can," although I knew that I would probably get as much or more from Dr. Demir. "May I return?"

"Of course," Corwin said, raising his glass to me. But his eyes had a faraway look that convinced me that he was focused on the cache of coins that had been stolen, or that Dielman may have reburied, and how he might get them for himself.

"Beware, my friend," he said as I pulled on the door handle. "Beware of the Curse of Croesus."

I released my grip and let the door swing shut.

"And what is that?"

"Please, sit down and have another glass of wine."

I sat, and he poured another portion into my glass.

"The Curse of Croesus is like the curse of the Pharaohs, a curse that warns against disturbing the remains of a burial."

"Is this a myth?" I asked.

"You'll have to decide that for yourself. It originates from the discovery of the Karun Treasure found in the Uşak Province of western Turkey, near the village of Güre. It is sometimes called the Lydian Hoard or the Croesus Treasure because it contained many priceless urns and metalwork from Croesus's reign. Signs point to its origins in the tomb of a Lydian princess.

"A scandal erupted in the 1980s when the New York Metropolitan Museum of Art obtained the artifacts, probably without admitting that they were acquired through—let's say—extralegal means. After a lengthy legal battle, the Turkish government was able to prove not only that the hoard belonged to Turkey—in accordance with a 1983 law of repatriation—but that the New York museum knew they were illegally obtained when they bought them."

"That 1983 law," I interjected. "That's the one that empowers Turkey to petition for the return of artifacts that they believe originated in their country?"

"Yes, precisely," Corwin responded with a note of surprise.

"Anyway, the treasure was first stolen during a grave robbery scheme back in the 1960s," he continued. "Supposedly, seven of the men involved died violent deaths not long after the theft. According to local stories, one of the men also lost three of his sons, including a gruesome murder where a throat was slit. The other sons died in violent and unexplained traffic deaths. Another robber lost his son in a knife fight, and he, the father, committed suicide himself. A smuggler from İzmir named Ali Bayırlar sold some of the treasures on the international market, and he, too, died a terrible, painful death.

"The treasure was returned to Turkey in 1993, but there are still stories of revenge carried out by the spirit of Croesus on those who would attempt to claim part of the hoard."

"Sounds intriguing," I added, but I remained skeptical of this and any other conspiracy theory. "I will remain alert," and with that, I stood once again and offered my hand to Corwin in farewell.

At the door, I paused and turned to look back at the man. He was staring in my direction, but I could tell that he was deep in thought.

"You said you had been bitten," I began, "and I assume you mean by the coin collecting bug."

He nodded with a slight smile.

"With all these coins you have here in Croesus Gold, have you ever been bitten by the curse?"

"Not so far."

I started once again toward the door, but Corwin held up his hand.

"Dielman," he said. "He found coins," and he paused for obvious effect. "Do you think he died because of the Croesus Curse?"

I didn't smile or in any other way acknowledge his question. It seemed a lot like the diversionary tactics used by suspects I had dealt with in my career.

## ALBERGO DEI FIORI

It was nearing supper time, and without Alana, I didn't care to dine in Rome. So, I retrieved the rental car and worked my way through the city's rush hour traffic toward Route E80 north to Civitavecchia. Estimating an hour to get there, I figured to arrive just as the team was quitting for the day and would soon be ensconced in the lobby bar of the hotel.

I was the first to reach the Albergo dei Fiori, but only moments before others came in dusty from the day's work at the dig. They smiled and waved at me as they passed through the lobby; I could tell that a quick shower and clean clothes were uppermost in their minds. I was starting up the stairs when Tesa and Aggie arrived.

"Hey," he called. "How did it go with Corwin? I hear he's a curious guy?"

"If you mean he's curious about coins, that's a decided 'yes.' If you mean he acts in a curious way, well, I guess that's also a decided 'yes.'"

"We'll be done shortly," Tesa said, "if you want to meet in the bar."

"Perfect," I replied. I had no pressing need to retreat to my room, so I just turned around and took up a spot at the small table under the window in the lobby bar.

"*Buona sera, signore,*" said the desk clerk Giorgio as he approached me. Workers often performed multiple tasks in these small Italian hotels, so he abandoned his desk duties to serve me something from the bar.

"My friends and I would probably like wine, so I think I'll just order a bottle and let them join me. What Chianti do you have?"

"Badia a Coltibuono, Banfi, Castello di Gabbiano ..."

"Okay," I said, holding up my hand to stop him. "I'll take the Gabbiano."

I had visited the Castello di Gabbiano south of Florence on a previous wine tasting trip. The wines were consistently fantastic, the estate was an old castle surrounded by gardens, and there was a wonderful restaurant on the property. So, with such grand memories, I decided that this wine would be perfect.

While waiting for Giorgio to return, I stared out the window at this quiet neighborhood of Civitavecchia. The city itself was ancient and had served as a major port for centuries, but the Albergo dei Fiori was in a less-traveled section and enjoyed a relaxing quiet that the rest of Civitavecchia didn't have.

Why would Corwin be so interested in the coins? Of course, he was a merchant, an expert in ancient coins. Why would he *not* want a cache of ancient coins, possibly a cache of the earliest coins in the world? But did the collector's desire alone explain his interest? He didn't act like he knew Hamza Yavuz—from my years as an interrogator, I'm comfortable with my ability to spot subterfuge and would have picked up on signals. But he knew Yusuf Demir, and he knew of Charlie

Dielman's work. And he eagerly jumped into the mystery involving the missing coins. Did he know of the find and, more importantly, did he have any information of its whereabouts now?

And what did Corwin think of Yavuz being caught with a pair of coins, including a *stater*, the news of which obviously hit him hard? Did he already know, or suspect, that there were *staters* in the pit? Was he using me to find the cache of coins?

Giorgio returned with the bottle. It arrived with cork already drawn, not unusual in Italy, where bottles are often dressed and prepared in the back. In America, that might worry me, wondering what wine was really in the bottle, although my years as a wine critic would undoubtedly reveal any deception. But here, in the land of wine, they not only respected the product but honestly didn't see the point in deceiving the customer.

He poured an ounce in my glass and let me taste. Just as I suspected. The wine had the reddish-garnet glow of the Chianti from Castello di Gabbiano, an exciting blend of aromas and fruit flavors that could only be accomplished by an Old World winemaker who respected the advances of New World technology.

I nodded appreciation for the wine but saw he had only brought one glass.

"There will be two friends," I said, to which Giorgio nodded.

"Si, lo so," he said. "Yes, I know," as he reached toward the sidebar next to my table and grabbed two more tumblers, setting them on the table before excusing himself.

Just then, my phone rang.

"Darren," the voice said. It was Alana. "I'm here, home, I mean. How's everything there? I miss you."

I had to smile. Alana never had one thing, or one question,

to say. Her sentences always bounded out in triplets or quadruplets. I never knew which one to respond to first.

"I'm glad you're there," I replied, then added, "actually, I wish you were here." And I could imagine her smile.

"Everything is fine here. I met with Corwin this afternoon. You would find him very interesting."

"How do you mean?"

"He's a youngish Australian man ..."

"With an accent?"

"Yes. Why?"

"Because I always find youngish men with an accent interesting."

Hmmm, I thought. I guess I didn't fit into that category unless she considered an American accent to be sexy.

"Okay," I continued, "anyway. He was very interested in the coins and in what Yusuf Demir might have said."

"He knows him?"

"Not only knows him," I added quickly, "but possibly knows a connection—or suspects a connection—to the coins."

"So, we're trying to solve a possible murder investigation," she said, "but there are people cluttering the scene who apparently care more about coins."

"Yeah, so it seems."

"Can we separate the two things?" Alana asked.

"They might not be separable."

"Explain."

I had to organize my thoughts for a moment.

"Greed can be the essential ingredient," I began. "Hamza Yavuz appears to have stolen at least two of the coins. Yusuf Demir shows an informed interest in the meaning of these coins appearing in an Etruscan dig. Daniel Corwin is eager to get his hands on the stash."

"Don't forget Mehmet Arslan," she suggested.

"Wait," I needed a moment to refocus my attention. "He's the guy that Yavuz works for, right? The extremist son-slash-nephew, whatever of the guy at the Turkish Ministry of Culture?"

"Right. And Yavuz is known as the dirty jobs guy for Arslan. And then there's Antonin Peliatis."

"What? Who's that?" I asked.

"I used my contacts at Interpol," Alana said. "He's a low-order gold merchant. He wants whatever he can find, and he melts it down and sells it in bulk."

"How is he involved with this?"

"Interpol said they've picked up telecons with him talking about the gold stash found in Tarquinia and how it's untraceable."

"You mean that it's not gold bullion, so there would be no serial numbers or other means of finding out where it came from."

"Exactly," she said.

"Okay," I said, mulling over this new information. "Where is he? And how do we account for him?"

"Not sure yet, but I'm working on it."

"Then there's the death of Dr. Dielman," I continued. "Tesa is heartbroken and has lost a professional friend and colleague. Rafaela Indolfo is somewhat suspicious but still running down the leads. Hamza Yavuz can't be excused by any means; in fact, he should be the number one suspect."

"Maybe in league with Mehmet Arslan."

"Maybe even with Demir," I said.

"The question is ..." I began, just as Tesa and Aggie approached.

"The question is," Aggie cut in, "is the security of the coins and their whereabouts somehow connected to Dielman's death?"

Tesa's shoulders slumped when she heard him say this. Only slightly, but evident to me.

"Right," I concurred, and I could tell that Alana heard the comment. "Alana, let me call you back. Aggie and Tesa are here."

Aggie went for the bottle first, lifting it and reading the label before pouring some for himself and asking Tesa if she wanted some.

"Yes," she replied, sitting down.

"So, tell us about Corwin."

"He has cards to play, but he keeps them close to his vest," I replied. "He makes me suspicious, but I haven't been able to nail it down yet. Is he acting that way out of greed because he knows about the coins that were found, and he wants them for himself? Is he acting that way because he has some knowledge of how Yavuz came into possession of them? Or is he acting that way because he had something to do with the removal of the coins? He didn't make me think he knew where they were, though."

"If he was involved with Yavuz, the guy's arrest might have prevented Corwin from reaching him and getting the coins before they disappeared again," said Aggie.

"Alana called—that was her on the phone," I said, but they seemed to already have figured that out. "She mentioned someone called Antonin Peliatis that she found in Interpol files."

Tesa groaned at this.

"What's that about?" I asked.

"I've never met the guy, but you can't work in antiquities in Italy and not have heard his name," she replied. "He's a gold hoarder, can't really say he's a merchant. He finds what he can, collects abandoned jewelry, melts it down, and sells it off-market."

"Is there really a demand for that?"

"Sure, anyone who wants gold for cheap," she said. "He gets it from who-knows-where, sometimes without buying it, if you know what I mean, and converts it to bulk metal. There are side-street vendors who will take it off his hands and turn it into cheap knock-offs to sell to tourists."

"Where does he operate?"

"In Florence," she said. "gold capitol of the world. So, there are lots of unsuspecting buyers."

"Would he be involved with a theft of ancient coins?" I asked. "Or, more importantly, with a murder to procure them?"

"Hard to say. He's not well-liked or trusted. I guess that's how Alana found him in the Interpol files."

I decided to risk a sensitive area and switched topics.

"Have you heard from Rafaela about the tests on the exhumation?"

"No. Tomorrow morning, she said."

By then, members of the team began to filter into the lobby bar. We talked on for a while, and Aggie finished his glass of wine. They invited me to dinner afterward, but I begged off, saying I needed to call Alana back and they should have some time to themselves.

As I was headed up the stairs to the room, my phone rang again.

"I just got something else," Alana said into my ear.

"What?"

"It's about Yavuz. Interpol has records of investigations, even some when no charges are filed."

"And?"

"He's not a very nice guy. Yavuz has been convicted of fraud, theft, even some assaults with a deadly weapon."

"That makes him a clear suspect," I said, pausing with one foot on a higher step. "But you said Interpol has files even when no charges were filed. Those are all convictions. What are you not telling me?"

"They keep information on known people, such as people who already have a record. Because there's a file on them, like on Hamza Yavuz, they just keep adding information they get in case it comes in handy later."

"Like what?"

There was a long pause on the line before she replied.

"Some investigators in Italy wondered about Olivia d'Alantonio's death. At least some thought there was foul play. Her death was unexplained, despite that *idiopathic* conclusion on her death certificate."

"Your friend, Rafaela, had the body exhumed today. We'll get the results tomorrow."

"Yeah, well, it seems like Yavuz was one of the suspects."

"One of?" I asked.

"Well, more like *the* suspect."

"What happened?"

"They didn't have enough to charge him, but their notes went into the Interpol files."

"Why would Dielman and Tesa allow him to continue working there?"

"In Italy, the investigators have a policy of not telling anyone if they don't file charges."

I was dumbfounded. In my experience, the associates of a suspect would know something was up. How could the people at the dig, especially Dielman and Tesa, not know?

"I still don't understand. It was Tesa's mother who died, perhaps by some nefarious act. Tesa couldn't have let Yavuz stay on if she suspected anything."

"Apparently, she didn't suspect anything."

"Okay, I'm going up to my room to look through some notes. Kiss little Kia goodnight for me, okay?"

"I sure will. Thanks," she said.

"Oh, wait," I said before clicking off. "One more thing. Did you check on trains to Rome for Friday?"

"I sure did!"

# ALSIUM

## 610 BCE

THE SEAS WERE CALM AS THE BOATS APPROACHED THE SHORE *of Italia. Tyrrhenus had conducted the voyage as planned, stopping for two days of trading with the Ostians, then pushing off and turning north just when prevailing winds dictated it. This misdirection would allay concerns that their local hosts might have about the direction of the fleet, and it allowed Tyrrhenus to steer his people north to a relatively virgin area surrounding the small settlements of Alsium.*

*The boats that he commanded were designed for shallow draft, so they could approach coastlines that had no ports or docks. He knew that his passengers could wade ashore, but they were also bringing trading goods of their own as well as more that they had secured from their previous stop, so he sought out inlets that might allow them to come close to the shore and protect the goods during conveyance onto the beach.*

*There was no one to greet them when they landed, which was exactly as Tyrrhenus wanted it. He knew the Pelasgians only barely, and although he was not suspicious of them, he* didn't want to encounter them more than was necessary and possibly raise questions that he was not ready to answer.

He spotted a tributary that ran from the calm waters of a shallow river down the slope and emptied into the waters off the coast where his ships bobbed on the waves. The tributary met the coast at a low-lying area and therefore spread its waters into a wide delta, calming the flow of the waters as it emptied into the larger sea. The winds would be still too unruly to manage a soft landing by sail, so he had the men stow them and take up the oars, giving Lutus more control over the helm to steer the ship into the white foamy wash of water near the shore.

Tyrrhenus and his people in all five ships spent the remainder of the day tying down the vessels and unloading the cargo. He had hidden some of his own load from the Ostians, things like timber and canvas that would have revealed their intention to establish a settlement, but now these materials were off-loaded onto the shore along with the grain and other food-stuffs they had gotten in trade from the Ostians. He counted on access to more raw materials after landing but wanted his people to have the starting essentials as soon as they landed.

"We will camp here on the shore tonight," Tyrrhenus told Xenus, who nodded. "Tomorrow, we will look farther from shore and see what is beyond the coast."

"Have you been here before?" Xenus asked.

"Yes, but only on the edge. We would occasionally sail by, put in to shore, and look about. Not with the goal that we have now of settling, so I can say little about this as a proper place to set up."

Lutus approached and asked about the plans for the hundred-plus people in the expedition.

"We will sleep here tonight and explore tomorrow. Tell the men to build fires and the women to make arrangements for the food."

All set about their work as directed, but Tyrrhenus remained on the fringes of the activity. As the leader—in fact, acting as the king in these distant parts—he was responsible only for guiding the plan and the effort. He stood in the small waves at the shore and looked west toward the setting sun, trying to imagine this being his new kingdom. Then he turned fully around and looked at the blackness of the sky that approached from the east, the nightfall that had just begun to reveal the twinkling lights of the firmament above.

"It is a good spot, no?" asked Xenus.

The king's advisor had his own opinion, but he knew nothing about establishing a community and awaited the opinion of his liege.

"Yes, possibly. But we have not yet explored the lands beyond. We will do that and then know more."

———

The weather was calm and the night sky dark, and the crew and passengers of Tyrrhenus's fleet rested well after a satisfying meal of pork roasted over a seasoned fire, potatoes, and long greens. By morning, they seemed to have recovered from the arduous work of sailing, even though they were forced to sleep on make-shift bedding under the stars.

The next day, Tyrrhenus rose early, according to his custom, but Lutus was already milling about, waiting for his leader and captain to be approachable. Xenus was awake, but his arm was spread across his forehead and eyes to hold back the light of the rising sun at this early hour. Opening his eyelids a bit, he saw that Tyrrhenus was up and about, so he rose.

The camp would be maintained for the time being, so the women set about building morning fires and collecting the remnants of the food from the night before to be served to those *still hungry. The men who had managed the ships bobbing in the gentle surf gathered to decide what they might do to be necessary and helpful.*

*"What would you have the men prepare?" Xenus asked Tyrrhenus, now acting more supplicant than critic.*

*"They should prepare this landing place for long habitation, but we will also consider the places inland, or shortly far from this spot near the water, to create a permanent place for the Lydian people. If it is suitable, we will transform this landing spot to a proper bay for sailing in and out of."*

*The men and women of the expedition set about organized chores to establish a settlement there so that they could survive and thrive until more permanent solutions presented themselves.*

*Tyrrhenus chose a small team of men to explore the area beyond the shore, an area that would cling to the banks of the small river that emptied into the delta where they had landed. The plan was to keep them close to water, a source that would offer the opportunity to move among the fertile plains and animal herds of the inner coast.*

*They gathered for a morning meal of pork scraps from the night before, eggs from the hens brought from Lydia, and scrub greens picked by the women the night before. They didn't have herbs or garlic to flavor the food—these would have to be planted and grown. But it was enough to satisfy a people accustomed to sacrifice.*

*After eating, Tyrrhenus gathered his team, armed the men with spears and bows to fend off any surprise by a wild beast, and turned his attention to the lowlands that spread from the beach to the inland area. Xenus asked for permission to go with him and was allowed; Lutus remained at the camp as the leader in Tyrrhenus's absence.*

*Trudging through the sandy beach in leather footwear still* damp from the voyage was slow, but once the squad of men reached the grassy dunes, the going became easier. They leaned on their spears to steady themselves but kept their eyes forward since they were advancing into unexplored territory.

Tyrrhenus steered his fleet to what appeared to be an unoccupied area. He would present himself to the locals soon enough, but he wanted to avoid them at first, at least until he understood the area that he was exploring. If it was unsuitable for a lengthy habitation, he would answer the locals' questions one way. If he liked the area and wanted to establish a settlement there, his replies would be more guarded.

Beyond the dunes, the land flattened out again. Some low spots had pools of water, but mostly it appeared to him that the region was hilly and green. Fields of fertile soils were broken occasionally by long disorderly lines of spiny trees, and lush green grass and rooted plants filled the spaces between. They mainly saw wild pigs and short four-legged animals with shiny coats and fluffy manes of hair on their necks. At their feet, they occasionally saw small rodents scurrying past, and wild chickens and turkeys abounded. Birds of many kinds flew overhead, cawing their messages to their fellows.

"They are warning the brothers," Xenus said with a smile.

Tyrrhenus smiled back.

"But they have nothing to fear from us," he replied.

"Not from me," Xenus said with a chuckle, "but you have a bow and many arrows!"

"Oh, no, I'm not sure they know this weapon yet," the king said.

"No, but they will come to know it, by the will of Cybele," he said, calling up the goddess that his people worshipped back home in Sardis.

They continued to follow the stream to its source. It had cut a trough between the dunes and led them up a small hill from which a gurgle of fresh cool water emerged. Tyrrhenus stopped and looked back at the area they had covered. They had been exploring for several hours, past the time that the farmers in his homeland would have left their fields to return home to the village. He looked down from the hill toward the beach and saw that they had covered a great distance. From this elevated spot, he could see the dunes but also past them, seeing his small fleet of boats anchored in the shallow waters. He could see the dozens of men and women left behind to tend to their temporary settlement, and he tried to picture this as the future of Lydia.

Where he now stood would be a fortress, not for defense he hoped, but to serve as the gathering place for all his people. The flat plateau of the hill on which he stood would make a good position, and the many rocky outcroppings around him would provide the raw materials to build his seat of power. The homes for all the others would be erected in concentric circles around his fortress, with room for markets and artisan shops and fenced corrals for their animals. Tyrrhenus nodded in anticipation but also in appreciation for what the area around Alsium provided.

"Xenus, what do you think of this area?"

Xenus had not expected to be asked for his opinion, but he was pleased that Tyrrhenus would seek it.

"This is a grand spot, sire. We will know more as we explore further."

"Yes, we will, and our people will spread. I like being close to the shore, close to a river, and upon a hill. We can discover other places in time, but I want to move our day camp," he added, pointing to the base they had established overnight, "to here. This will be where we begin."

# THE SEARCH

Alana had left for Vienna yesterday, Monday, although her access to Interpol records would still keep her involved as a valuable part of our investigation. She promised to find out more, and I knew that I could use her to research other evidence that we might find. Rafaela had similar access, but I preferred to count on my personal connections.

I joined the dig team in the breakfast room soon after dawn. They signaled to me, and I prepared to join them when Aggie and Tesa entered the room.

"Hey, everybody," said Aggie with a morning brightness. Then, to me, "We're over here," pointing to a table under the window.

I saw that there were already emptied coffee cups and half-eaten rolls there, and then I noticed that the pair already had their shoulder bags on the chairs. "Early to rise ..." I almost said out loud.

I collected my double espresso, two rolls, and a small bowl of fruit and joined them at the table. I intended to hurry my meal, so I could leave with them to reach the site, but Tesa told me not to bother.

"I have some paperwork to do there first, organizing the panoramic photos of the dig. It's not very interesting. Relax, have your breakfast, and join us when you're done."

"I'll stay with Darren," Aggie said. "To make sure he doesn't get lost," followed by a chuckle. But I was glad to have a little one-on-one time with him.

After Tesa left the room, Aggie didn't waste any time.

"This Yavuz guy. He's bad news, that's obvious. He stole the coins, lied during the police investigation, and ..."

"... and was the suspect in Olivia's death," I added.

"What!?"

"Yeah. Alana called me last night after you and Tesa left for dinner. She got into some Interpol files and found—not only his lengthy history of arrests—but also some reference to Olivia d'Alantonio. Reading between the lines, she concluded that Yavuz was at least one of the suspects in her death."

"Reading between the lines, huh?" he replied.

"Well, it's not terribly clear, and the inference was slight enough to prevent them from bringing charges."

"Then why in hell ..."

"... didn't they tell Dielman and Tesa who employed the guy at the dig? Exactly what I asked her. She told me that the police in Italy don't like to talk to a suspect's associates unless they bring charges. They didn't, so there was nothing to tell Charlie and Tesa."

"Shit! And if he did it, and he continued working here for the last four years, there's no way to tell what else he may have done."

Just then, Aggie's phone rang.

"*Pronto*," he said brightly into the mouthpiece. "Who is it?"

"Signor Darwin, Aggie, this is Rafaela. I tried to reach Tesa, but the call didn't go through."

"She's on the way to the dig, and reception might be spotty. Anything I can do for you?"

"Yes, but I'd like to speak with her also."

This was followed by a long pause.

"Is the cell phone reception good at the dig?" she asked.

"Not terribly. Comes and goes," he replied.

"Okay, then. Let me tell you what I know in case I can't reach her. We exhumed the remains of Olivia d'Alantonio yesterday."

"Uh-huh," mumbled Aggie.

"Tests were conducted immediately, and tissue samples indicated the presence of wolfsbane."

"What the heck is that?" he asked.

"It's a poison, a bit Medieval if you ask me. It's a plant, officially called *aconitum*, that is very strong and usually lethal if ingested in large quantities. The symptoms are not easy to diagnose because they present much like intestinal nausea or, at worst, simple food poisoning. After four years interred, it's hard to tell for sure, but it seems there was enough in her system to cause her death."

"Could she have ingested it accidentally?" he asked.

"Not likely. It's a flower, and it can be chopped up and swallowed, but one doesn't accidentally chop up flowers for a meal."

Aggie spent a moment to consider this, then looked at me and back at the phone.

"Darren is with me. He told me something he heard from Alana," then he handed me the phone.

"Yeah, hi, Rafaela. Alana got something from Interpol last night ..."

"Yes, I know. I queried Interpol on Yavuz also."

"So, you know he was a suspect in Olivia's death."

"Yes," then a pause. "I've already requested a search warrant for his hotel room. I suggest you stay where you are and call Tesa back from the dig as soon as you can. I'll be there in about an hour."

Aggie tried immediately to call Tesa, and the call went through. Fortunately, the earlier reception problem was only because she was driving. He told her what Rafaela had said and filled her in on what Alana found from Interpol. His call wasn't on speaker, but I could hear the conversation anyway. And I could tell that Tesa was very quiet with this news.

"I'm coming back right now," she said and hung up before Aggie could reply.

———

As expected, it took Tesa only half an hour to return to the hotel, where she joined us in the breakfast room. The rest of the team had departed, so the room was otherwise empty. Rafaela would still be a while away, so we had time to go over what we knew.

Tesa was visibly upset, learning that her mother was probably murdered and possibly by someone who worked alongside her. And Charlie's death might have been caused by the same person. Not to mention the ongoing threat to the dig and the likely theft of rare coins from the excavation.

Her skin color was pink, and her eyes were wider than usual. I could even detect a slight tingling of her skin from the rise in the hair on her forearms. We gave her a few moments to collect herself, but then she blurted out news that I never saw coming.

"He killed my mother..." she began, but Aggie intervened.

"We still don't know that for sure."

Tesa looked at him, and the fire in her eyes was enough to shut down any further comment from Aggie.

"He killed my mother, and now he has killed my father."

I was completely confused, looked at Aggie, but he also seemed baffled by what Tesa had just said.

"Your mother," he began, then stuttered, "and your father? Your father is in New York."

Tesa looked down at the table and laced her fingers together. Whiteness appeared at her knuckles.

"Charlie Dielman was my father."

I sat back in the chair and decided to say nothing, just waited for more explanation. Aggie reached out for Tesa's hand, but she reflexively pulled it away. He wanted an explanation, so did I, but as the seconds ticked by, it became obvious that we didn't need an explanation. Olivia d'Alantonio and Charlie Dielman had worked together for many years. They were both revered experts in their field, and they went from one archeological site to another. She spent long periods away from her husband, Edoardo Richietta, who was quite content to remain in New York teaching literature at NYU. This was not the time to wonder about their relationship or to doubt whether they loved each other.

But it did seem like the time to realize that Charlie and Olivia shared an intimacy that was kept secret all these years.

Still, she became pregnant twenty-six or so years ago and delivered a baby, Tesa. Would either of the men wonder whose child it was?

"Does your father, I mean, your father in New York, know this?" Aggie asked.

"I think so," she replied, "but he is too much a gentleman to make something of it. I think my parents, that is, Edoardo and my mom, loved each other. I think he guessed at the relationship that might have developed between my mom and Charlie.

But they lived apart most of the time anyway. Dad, Edoardo, I mean, wasn't going to leave New York, and he wasn't going to make a pitch for my mom to return home. They reached an understanding. I was born, then raised in New York and Baltimore, attended school in the States, but came to work with my mother whenever I could be here in Europe. And, lately, here in Tarquinia."

"How do you know that Charlie is your father?" I asked.

"When she became sick, mom lingered for days. Here, in this hotel. I took time off from the dig to care for her. We had some very intimate conversations. I assumed she would recover —it was some kind of food poisoning, I told myself. But she acted as though she knew she was dying. She said she wanted to tell me things about myself. I didn't think I needed to know anything. I knew who I was. But her eyes stared into mine, and a sweet smile came over her lips. 'There's more,' she said. She went on to explain the attraction some people have for each other—it seemed like she was talking to a ten-year-old child—about the irresistibility of it, the inevitability of it. She even described their sexual relationship with a bit of reserve. She said they bonded, there was 'a union,' as if I didn't know at twenty-two years old what all this meant.

"I asked her about Dad, Edoardo-dad, in New York. She told me how much she loved him, what a wonderful man he was, but that they had married when they were 'kids.' That was her word. They were both brilliant students and had ambitious plans for their future, but his was in literature in New York, and hers was in the ancient dig sites of Europe. She never stopped loving him, she said, but Charlie was her perfect mate."

At that, Tesa grew quiet; Aggie and I had nothing to say.

Just then, Rafaela strode quickly into the room and stopped suddenly when she saw the sullen scene before her.

"Did somebody die?" she asked.

But none of us could respond to the comment.

———

I didn't want to leave it to Tesa to repeat all these reminiscences to Rafaela, but I also knew that it wouldn't seem right for Aggie or me to offer them. So, I grabbed him by the shirtsleeve and tugged him to his feet, suggesting that we get another coffee. We lingered over the espresso machine for some time. I looked back occasionally, seeing Tesa crying into the palms of her hands and Rafaela reaching out to comfort her.

Aggie looked forlorn, unable to fully understand and unable to comfort this woman he loved.

"Let them be," I said, pointing to another small table that we could sit at.

I knew that, in addition to Tesa's revelation about her parentage, Rafaela would want to put the possible poisoning into perspective, so they had a lot to discuss.

After another twenty to thirty minutes, uniformed officers came through the door of the hotel lobby and stopped a few feet back from Rafaela. By that time, Tesa's active crying had receded, and Rafaela was ready to proceed with the search of Yavuz's room.

We—me, Aggie, Rafaela, Tesa, and the officers—climbed the steps just behind the desk clerk who jangled a ring of keys at his side. At the door to Yavuz's room, we paused and waited for him to unlock it. Rafaela was the first to enter, followed by the officers she had summoned. Aggie, Tesa, and I followed.

The search was conducted quickly and completely. Bedding was upended, drawers were searched top and bottom, even the interior of the cabinetry that held them. The closet was disrobed of Yavuz's clothes, and the paneling behind the hangers tapped and inspected. The rug was rolled up, the drapes were smoothed down in search of secret hiding places, and even the light fixtures were examined for possible contraband.

We, the non-police threesome, mostly stayed back.

When Tesa followed one of the officers into the bathroom, he asked her to stand farther back. She followed him in anyway.

Tesa was the first to find a packet of soft material in Yavuz's toilet kit. She examined it herself, and I noticed her throwing a look in my direction as her hand reached into the kit. I shook my head as if to suggest that she leave evidence alone, but she gave me a cold stare in return. Then she handed the kit to the officer standing beside her, but not before I saw her jamming her hand into the pocket of her jeans.

"Inspector Indolfo," the officer called out. "Come look at this."

He presented the toilet kit to Rafaela and let her consider the contents. She looked surprised at first, then smiled as she withdrew the soft packet I had seen in Tesa's hands. Smelling it, she asked the officer to have it bagged and tested.

"No need, inspector," he replied. "Strange as it seems, I know this one. It's a natural flowering plant, a poison. It's called wolfsbane, sometimes 'queen of poisons.' It was popular in the Middle Ages as a way to silence one's enemy. If ingested in small quantities over time, it causes nausea and weight loss. If ingested in larger quantities, it can lead to hallucinations and rapid death."

I glanced at Tesa. She still had her hands dug deep into the pockets of her jeans.

"Save it," Rafaela said. "Test it, and have Hamza Yavuz held on double murder charges. Do not, I repeat, do not let him out."

# PIECING IT TOGETHER

The rest of Tuesday was a wash. We weren't going to get much done at the dig, and the search—and Tesa's revelations—left our heads spinning. Rafaela and her officers departed the hotel to continue with their investigation. We remained at the hotel—Aggie and Tesa to their room so that she could recover; me to my room to contact Alana and catch her up on the story.

"This is incredible," was Alana's immediate reply. "Tesa, Charlie, Olivia. Wow, I never put that into this narrative."

"And it changes how we analyze the evidence. I don't mean that Yavuz knew the link between Charlie and Olivia but think back to what Tesa told us about her mother."

"When? You mean a couple of days ago?"

"Yeah."

"Let's see, she described her as devoted to her discipline and to the archeological digs she was working on. And that she welcomed Tesa during summers off from school."

"More," I said, encouraging her recollection.

Alana paused to consider.

"What about her area of study?" I asked.

"Olivia? She was a philologist."

"Right, an expert in linguistics. In her case, an expert in tracing the roots of people through their language."

"Through the evolution of their language," Alana corrected.

"Precisely. And what did Olivia have to say about the Lydian-Etruscan connection?"

"Well, that the lineage of languages didn't support the conclusion that there even was a connection."

"Right," I said. "Olivia's conclusion was that there was no link, or at best only a tenuous link, between the Lydian people and the early Etruscans."

"Why does that matter?" Alana asked, but I knew how intuitive she was. I didn't answer, giving her time to piece it together.

"Wait a minute," she came back. "Olivia's view cast doubt on the Lydian origins of the Etruscan civilization."

"Uh, huh."

"That wouldn't be a popular view with the Turkish government that wants to claim such a connection."

"And Olivia's conclusion, which Tesa told me she was ready to publish in a scientific journal, would have cast doubt on the right of the government of Turkey to use the 1983 law to reclaim artifacts and elements of the Etruscans."

"Yavuz killed her to prevent publication of a paper?" Alana said. "That's a bit of an overreaction, don't you think?"

"You told me the Interpol files had things like that on Yavuz. 'Overreaction' seems to be in his DNA."

"If Yavuz poisoned Olivia to prevent her from publishing a paper, one that weakened the Turkish government's argument," Alana asked, "why would he kill Dr. Dielman, who was on the opposite side of the debate? According to Tesa, Dielman relied on physical evidence..."

"As a physical anthropologist," I interjected.

"Yes. He relied on physical evidence and thought that there was a connection between the Lydians and the Etruscans. Why would he kill him, too?"

"Don't know," I thought out loud. "Of course, we have Charlie's notes which indicate that he found as many as a couple dozen Lydian coins."

"It would have strengthened his case for a connection. And strengthened the Turkish case for repatriation of the artifacts."

"Then there is the intrinsic value of the cache of coins," I said, "possibly a very attractive opportunity for a young guy whose past indicates a willingness to break the law for profit."

We continued to discuss the variations on the story but kept coming back to Hamza Yavuz. He acted suspiciously from the time he left the dig site, to the time he was arrested in Pescara, to the time we interviewed him in the jail. He appeared to have lots to hide. In fact, he was hiding the *stater* that was found in his pat-down. And he had since refused to talk.

There was no evidence in his favor, but then again, we might not have enough to prove his involvement in Charlie's death. However, finding the same poison in Olivia's remains and in Yavuz's hotel room was mighty strong evidence against him.

"What's next?" Alana asked.

"Well, it's Tuesday, and Rafaela has him locked down in jail. Tesa is pretty distraught and probably won't be going back to the dig today ..."

"Maybe even tomorrow."

"Yeah, maybe. I'll check with Aggie later this afternoon and see how she's doing."

"Okay. Sounds good."

Just as we were signing off, Alana grabbed my attention with another tidbit.

"Darren, one more thing. I asked Interpol to check the phone records of Hamza Yavuz. He's been in regular contact with Mehmet Arslan ..."

"The guy in Turkey who seems to be ready to stretch the rules, let's say, to get artifacts returned. No surprise there. He works for him."

"But there have also been a number of phone calls to Yusuf Demir."

"Demir? The guy we met with in Cerveteri."

"Yes. Most of the calls were brief, but there have been more than thirty in the last two months."

"Demir said he didn't know Yavuz," I said.

"Exactly. That's what I thought he said."

We wound up the call quickly because I was now ready to start off in a different direction.

# CATCHING UP ON CALLS

I wanted to use the afternoon to check all my notes and make some contacts. I called a friend in the States about *staters,* and he confirmed their rarity and value.

"You mean *trites*, right?" he asked for confirmation.

"No. Full *staters.*"

"Oh, yeah, wow. Those are really rare. Did you find some?"

"I'll get to that later."

I asked him about the cultural meaning that might attach to them, but he had no direct answer.

"Ancient coins and their value—that's my field, Darren. Questions about their importance to the countries and cultures from whence they came is out of my league. Why do you ask?"

I filled him in on what Yusuf Demir told me, what I learned of coins from Daniel Thomas Corwin, and what we pieced together about connections between the Lydians and the Etruscans. I didn't go into the death of Charlie Dielman or the mystery surrounding Olivia d'Alantonio's death. And I certainly didn't go into Tesa's parentage.

"I'm not a cultural anthropologist," he repeated, "and

certainly not a geneticist. I can see how ancient tribes like the Lydians would migrate, intermix with distant indigenous peoples, and create new hybrids of both tribes. And I can see why modern nations might like to research that and understand these ancient bonds. But what does it benefit Turkey?"

"The benefits are doubtful. Except on two counts. The Turkish legislature passed a law in 1983 that claimed the right to repatriate artifacts that originated in their country. Anatolia, that is, and Lydia back in the sixth century BCE."

"Repatriating artifacts means, if I may be so blunt, to take them from the museums where they are exhibited," he mused.

"Yeah. Exactly. In fact, there's famous litigation on that score, specifically between the Turkish government and the New York Metropolitan Museum. It seems that some ancient artifacts, known as the Croesus Hoard, had been gained by extra-legal means by NY and Turkey petitioned for their return."

"Did they get them?"

"Yes, but it took a while. Then there's the whole thing about the Curse of Croesus ..."

"Wait. What?"

"Long story. Basically, the Croesus Hoard was traced back to a *tumulus*, a burial crypt for a Lydian princess, and the grave-robbers were among the first to suffer tragic deaths for stealing it."

"The first?" he asked.

"Yeah. Others who have been associated with the jewels and gold of that hoard have suffered the Curse of Croesus. Or so people say."

"Okay. Wow," he replied. "You said the benefits to Turkey are on two counts. What's the second?"

"If the Lydians are shown to have been the progenitors of the Etruscans, and the Etruscans begat the Romans ..."

"Wait!" he exclaimed. "The Romans? You're piling a lot on here, Darren."

"Yes, I am. If the Lydians are shown to have been the progenitors of the Etruscans, and the Etruscans begat the Romans—and two of the late-Roman kings were Etruscan ..."

I heard my friend exhale deeply at that.

"...then the modern Turkish people could claim that their ancestors, the Lydians, produced the Etruscans, and therefore produced the Romans, and therefore were the rightful ancestors and heirs of the Roman Empire."

There was a long silence on the phone.

"So, the Turkish people want to say that they were the real Romans. That's all fascinating, Darren," he responded after a moment, "but let's get back to my area, the coins. If you have found *staters* in a dig in Tarquinia, as you indicate that you have, they had to come from the Lydians."

"And if they did," I added, "it proves that the Lydians were in central Italy at about the time of the rise of the Etruscan people."

"Again," my friend pleaded, "I'm not a cultural anthropologist, but that sounds very interesting. Historically, I mean."

———

Not long after the call to the States, my phone rang again.

"Mister Priest," came the husky voice of Dr. Yusuf Demir. "How are you? I've been thinking about our conversation and wanted to speak with you again."

At our dinner, we had covered much of the history of the Lydians and Etruscans, including their links to the Turkish people. At that time, I told him about catching Yavuz with a *trite*, but we didn't yet know that he also had a *stater* in his possession. Or that perhaps a couple dozen Lydian coins had been found. Or that Olivia apparently was poisoned.

"Yes, certainly," I replied. "We enjoyed the conversation very much. Alana has returned to Vienna, now," and I decided to risk a bit more information. "She is a police inspector there, and work called."

The brief silence on the line convinced me that Demir was considering that bit of news and how it might affect him.

"I'd like to see the coins," he said.

"I doubt that that would be possible because the *polizia* are holding it as evidence." I stressed the singular word "it" because I didn't think Demir should have known that there were multiple coins.

"Besides," I continued, "I thought you didn't care about coins."

"I care about all things that are of Turkish origin," he replied a bit assertively. "And why are the police holding the coins?"

"As evidence in a murder. Possibly a double murder."

Another silence on the line, this one longer than the last.

"Thank you, Mr. Priest. I guess we have nothing to talk about then."

"Hold it. Why do you want to see the coin?"

"I told you. I care about all things that are of Turkish origin."

"And how far does your care go? To repatriation?"

"That is not a conversation we're going to have."

"You said you didn't know Hamza Yavuz."

Another long silence. I weighed how many seconds to let pass before I pressed him.

"It's a curious thing," I said, testing to see if I could keep him on the line.

"What is that, Mr. Priest?"

"How many calls you could place to and receive from a cell phone owned by Hamza Yavuz, and yet still claim to not know him."

There was no audible click on the line, but I could tell that it went dead. Demir's interest in the coins and his apparent relationship with Yavuz put him in the scope of the investigation. I thought about it for a minute but decided to call him back and press the point.

"*Pronto*," he replied when he answered the call. He would have known that it was me from the caller ID, but he still decided to answer.

"My apologies," he continued. "It seems that the reception was lost."

"Dr. Demir, let me ask you again, do you know Hamza Yavuz, and were you aware of his theft of coins from the Tarquinia excavation?"

It was a sudden decision on my part, and I still wondered whether taking a blunt approach was the best strategy. Demir didn't respond for the longest time, although I could still hear the faint sounds of his breathing, so I knew the connection was still there.

"I'm not in the habit of answering multiple questions at once," he said, and I couldn't help but smile about Alana's tendency to do that. It was a way of confusing the witness, and I, too, employed the tactic.

"Besides," he continued, "we are in Italy. You are an American, and you have no right to question people here."

"No, but Inspector Rafaela Indolfo does, from the *Polizia di Stato* in Rome." I paused for effect. "Shall I have her call you?"

Another long pause.

"I told you that I work for the government of Turkey, that I have contacts—unfortunate, at times—with Mehmet Arslan, who has close ties with the Ministry of Culture. I speak with him often and, at times, with his underlings."

"Hamza Yavuz is Arslan's underling?"

"He is what he is, a semi-human, brutish bottom feeder."

"Okay," I said, "so you like him."

"No. I do not like him," he said emphatically, with a tinge of anger in his voice. "Do you suspect that I had anything to do with Charlie Dielman's death?"

"The first question might be, 'Did you have anything to do with diverting the coins found in the dig?'"

"I am not a criminal, Darren. Although I don't believe I have any reason to explain myself to you. I am an official of the Turkish government, a noted expert in cultural matters, particularly those dating back to ancient times. And I am well aware of the cultural diaspora of my people. That doesn't mean I would involve myself in seedy behavior, certainly not illegal behavior, and most definitely not murder."

"But one thing leads to another," I replied. "If someone had an interest in certain things, coins let's say, and, to acquire them, another person had to resort to—what did you say, seedy behavior?—to get them. Would that first person be implicated?"

There was a long silence on the phone.

"Mr. Priest," he said, abandoning the familiar "Darren," "I need to make sure you know that I would not, did not, and could not, be involved in illegal behavior. I am a respectable man, an official of my country's government, someone with an esteemed reputation for honesty. I would not be associated with someone like Hamza Yavuz and his dealings."

The self-defense seemed a little over the top.

"But you are associated with Mehmet Arslan, right?"

"Not associated with him; I know him. And I do not approve of his methods."

This seemed like an unanticipated, but not to be wasted, opportunity.

"What methods are you referring to?" I asked.

Another long pause.

"Let me see if I can make this absolutely clear," Demir began. The Turkish government has a great interest in the expansion of our culture through ancient as well as modern times. We are a proud people, and we know that our ancestors contributed immensely to the literary and cultural wealth of the world. We understand and are pleased with how the people of Anatolia, Lydia, and now Turkey have influenced the development of civilization throughout the Mediterranean region, Europe, and the world."

I didn't know whether to stop him or not. It seemed like we had veered in the direction of a lecture that combined history and ethnic pride.

"We are also interested in all information that supports our belief that the Turkish people have had this impact on the world. Are we interested in the Turkish diaspora? Yes. Are we interested in proof of this impact? Yes. Do we believe that the early peoples from our region settled in parts of Europe and brought success to the indigenous tribes? Yes. Do we believe that proof of this impact can be seen in the archeological evidence? Yes."

I wasn't sure how long it would take for Demir to get back to the theft of the coins from the dig in Tarquinia.

"Do we believe that the ancient tribes from Anatolia settled central Italy and led to the emergence of the Etruscans?"

I held my breath because this was the crux of the whole story.

"Yes."

I wasn't surprised because Demir had always made his position clear on this subject. But his professorial delivery gave it added clarity. It still didn't settle whether he was involved with Yavuz, or even Arslan, in stealing the *staters* from the dig site.

"We found two coins in Yavuz's possession," I said. "Do you know where the other two dozen coins are?"

The phone call ended abruptly then.

———

I called Alana and briefed her on the call, and what more I knew or thought I knew. She told me about further contacts between Demir, Arslan, and Yavuz and how they were working more closely than we initially thought. Demir's persona as an educated man with high culture was all well and good, but it seemed that he occasionally met with people of a less desirable stature.

# CROESUS GOLD

I HAD TIME IN THE AFTERNOON TO RETURN TO ROME AND visit Corwin at Croesus Gold. I still wanted to know whether he had heard anything about a hoard of *staters* and if someone was hawking them on the market. Knowing what I did about Corwin and his not-always-legal approach to securing his treasures, I doubted that he would be willing to tell me much, but I trusted that I could see through any deflections.

It was about four in the afternoon when I walked up to Croesus Gold. Pushing the door open, I heard the slight jingle of the bell overhead and saw Corwin, this time standing behind and leaning over the glass counter; he looked up at me with a smile.

"Back so soon?" he asked. "I hope now I can show you some of these old beauties that I have collected," he said, pointing to the glass top and to the contents below.

I approached the counter and leaned forward to examine the collection. I'm not a coin collector and wouldn't really know much beyond the Liberty Head and Buffalo nickels in the U.S. But I had to marvel at the satiny finish of some of the coins resting on the soft white satin cushions in the case. Some were slightly chipped or uneven in their edges, but all were clearly very old. I could make out images on some—recognizing wheat stalks, protruding noses on worn faces, and a nautilus or two—but the letters were etched in shapes that reminded me of Greek or other long-ago alphabets and were beyond my understanding.

"This one," Corwin indicated by pointing, "was struck during the time of Vespasian." I recognized the name of this first-century Roman emperor as well as the crown of laurel and the flabby neck and chin of the ancient ruler.

"This one," he said, motioning toward another coin, "comes from the area around Athens." The image on the coin was obvious, the grinning face of some mythical character. "Around 500 BCE," he continued, "and these are Lydian coins," sweeping his hand across a line of three shiny coins. "*Hektes*, one-sixth of a *stater*."

"Do you have any *staters?*" I asked.

"Not yet," he said quickly. I focused on the "yet."

They had a silvery-golden hue, not quite fully either color, but the surface of each had been buffed to bring out the ridges on the engraving and express the image of the lion heads.

Corwin bent down as I had seen him do the previous afternoon, once again reaching for a bottle of wine, a corkscrew, and two glasses. He moved these to the little table by the window and invited me to sit, but before joining me, he returned to the glass case and withdrew the palette of Lydian coins from the case, setting it on the table between the wine glasses. Passing his open hand over them, palm down, he gestured that I should not touch the coins.

"These coins are electrum. Remember that?"

I nodded.

"So, you know then that these predate the reign of Croesus himself, since he had his smiths separate the metals and create coins of gold and silver, individually."

"So, these," I said, pointing to the tray before me, "are older than that. From ...?"

"About 610 to 650 BCE," Corwin said, completing my comment.

"Does that make them more valuable?"

"Yes, and no. Older is usually rarer, but coins struck from an alloy are also not 'pure' in the sense of a collection. But there's a more important reason why the coins of Croesus might be considered more valuable than anything that preceded it."

I waited for him to continue, but my host seemed to enjoy letting the excitement grow on its own.

"You're familiar with gold and silver coins, no?" he asked.

"Of course. Most of the world's currency, at least the non-paper currency, consists of these two metals."

"Correct. And copper?"

"American pennies."

"Exactly. There were some others, like the copper coin of King George IV of Georgia, dating back to the thirteenth century, but otherwise, copper has been a tiny fragment of the bimetallic system. This is very significant for world coinage. It was in Croesus's time or, more specifically, because of Croesus that the gold and silver metals were separated. Value at that time was a matter of supply, or scarcity if you will, and gold was more precious than silver."

"You said that electrum contained gold and silver in a ratio of about ten to one. That would make silver more precious."

Corwin smiled, seeming to enjoy my clarity of the subject.

"Yes, but these same metals occur elsewhere in the environment. Not just mixed in electrum. Overall, gold is in smaller supply than silver, so it is more valuable. Therefore, coins could be struck of each metal individually, allowing a system of monetary exchange with more denominations."

I was processing this and deciding where to go next, but Corwin now seemed impatient with my thinking.

"Different denominations of coins—long before there was paper money—were crucial to establishing an exchange market so that more products could be bought and sold within the range of their own value. Even though gold and silver had intrinsic value, they were still considered a symbolic form of exchange in a marketplace that had been dominated for thousands of years by a barter system. You know, two sheep for one axe, and so forth."

"Coins," I offered, "would allow someone to buy sheep even if he didn't have an axe to trade."

"Exactly. For the last two and a half millennia, the world market has functioned on the basis of the bimetallic system first created by Croesus."

"Well, no," I interjected. "Now, we have paper money ..."

"All of it worthless," he said with a sneer and a dismissive wave of his hand.

"... and e-money," I continued, "whatever that is."

"Numismatists don't collect bits and bytes," he said with a similar level of derision, "and neither will history."

We both smiled at this and sat in silence for a moment, sipping the wine and me studying the coins on the plate in front of me.

"Is this why you are so partial to Croesus gold?" I asked. "So partial that you named your shop after him?"

"Yes, I suppose so, but Croesus was more than the inventor of the bimetallic system. Under his watch, the Mermnad line of kings in Lydia ..."

My hand went up, and Corwin smiled.

"That's what they were called, from Gyges, who reigned from 687 BCE for nearly thirty-five years, to the last king, Croesus, who reigned from 560 to 546 BCE. The Mermnadae were the most successful line of kings, succeeding the Heraclidae, and Croesus became so wealthy that a phrase was coined—uh, sorry for the pun," at that, we both laughed, "a phrase was coined to 'be as rich as Croesus.'"

This didn't get me any closer to Charles Dielman's death or the dig at Tarquinia or the Etruscans—or whether Corwin had an abiding interest in the *staters* found in Tarquinia, but I was fascinated. One thing was nagging at me, though, and then it surfaced in an epiphany.

"Wait," I begged. "The ... what did you call the kings?"

"The Mermnadae."

"Okay, the Mermnadae were fabulously wealthy, right?"

Corwin nodded.

"And a phrase was coined to call such fabulously wealthy people 'as rich as Croesus,' right?"

Again, he nodded.

"Then why was Croesus the last king of Lydia?"

"Let's just say that that was due to speculation of a non-monetary sense," he said. "But we'll save that for another day."

The little bell above the door jingled just as another customer entered the shop.

At the arrival of this new guest, I stood and bid to take my leave, but I had one more question for Corwin.

"What of the bull's head? I thought the *staters* had both lion and bull?"

"That, my friend, will have to wait till later," he said and then turned his attention to the dark-haired woman who had just come into the shop.

On my way out, I stopped to look at an old-looking note in a gilded frame.

"Mark Twain," I mused, reading the signature. Another frame included two short notes, one bearing an indecipherable signature and date of 1750, with the seal of Eton College at the top, regretting an eye injury to a young Charles Cornwallis and assessing his future as bleak due to the loss of sight. The note next to it was signed by General Cornwallis himself, dated 1801, poking fun at the quick dismissal of his opportunities by the gentleman at Eton.

Next to it hung a painting of an old man with long white hair and beard, bent at the knee and leaning toward the bright waters of a stream. I was studying this when Corwin turned his attention to me.

"Remarkable, isn't it?" he inquired.

"Who is it?"

"That's Midas."

"The man whose touch turned everything to gold?"

"Yes, but it was a curse, not a blessing," he said.

"How so?"

"Everything he touched turned to gold," he repeated, to which I nodded.

"He was a mythical figure, of course," Corwin continued, "and so there are many stories about him. I like the one told by Nathaniel Hawthorne in a book he wrote in 1852 called *A Wonder Book for Girls and Boys*. In it, he told of the scene when Midas's daughter came to him distraught that the beautiful roses had turned hard at his touch. When he reached out to comfort her, Midas' daughter also turned to gold."

I knew the story, nodded in Corwin's direction, then pulled the door open. But before exiting, I stopped.

"You know of the coins mentioned in Dr. Dielman's journal."

Corwin nodded.

"You will tell me if you hear anything about them, won't you?"

Corwin just smiled, then turned his attention to the woman who had entered the shop.

# THE DIG

I FILLED MOST OF TUESDAY WITH CALLS AND THE VISIT TO Corwin at Croesus Gold. Cerveteri was a little over halfway from Rome to the hotel in Civitavecchia, so I decided to take my time and stop for a meal.

Eioli Osteria wouldn't be wise since Dr. Demir seemed to be a regular there. But while wandering through the city with Alana the other day, we found some other spots that might be worth looking into. La Cantina di Margherita was the one I chose, and I had a fabulous meal without the demands of a conversation about Charlie's death and the coin theft to distract me.

Seafood was the specialty at Margherita's, so I opted for all three courses in that vein. *Crostini di provatura e alici* began the meal, little toasted rounds of bread topped with butter-fried anchovies. I was amused to see *ciufulitti* on the menu. It was not a seafood dish, but it dated back to ancient Roman times, favored by the old Sabini tribe. It featured fusilli pasta and, here, was served in a light, oil and butter sauce.

*Stracciatella alla romana* came next. Typically, this broth soup is relatively plain, dressed up only with a spoonful of grated Parmesan as a topping. But at Margherita's, they added tiny sea urchins to the sauce to introduce the flavor of this amazing shellfish that is prominent in the Mediterranean Sea. As a finale, I ordered *mazzancolle al coccio,* jumbo shrimp cooked with garlic, olive oil, white wine, pepper, lemon, and chopped parsley.

I also managed to finish off most of the carafe of Velletri wine that they presented to the table. It was a full carafe when my meal began and somewhat less when I finished, but I wasn't sure how this would be charged. The bill came with the words, "*vino per uno,*" that is, "wine for one," and I was reminded of how in Italy, wine was considered a necessary condiment, so there was little pretense or formality around it.

But this morning, now Wednesday, I woke and showered, planning to meet Aggie, Tesa, and the team in the breakfast room. I did so, although later than usual, and most of the others had already left for the dig. Aggie was still there, but not with Tesa.

"You're alone this morning," I said.

"Yeah. Tesa said she had some business to take care of. I thought I'd wait for you, and we could go to the site together."

"Sure."

I filled Aggie in on my phone calls from the day before and my visit to Corwin.

"What's he like?" he asked.

"He's odd, pretty sure of himself, and obviously smitten with coins."

"Smitten enough to do illegal things to get them?" Aggie wondered aloud.

"Yeah, probably. Although I don't know whether these things include murder. I asked him if he knew anything about the coins mentioned in Charlie's journal."

"And?"

"He just smiled at me. Didn't have an answer. And there was someone in the shop, so I couldn't press him."

"What about Demir?" Aggie asked.

"I talked to him too. He seemed interested in the coins and what we were doing. But he was evasive. When I probed too much, he turned off."

"Turned off? Explain."

"He literally hung up on me."

We finished our coffee and rolls, with a side helping of orange wedges to tide us over until a later lunch, then we went out to the car Aggie used. It was an absolute heap, an old Jeep that had seen better days, but he slipped behind the wheel with a comfort based on familiarity, and I slid into the seat beside him. Feeling the bumpy ride offered by obviously worn shocks, I was glad I had fastened my seatbelt for the ride.

We talked about the events so far, including the meeting with Yavuz in the jail while riding to the dig. When Aggie parked the car at the fence line that defined the dig site, he looked to the left and seemed concerned and surprised.

"Tesa's not here yet," he said. "Hmmm."

"Do you know where she is?"

"No."

We joined the team in the mess tent, got another espresso and slice of bread, and went out to the excavation. About an hour later, Tesa walked up from the parking lot to join us.

"Where have you been?" Aggie asked.

She didn't respond right away, just settled the broad-brimmed hat on her head and entered the dig.

"To see Yavuz," she said finally.

Aggie looked at me and I at him, surprised by her reply and not knowing what to say at first.

"Why would you do that?"

"He's one of my employees. He's jailed for some serious things, but we don't know yet what will turn out," she replied. "I wanted to make sure he is getting enough to eat."

I was having trouble taking her at her word.

"I wanted to make sure he was alright. What if he did steal the coins for his daughter? What if he is telling the truth?"

"And," interjected Aggie, "what if he did kill Charlie?"

The very forward comment shut down Tesa's explanation for a moment, then she replied.

"We don't know that yet."

"And what of the poison that was found in his hotel room," I asked, "matching the same poison found in your mother's remains?"

Tesa turned her attention to the dig site as she stepped down the layers toward the bottom of the pit. She did not respond to my question.

I hadn't spoken to Tesa about what I saw her do in Yavuz's hotel room when she seemed to be hiding something in her pocket. And I hadn't talked to Aggie about it yet, although it seemed very suspicious—Tesa finding the bag that we found out contained the same poison discovered in her mother's remains. Finding it and then seeming to put something in her pocket.

"Well, if you ask me," said Aggie, "I don't think that was a very good idea."

"Nobody's asking you," she replied, with a tinge of anger.

"What did he say?" I asked.

Tesa stalled for a moment but then responded.

"He was startled too," she said, addressing Aggie as if in apology for her impatient reply. "He didn't know why I was there, but I told him that I still consider him part of the team. Charlie always said we were a family, and we had to look out for each other. I know jails around here aren't that comfortable, so I brought him some food to make sure he was eating well enough."

That didn't sound right at all to me. Yeah, maybe the jails don't feed their prisoners well, although that was doubtful considering we were in Italy where food was as essential as air. But Tesa catering to Yavuz's needs like that? I had to wonder.

"Isn't a bit odd that you would go to see him," I said, "after telling us what you did about him?"

Tesa was slow to respond, obviously looking for the right way to phrase it.

"I don't like him, but I thought later about what I said. I might have jumped to conclusions, and my guilty conscience got to me. I had to be true to Charlie's teaching. We are a family here."

Aggie gave me a look that showed that he was as doubtful as I was about her excuse.

"I asked him if he knew where Charlie put the coins," she continued. "He didn't know."

"He didn't know," I asked, "or wouldn't tell."

Tesa just shrugged her shoulders. I couldn't accept what she was reporting and began to doubt every statement of hers. Then she turned her attention to the dig and the workers who were standing silently watching this conversation, telling them to get back to work. From that point on, she didn't talk about her visit to Yavuz in the prison cell.

I even wondered what she really meant about questioning Yavuz. When she asked if he knew where the coins were, why didn't he just deny knowing about other coins? It was a good question, framed the way an interrogator would frame it. If Tesa actually said, "Do you know where the coins are?" she was leading the witness, like the famous police quip about "When did you stop beating your wife?" If those were her words, and if Yavuz simply said he didn't know, then he was confirming Charlie's notes and that there were more coins found in the dig.

My phone rang. It was Yusuf Demir.

"Darren," he said slowly, "I want to apologize. I'm sure that I came across as sounding guilty, at least of prevarication, when we spoke last."

"Yes, you did."

"I didn't mean to. Frankly, I was put off by your suggestion that I might be involved in a murder."

"I didn't say anything about murder, only the theft of the coins."

"Yes, but it seems like the disappearance of the coins is tied to the death of Charlie Dielman."

"In a way," I said, "but I wasn't going there."

"Anyway," Demir continued, "I want to assure you that I, and the Turkish government, will assist you in any way we can."

"Two things," I remarked. "Since Mehmet Arslan and his goon, Hamza Yavuz, are tied up in this, I wouldn't expect much cooperation from the Turkish government. Secondly, I'm not sure that—whatever your good intentions—you can promise the assistance from the Ministry of Culture in recovering the coins that were found and are, now, gone."

"Fair enough. But I will help." He paused. "You say they are gone, the coins that is. Are you sure of that?"

"What do you know?" I replied.

"I'm just asking." Another pause.

"Are you familiar with the Curse of Croesus?" he asked.

"Yes, I am, at least recently. I understand it has something to do with the Croesus Hoard that was taken from a Lydian princess's tomb and the unexplained deaths of many people associated with it afterward."

"Well, that's the folklore," he said. "Some people think that the curse still thrives and that anyone who tampers with the jewels, gold, or coins of Croesus will suffer unspeakable harm."

"Okay," I mused, but I had little more to say.

"Charlie Dielman found the coins. How do we know that he didn't suffer the Curse of Croesus?" Demir asked.

"Yeah, sure. Possibly at the hands of someone who felt empowered to carry out the curse?" I responded with derision.

"You don't know whether Dr. Dielman was killed, do you?"

I decided not to answer the question, but let it hang.

"Thank you, Dr. Demir. I will get back to you. Please let me know if you plan to leave Cerveteri to return to Turkey."

"I don't owe you that courtesy, Darren. You're not an officer of the law in this country. But just to show that I have nothing to hide, I'll be sure to let Inspector Indolfo know if I return home."

————

"What was that about?" Aggie asked.

I tried to summarize it without making assumptions about the meaning of Demir's explanation, but then I decided that I had to speak with Corwin. There's something about the curse that didn't seem right. My own words captured it: Is it cover for someone to commit murder under the guise of some ancient ghost of Croesus?

"Mr. Corwin," I said into the phone. "This is Darren Priest. Sorry to bother you again."

"No, not a problem. What can I do for you?"

"I wonder, considering your close connection to the world of ancient coins, have you heard anything about Lydian coins recently found at the dig in Tarquinia?"

I counted ten seconds before Corwin could figure out the best way to answer this. I also knew that Alana had found telephone records tying Corwin to Arslan, once removed from Yavuz, and possibly the theft of the coins.

"No, I haven't. I certainly am interested. Do you have them?" he asked, sounding clearly like a diversion.

"No, I do not. Just thought I'd ask. Would you let me know if you hear anything?"

I knew it was a useless request. If Corwin got word of the *staters* and *trites* showing up, on or off the market, he would be the first one in line to get them. And he wouldn't stop to call me first.

"Sure, I will certainly do that."

I told Aggie that I wanted to return to the hotel and asked if I could take his Jeep. Tesa was at the dig, and they could ride back together. He handed me the keys, and I left.

I was anxious to bring Alana up to speed on the news and trusted that she could use her contacts in the police department in Vienna and Interpol, so I called her while I was still driving away. I told her what I knew, but the assembly of facts left enough holes in the narrative that we both wondered where it would go. Then she struck quickly on the one thing that bothered me most.

"What do you mean Tesa went to the jail cell?" Alana said in amazement.

"Yeah, I couldn't believe that either. She can't really think that Yavuz is not a—possibly 'the'—suspect. Remember, she said that he killed both her mother and her father. That was right after we found out about the poisoning."

"Maybe she went to try to pry information out of him about the coins," Alana suggested.

"Yeah, but I don't think she's that interested in the coins."

"What then? Do you think she was leaning on him to get a confession?"

"I hope not," I answered. "That technique is not for amateurs."

We considered the possibilities while I drove to the hotel but came up with zero.

"I'll keep you posted," I said, getting out of the Jeep. "Stay in touch. Love you."

Just then, I realized that I had never said that before, used the "L" word. It just slipped out so naturally.

I couldn't see Alana on the other end of the phone line, but I could hear the sudden intake of breath. She heard it, too, and her soft reply was enough.

"Yeah," she said quietly. "Me too."

# ONE
## THE DIG

AFTER A QUICK BREAKFAST, THURSDAY, WE HEADED TO THE dig. I was focused on the suspicious behavior of Demir and Corwin, the jailing of Yavuz, and Tesa's inexplicable behavior. But the work continued, and there seemed little else to do while we waited for Rafaela Indolfo and the wheels of Italian justice to turn. I was not much help at the archeological site, so I focused on watching and learning.

It had only been a couple of days since I arrived in Tarquinia, and progress at dig sites was traditionally very slow. I wondered whether I would have the patience to continue day in and day out the way these workers did, spending hours sometimes unearthing a single buried artifact, coaxing it from the ancient earth without risking damage to it. Several team members were assigned to recording the finds, some with hand-drawn sketches and some with cameras. The sketches were a throwback to centuries of exploration before analog cameras, certainly before digital cameras came along. But Charlie warned Tesa and the team that a hand-drawn sketch sometimes captured an essential element of the find, sometimes as little as a shadow that might indicate an indention or scratch in the object, that a camera image might not.

The young people on this dig—and they were primarily young, ambitious archeology students—accepted the old ways, embracing them as a connection to the scientists who came before them. So sketches and photographs both made their way into the journals and official record of the dig.

Once again, I thought of volunteering my help, although I knew that the type of photography I had practiced with a hi-res cell phone wouldn't suit this particular project. So, I stepped back, made room for the experts, and watched.

I worked my way around the periphery of the dig. It was a rectangular excavation marked by four levels. Each level was a tier or broad step, from two to maybe ten feet wide and less than a foot deep, depending on the nature of the earth and the elements below it. Each tier had been cleared and swept mostly clean. Tesa's instructions to the team were to inspect each tier, capture and document the artifacts at each level, and create a flat platform before moving below it to the next level. In that way, she said, they would record the findings in a chronological format, what archeologists referred to as "association," where one artifact is collocated with another and, therefore, assumed to be of similar age. Finds appearing above others were assumed to be younger according to the "law of superposition." This plateauing effect made it easier to assess the age and chronology of the site and correlate the findings within the cultural context in which they were found.

My cell phone rang, and I smiled as I saw Alana's number come up.

"Hey! How are you?" I asked.

"Not altogether well," she said.

"Why? What's the matter? Are you sick? Is Kia okay?"

"Yeah, sure. All that. But Rafaela just called me."

"And?"

I couldn't understand why Alana was hesitating.

"Yavuz is dead."

"Oh, shit!" I exclaimed. "What happened?"

"Rafaela said that he was found in his cell with froth at his lips and his eyes open."

I didn't have to say anything but was sure that my thoughts and Alana's went directly to Tesa. What did she feed him?

"This is really bad," Alana said.

"You mean that he is dead, that he might have been murdered, or that we won't be able to find out what he knows about the missing coins?"

"Yeah," she said, "all that. I don't know why Rafaela told me first, maybe because she knows that I'm a cop and I'm back in Vienna. But she said she would be coming to the dig today."

"Has she told Tesa yet?"

"No. I think she wants to do it in person."

"So, I shouldn't say anything."

"I wouldn't."

We hung up the connection, and I turned to look at the dig site. Tesa stood at the lip of the excavation, hands on her hips, as she watched the work going on below. Aggie was still in the mess tent, under the awning and in the shade, so I turned in that direction. I knew it would be inadvisable to tell him what I knew, but I also wanted to warn my friend of big news to come when Rafaela paid us a visit. I walked over to the mess tent and straight up to the coffee machine.

"Hey, Darren," Aggie said, raising his coffee cup in salute.

I sat down across the table from him, bringing the cup to my lips and staring at him over the edge of it.

"What's up?" he asked. "Looks like you've got something on your mind."

"Yeah, sort of," I stalled. "Alana called to tell me that she found something out."

"What?"

"I'd rather wait for you to hear it from Rafaela."

"From Rafaela? Really? What is it? Can't you tell me?"

"No. She'll be here soon, but her news is specific to Tesa. When she arrives, you should join her at the dig."

It was awkward to sit there across from my friend without speaking, and the unrevealed news cast a pall over our conversation. I sipped at the coffee and waited for Rafaela. Fortunately, we didn't have long to wait. The sound of her Alfa Romeo announced her arrival, as did the small cloud of dust that followed the sports car. I heard the solid sound of a car door shutting and then saw Rafaela—surprisingly appearing in uniform—climb over the rise of the hill and approach us in the tent.

"*Buon giorno*," she began. "Is Tesa here?"

"Yes," Aggie said, pointing toward the dig site. "Over there."

When Rafaela started off in that direction, we followed.

"Signorina Richietta," the inspector said to Tesa. I was surprised by the formality of the greeting. "I was recently contacted by the officers at *Casa di Reclusione* in Civitavecchia."

"Yes?" Tesa responded.

"Signor Hamza Yavuz was found dead in his cell this morning."

"Oh, fuck," I heard Aggie mutter under his breath.

Rafaela waited several beats for a reaction from Tesa, who looked down at the ground but didn't speak.

"You visited him yesterday," Rafaela continued. "Did you notice anything unusual about Signor Yavuz?"

"No."

"Did you bring him anything?"

Tesa was slow to respond to this, and my mind fixated on the image of her thrusting her hands into her pockets after the plastic bag of something was discovered in his hotel room—the bag that was later determined to contain remnants of the same poison found in Olivia's remains. Did Tesa take some of it? Rafaela hadn't seen Tesa's action back there in the hotel room, and I wasn't sure if I should bring it up.

"Curse!" was uttered by a worker at the dig, and Rafaela gave him a dirty look. Turning her attention back to Tesa, she repeated her question.

"Did you bring him anything?"

"No," she said, although Tesa had openly admitted to me and Aggie that she brought Yavuz some food. I kept my silence.

There were mumblings from the diggers who were collecting around this conversation. I heard the word "curse" uttered again, less by the American students on the team and more by the local Italian workers.

"What are you saying?" the inspector asked the assembly.

"There's a curse," one of them said. "The Curse of Croesus. Anyone who tampers with the riches of the Lydian hoard will die. That's what happened to Dr. Dielman, and now it has happened to Hamza."

"Why do you think that?" Rafaela asked.

"You said that Hamza maybe stole the coins."

"I didn't say that, but I know that is what you have heard."

The digger persisted.

"If Hamza stole the coins, the curse would strike him dead."

Rafaela just stared at the man and sighed in a disgusted, impatient way before turning her attention back to Tesa.

"You didn't bring him anything?" she repeated.

"No."

I heard someone in the dig mumble, "It's the curse." But I kept my attention on the conversation between Rafaela and Tesa.

"The Medical Examiner will tell us how Signor Yavuz died, including whether there was foul play. His death does not seem to be of natural causes," Rafaela said.

"You found poison in his hotel room," Aggie offered to Rafaela. I was sure he was suggesting this to take the attention off his girlfriend.

"Yes, we did," Rafaela responded.

"If the ME finds that he died of unnatural causes," Aggie continued, "you should consider whether he ingested any of it."

"That's a conjecture that I'm not ready to make," Rafaela said, staring intently at Tesa. Turning back to Aggie, she continued, "You're suggesting that Yavuz committed suicide."

"Well, he was in jail and being held on murder charges."

"But the poison—if he even took any—was back in his hotel room," the inspector clarified.

"The prison guards didn't even find the *stater* sewn into his cargo shorts," Aggie continued. "Seems like he could have also secretly kept a poison available as a suicide pill."

It was a leap, but I was impressed with my friend's agile attempt.

"I will be in touch," Rafaela said in a stern voice, clearly not as friendly as she had been on earlier visits.

She turned to leave just as one of the diggers stepped quickly out of the excavation.

"Signora?" he said, holding out his hand to keep Rafaela from leaving. "May I say something?"

"Yes, certainly. And you are?"

"I am Ibrahim al Safita. I am a worker here at the dig and have been for a few years. I knew Hamza well, and Dr. Dielman, and of course Dr. Richietta, here."

"And what do you have to say?" Rafaela asked.

"I was going to tell Tesa this—Dr. Richietta, I mean," he said, "this morning, but then all this started."

"Tell her what?"

"We have security cameras for the site. It's meant not only to ward off scavengers but also to record actions in case we found tampering with the dig site."

Rafaela waited.

"The night that Dr. Dielman died, we all were leaving the site. He stayed behind because he was excited about a find. Possibly having to do with the coins."

"Yes?" Rafaela showed impatience. "I know all this. What about it?"

"Well, I am responsible for the security cameras. They don't run during the day, but we turn them on when we leave at night. Everyone was going back to the hotel, including me. So, by custom, I turned on the security cameras before leaving myself."

"Was Dr. Dielman still here?"

"Yes, and I didn't really think about that. But now, I realize that the recording might shed some light on what happened at the dig while he was here alone."

Rafaela turned back to Tesa.

"Didn't you say earlier that Yavuz didn't show up at the hotel that evening?"

"Yes. Not until later, and only briefly before leaving again."

The inspector then turned back to Ibrahim.

"Do you have the tapes from the cameras?"

"They're on one-week loops," Ibrahim responded.

"Yes, or no?" Rafaela was impatient.

"Yes. Dr. Dielman fell into the pit last Thursday night. Today, it's Thursday, but still morning. The camera recordings are still good but would only be kept in the system until this evening, when the tape will be written over."

"Where are they?" Rafaela asked.

"In the tent," said Ibrahim. "Would you like to see them?"

The question was too obvious for her to answer, so she pushed Ibrahim in the direction of the mess tent to begin the review process. We all followed.

―――――

Tesa, Rafaela, Aggie, and I sat around one table while the rest of the team found seats at other tables. Ibrahim brought a laptop to the middle of the room and began striking keys and staring at the screen, occasionally tapping something more until he was satisfied that he had found what he was looking for. He spun the laptop around so that it faced our table as the rest of the team moved over and resettled themselves at a bench and table behind us so that they could see.

The image on the screen was dark, but it held the entire dig site in the frame. Two lights glowed dimly in the background, and the edges of darkness and shadows filled most of the picture.

"This is set for the time when we were leaving the site," Ibrahim explained. "It is when I first turned on the security camera. Well, I turned all of them on, but this is the camera that is focused on the dig site where we found Dr. Dielman."

He pressed a few more keys, then swung the laptop back around to face us.

"I'm sorry it's dark, but it will brighten up a bit when the camera begins to roll. It's like that. It's something about the technology ..."

"Doesn't matter," Rafaela interrupted impatiently. "Just run the video."

Ibrahim acted a little frightened, as if he feared that he would be criticized for withholding evidence, so his movements were tentative.

"Just run the video," Rafaela repeated, sitting at the closer side of the table toward the laptop.

Ibrahim punched a key, and the recording began to run. Just as he said, the brightness improved as the video rolled, and it was easier to make out the images in the frame.

The camera was pointed at the dig site where Charlie Dielman was working, at a spot perhaps twenty feet away. Charlie's head was to the left of the frame and feet to the right; he was lying on his stomach with his left arm splayed outside of the dig with his right arm reaching down into it. He had his usual canvas hat on even though the sun had long since retreated to the horizon—a stylistic attribute that he seldom abandoned, even indoors, I was told.

The video showed him at work on something, reaching down below, but the "something" was not identifiable in the frame of the camera. Another man showed up behind him, standing behind Charlie, dressed in a worn t-shirt and cargo pants. It wasn't hard to identify this new person as Hamza Yavuz, from his clothing and the close-cropped black curly hair. He stood near Charlie, at his feet on the right side of the image, and leaned toward the pit as if to inspect the thing or things that had caught Charlie's attention.

Charlie raised his head, twisted it over his right shoulder, and talked to Yavuz—the video had no sound, so we had to imagine what was being said—then Yavuz walked away, disappearing from camera view.

Charlie returned his attention to the dig, reaching farther and farther into it, leaning into the hole so that his right shoulder was tipped forward and beyond the view of the camera. His head was still above ground, but he contorted his body to reach something below.

Suddenly, his left hand grabbed convulsively at the dirt as his feet dug into the ground and his body began to slip. It was as if we were watching in slow motion as Charlie slid over the edge, grasping for the turf, yet falling and rolling on his right side into the darkened pit below.

Another few seconds and Yavuz returned to the dig and came into camera view. He peered down into the pit for a moment, then left the area again, returning not long afterward carrying a limp canvas bag. At that point, he stepped carefully down into the pit where Charlie had fallen and, step by step, disappeared from view.

Several seconds went by before anything else appeared in the film.

Then, two hands appeared at the edge, pushing a soft bag over the lip of the dig. It landed on the edge of the excavation with a thud, then the hands let loose their grip on it and disappeared from view. Another few seconds and Yavuz climbed out of the pit a few feet away. He stood on the edge of the dig, bent over and looking down into it; it was easy to conclude that his attention was on the body of Charlie Dielman at the bottom of the pit. He then picked up the bag, looked around a bit, and exited the area.

The rest of the video was a blank view of the edge of the pit devoid of people or activity.

Ibrahim waited a few seconds before reaching for the laptop and punching a button, turning the video off. Everyone was silent. I looked at Tesa first, then at Rafaela. Aggie poked at my arm to get my attention, and I looked over at him. His eyebrows raised, and he lifted his hands, palms up, in a gesture of confusion.

"Oh, fuck!" he said again.

More would have to be seen, but the video from the security cameras seemed to confirm that Charlie's death had been an accident, that Hamza Yavuz was on the scene at the time, and that he had left the site with a bag of something. The coins mentioned in Charlie's journal? It was hard to say, but it seemed like that was the easiest explanation.

The video also confirmed that Yavuz was not responsible for Charlie's death.

Aggie looked at Tesa, who sat white-faced after the laptop screen went blank.

Rafaela sat quietly by, looking slightly downward as if she was trying to process all the facts.

I had little doubt that Tesa was somehow involved with the death of Yavuz, and I assumed that Aggie knew that too. As did Rafaela. Was she now going to be implicated in the murder of the man? It was easy to tell that Charlie's death was an accident but that Yavuz's death was not. Perhaps even Olivia's death was no accident.

"Does anyone know what that sack contained?" Rafaela asked the team assembled under the tent.

Lots of shaking heads, looks of confusion and dismay. Scanning the gathering, I couldn't find anyone who had a sense of what had happened. From what I could see, the sack disappeared with Yavuz.

"The curse of Croesus," I heard someone say but couldn't identify who said it.

"Bullshit," Rafaela said to no one in particular. "This is no curse."

But others gathered at the tables under the tent were not so sure.

"I want that laptop," said Rafaela.

"Madam, I'm sorry," replied Ibrahim, "but we need that for our work."

"Then download a copy of that video for me. Now! And don't erase that segment until I call you."

Ibrahim did as he was commanded and gave a small thumb drive to the inspector when the file was downloaded.

Rafaela moved toward the edge of the tent enclosure, then stopped, turning back toward Tesa.

"I will need to look into this further. I want to find out where that sack went." Then, pausing for a thought, she continued.

"And I want to find out how Yavuz died in the custody of the Italian police."

Then she left with deliberate strides toward her Alfa Romeo and left the site, dust clouds circling behind the vehicle.

We remained in the tent, speechless. Tesa seemed very anxious; Aggie had a mix of relief and worry on his face. The rest of the team whispered quietly among themselves.

After her departure, another car appeared over the horizon. Coming quickly to a stop, carelessly parked at an angle near the fence line, a door slam indicated the arrival of another visitor.

Still reeling from the events of the morning, the team had remained in the tent, and this new arrival held them in place. After several seconds, Corwin appeared over the hill, dressed in suit pants but with no jacket, his starched shirt collar bearing no tie. He went straight to Darren and extended his hand.

"I don't believe I know any of these people," he said with a friendly smile.

I assumed he didn't know about Yavuz since Rafaela had kept the man's death quiet until she could tell Tesa. And I was very sure that Corwin didn't know what the video just played told us about the evening Charlie died.

I introduced him around, and his eyebrows went up when he was introduced to Tesa.

"So, it was an accident," he said confidently.

"I assume you mean Dr. Dielman's death," I said, "Why do you think that?"

"Man's working in a deep pit, late at night, no lights. He lost his balance and fell into the pit."

I felt that Corwin was giving up too much information and, when Aggie started to speak, I touched his arm to allay his inquiry.

"He wasn't pushed?" I asked. "Why do you conclude that?"

"Doubtful, under the circumstances."

"What about the coins?"

"The coins?" he responded with a smile. "You mean the coins that Dr. Dielman took from this dig?"

Tesa started forward toward Corwin, and it took Aggie's strong arm to prevent her from taking a swing at him.

"Those coins will never be found," Corwin continued. "They're gone."

This amounted to a confession of the theft, I concluded, but I had too little to prove it. Perhaps if we found the coins—particularly if we found them in his possession. But the man who took them—Yavuz, not Dielman—was now dead, and we had lost a witness who could help us connect the dots and unravel this mystery.

Corwin turned around and went toward his car. I wondered why he came to the dig unless it was an inadvisable attempt to boast. Then again, knowing criminals the way I did, I figured it was simply the perpetrator returning to the scene of the crime.

My phone rang. It was Alana, who knew the information that Rafaela would pass on and was probably very impatient to find out how it had gone.

I signaled to Aggie that I was headed toward the car and took the call while walking to the lot. I filled Alana in on Rafaela's report and, more importantly, on the security video that Ibrahim had shown us. An audible gasp came across the phone line. I let some of that settle in, then briefed Alana on Corwin's visit and his haughty display in coming to the site and proclaiming that Charlie's death was a simple accident.

"That much I probably have to agree with," I told her, "but he has the coins."

"Really?"

"Either he has the *staters*, or he knows where they are."

# ALSIUM

## 580 BCE

Tyrrhenus's expedition had been very successful. They identified some unsettled land near the coastline, land that rose to a low peak in the hills beyond the shore that made a perfect spot for their planned city.

He chose the highest of three hills, laying out the footprint for his castle and city on the highest, and assigning the military to the other two hills to construct fortifications to defend the king's village. Construction proceeded quickly, at first based on the timber and other building materials that the Lydians had brought with them on the voyage, then supplemented by the natural resources of the area in central Italia.

There were other tribes in the surrounding area. They called themselves both Pelasgians and Villanovans, and the Lydians established treaties of consent between them. Tyrrhenus didn't intend to take their land or rob their resources; he set out to share what was there and build a consensus with these local tribes. In just the three years since their first landing, the Lydian people mingled with the Villanovans. This was especially important since the first sailing from Anatolia included mostly men at a ratio of ten men to one woman, so fertile local stock among the Villanovan tribes would be critical to establishing a thriving community.

Once the plan for the new city was laid out, Tyrrhenus sent the fleet of ships back to Lydia. Lutus worried that one or more vessels should remain, but his king disagreed.

"What will we do with one ship?" Tyrrhenus asked. "We couldn't fend off an attack, and one ship would be too small to arrange an escape for our people. No, it is better to send all the ships back to Ardys and hope to bring more of our people here on the next voyage."

And so, the ships departed for their home shores, returning in a few months with another hundred Lydians, and back again every few months until Tyrrhenus fulfilled his father's plan to emigrate half of their homeland population to the new world, here in central Italia.

They brought their people, their traditions, and their culture. And they brought their money. Staters had been a successful unit of exchange over the years that the Lydians had plied the waters of the Middle Sea, and staters would be the instrument of exchange for this new economy, based on the electrum coins that had been struck in Ardys's empire. With each voyage arriving on the shores of Alsium came more staters and trites, each to be used by Lydian people in this new land that they claimed as their own. These would be the coin of the realm for the new Lydian empire, settled here on the western coastline of Italia.

––––––

The sons of Tyrrhenus continued what he had begun. The Lydian settlements in central Italia grew, they mingled with the Villanovans and produced new generations, and they built their cities and economies based on the electrum coins that were the foundation of the financial empire of the Lydians back in Anatolia. It became a new Lydian empire here in this new land, and their coins served as the instrument of exchange, a symbolic form worth far more than the market value of the electrum, gold, and silver that could be melted down and traded in bulk.

In time, over many years, the generations that were born from the mingling of Lydian and Villanovan blood came to be known as Etruscans. Cultures merged and evolved, and traces of each were visible in the new society. But the coinage remained truly and faithfully Lydian. Instead of seizing the electrum coins and melting them down, the Etruscan cities that grew from this early birth maintained them as the system of monetary exchange. Lydian coins were used to buy and sell, and they remained as King Ardys had intended: As the coin of the realm and representative of the royal power which established them.

Melting the electrum coins had a certain attraction, to be traded for their market value. But that value paled in comparison to the face value of the coins—the staters, trites, hektes, and hemihektes—that were the basis of the great mercantile empire that the Lydians had established throughout the Mediterranean region.

Tyrrhenus's brother, Sadyattes, didn't follow him to Alsium, to the cities then known as Tarchon, but Sadyattes's son Alyattes did, and he continued the path begun by Tyrrhenus. Staters and trites remained their medium of exchange and commanded great respect, carrying uncommonly great value in the market for many years to come.

# ALBERGO DEI FIORI

I took Aggie's Jeep and returned to the hotel, talking to Alana for nearly the entire thirty minutes about what had transpired. The facts were coming together, and today, now that it was Thursday, I needed to start thinking about meeting Alana in Naples tomorrow so we could return to the Villa Poesia in Praiano.

"Let me run this down," I heard her say into the phone. 'Olivia's death was probably by poisoning. Charlie's death was probably an accident. Yavuz's death was by poisoning."

"Right."

"The poison connected to Olivia's death was found in Yavuz's hotel room ..."

"Not the specific samples," I corrected in my nerdy attention to detail. "The same kind of poison."

"Okay," she replied. "Now, the coins—if in fact Charlie's notes are correct and he actually found some—are nowhere to be found."

"Right."

"But Corwin is acting smug as if he knows where they are."

"Right again.

"And Demir claims to be cooperating with the investigation but also has an official interest in artifacts tied to the early Lydian peoples."

"Sure," I said.

"So, where are the coins?"

Her question was too simple to have a ready answer.

"Looks like Hamza Yavuz took them, at least based on the video. But he's dead, and he couldn't have smuggled them into his jail cell. Either he got them to Corwin, or he reburied them somewhere."

"And they're worth a lot."

"Yes," I replied. "They are. But don't forget that the meaning behind the coins, the fact that they were Lydian coinage—not melted—lends credence to the theory that the Lydian people not only populated the central part of Italy about twenty-five hundred years ago but also that the condition of the coins, that they were preserved with their embossed images, suggests that they were the coin of the realm in the region."

"And that means what, exactly?" she asked.

"It could mean a lot of things. But one theory, from Demir, is that it proves that the Lydian people—the ancestors of the Turkish people—were the ancestors of the Etruscans and, therefore, of the Romans. Even their kings."

"Whew!" was all she could say.

I arrived back at the hotel and went straight to my room. It was only mid-afternoon, so too early to gather in the lobby bar. And I thought it best for me to collect my notes and record what I knew so far.

Alana had very well summed up the facts as we knew them. I had my own conclusions, which I thought she would agree with, but they included implicating Tesa in the death of

Hamza Yavuz. We didn't talk about her motivation—we didn't have to; Yavuz was a clear suspect in her mother's death—but killing someone, even your mother's murderer, was still against the law. No matter what country you were in.

Olivia's death was unfortunate but past tense. Charlie's death was an accident. Yavuz stealing the coins, and it certainly seemed that he had, was wrong, but he, too, was now dead.

We could put a watch on Corwin, but he was too smart to be caught so soon. If he had the coins, he would arrange to fence them on the dark market, and we wouldn't be able to trace them. Demir cared about the find but only in support of the Turkish government's theory about the origins of the Etruscans.

And there was Peliatis who, from most accounts, would just as well melt them down and sell them in bulk to gold merchants in the country.

Of the guilty, Yavuz was a likely suspect, but he was dead. Corwin could be implicated but only in theft. Demir was somewhere on the periphery of all this but not completely absolved of suspicion. Peliatis lurked in the shadows, and I couldn't assign any specific guilt to him yet.

Tesa was clearly at risk of a criminal charge.

"What next?" Alana asked.

"Don't know," I responded. And I really didn't.

# ENOTECA FILICORI

A FEW HOURS LATER, THE TEAM BEGAN TO ARRIVE AT THE
hotel. I had taken a shower and went down to the lobby just to
get out of my room, so I watched the parade of diggers as they
arrived.

Aggie and Tesa arrived last, in close conversation and whis-
pering between themselves. I waved to Aggie, and he saw me
sitting there in the room lit by the afternoon sun. Raising his
index finger in the air and making small circles with it, I recognized the signal as him promising to return soon.

They went up the stairs and disappeared from view. I sat
with a coffee and my notes but soon heard the sound of Aggie's
heavy boots clomp down the steps as he entered the room
alone.

"Hey," he began. "Quite a day."

I didn't have anything to say right away.

"Is Tesa in trouble?" he asked.

"Yeah, I think so. I'm sorry."

"Will she be charged with poisoning Yavuz?"

"Don't know, but Rafaela seemed very official today."

"What if she charges Yavuz with theft of the coins?"

"That might sway a jury, but theft isn't a capital offense."

"What if she, Rafaela I mean, doesn't charge her?"

"Doesn't charge Tesa?" I asked. "Possible. Not likely."

"Fucker deserved it," he said.

"Not on point, I'm afraid."

At that moment, Tesa came down the stairs and joined us.

"How about we move to the Enoteca Filicori?" she said. "I need a drink."

"I agree," Aggie offered. "Is it too early?"

"Not on a day like this," she replied.

The three of us walked heavily out of the lobby bar and out the main door of the hotel, turned left then headed up the street to the wine bar, the *enoteca*, that she had mentioned. The restaurant area of Enoteca Filicori was set for dinner but still empty of guests, so we settled into chairs near the service bar and scanned the shelves of wines on service.

Then my phone rang.

"Darren," I heard Alana's voice say. "I'm coming into Naples tomorrow at noon. Is that okay?"

"Yeah, sure. In fact, it's perfect. I can't wait to see you. I'll be there an hour early. Just ring me when your train arrives."

There were only maybe six or seven other people in the wine bar. Luigi, the joyous bartender, came smiling up to us and waving his hand at the wines.

"Do you like Italian wines? We have many," he said exuberantly. "Even some from other countries."

"*Lui ha Barbaresco? Forse, da Pio Cesare?*" I asked.

"*Oh, certo! È il migliore!*" he responded. "Pio Cesare is the best, in my mind."

My favorite, too, although my personal wine cellar abounds in Barbarescos from many producers in Piedmont.

"*Sì, va bene,*" I replied. "That's good," although Tesa asked for her own drink, a Negroni. Stronger than wine and maybe more medicinal right now.

Luigi quickly returned to the bar area and came back a few moments later with the bottle, two wine glasses, and Tesa's Negroni. Before the barkeep could leave the table, Tesa ordered another round.

Conversation was slow for a while. Each of us wanted to avoid the obvious legal difficulties Tesa faced, but we really didn't know what else to talk about. I tried a hopeful comment about the cause of Charlie's death, but that only brought a darkened look to Tesa's face. Aggie said that Yavuz got what he deserved, but then the table went quiet, all of us contemplating whether Tesa would be forgiven for meting out justice on her own.

"Okay," I said in a serious tone, "let's talk about what we have."

"I'd rather not," Tesa replied, but Aggie put his hand on her forearm to calm her.

"I didn't poison Yavuz," she said defensively. "Maybe he got it himself. How do they know?"

I stared at her, recalled the scene in Yavuz's hotel room and the image of her shoving something into her pocket. I really didn't see what it was, and with nothing other than the guilty look she gave me, I had no information. No one else saw her do it. Why would she be a suspect? Even if someone did turn the glare on her—possibly tying the death of Yavuz to Olivia's poisoning—what basis would they have for a case?

And then, if they charged her and called me as a witness, what could I say? I saw her put her hands in her pockets. She gave me a searing, though guilty, look.

"Did you see what she had in her hand?" would go the questioning.

"No," would have to be my reply.

"Do you think she had taken some poison from the plastic bag?" another question.

"Objection!" the defense would say. "Requires conjecture. We're not interested in what Mr. Priest thinks, only what he saw. And he already answered that question."

The courtroom scene played out in my head, and I knew I wouldn't be a good witness for the prosecution. Not that I was trying to be, but I couldn't see how a case could be made.

About then, Tesa's phone rang. She looked at the screen, then her eyes went wide, and she looked up at Aggie and me.

"It's Inspector Indolfo."

"Are you going to answer it?" Aggie asked.

Tesa punched a key and lifted the phone to her ear.

"*Pronto*," she said without emotion.

I could hear Tesa's side of the conversation, but because Rafaela's voice was low, I couldn't pick out what she was saying. Tesa's eyes brightened at one point, then began to show tears forming on her lower eyelashes.

"Why is that?" she asked.

It was a formless question for me since I didn't know what prompted it.

"Okay," she added. "Yes, for now."

Some low mumbling from the other end of the phone line.

"I would. I know that," Tesa continued. "Of course. Thank you."

Then she lowered the phone, stared at the screen as if in disbelief, and punched the red "end" button.

"What is it?" Aggie asked.

Tesa paused for a moment, gulped down the first Negroni, and eagerly turned toward the second one that Luigi had just delivered. She swallowed half of that one, paused, and then drained the rest of the glass. Then, wiping her lips with the napkin, Tesa stared up at the ceiling for a moment before she began to shake, tears trickling down her cheeks.

"The Curse of Croesus, she said," Tesa commented. "That's what she said."

"What the heck are we talking about?"

"My mother and Hamza died of the same poison, and Charlie died falling into the pit of Croesus. Rafaela can't explain so many deaths related to the same place, without evidence of someone's actions. She said she has known about the Curse of Croesus for years and never believed it. Now she does."

Tears of relief streamed down Tesa's cheeks as Aggie grabbed her hand and smiled.

"Is that what she said?" he asked. "Is that what she believes?"

Tesa shrugged her shoulders and nodded her head.

"She can't put that on the official record," Tesa continued. "But Olivia's death was already listed as *idiopathic,* 'no known cause.' If Hamza died of the same thing, his would be listed as *idiopathic.* And we know from the security camera that Charlie simply fell to his death. Rafaela isn't blaming it on the Curse, but she said she will probably tell her friends and colleagues about Croesus when they are recounting the case."

"So," Aggie said haltingly, "she's not going to follow this anymore or charge someone?"

The "someone" he cared about was obviously Tesa, but he didn't want to refer to her in the sentence.

"Apparently not," Tesa replied. "She's closing the case. Her final words were 'the Curse of Croesus strikes again.'"

# VILLA POESIA

I waited in the Café Roma in the Naples train station on Friday morning for Alana to arrive. It had been an eventful week. I had an uneasy feeling about Tesa and what I knew—or thought I knew—about her involvement in the death of Hamza Yavuz. I didn't like glossing over someone's guilt, but I had learned from my career in military intelligence that truth was sometimes a flexible concept, and although we would like to deny it, it was also often situational.

The Curse of Croesus was simultaneously a gratifying way to end things and an unsettling conclusion.

When Aggie, Tesa, and I shared her news from Rafaela last evening at Enoteca Filicori, I drank deeply of the Pio Cesare Barbaresco but didn't stay for dinner. I would be hungry, I knew, but decided that I should find sustenance elsewhere and leave my two friends alone.

Before leaving the wine bar, I said my goodbyes to my old friend Aggie, reminding him to stay in touch, then stepped around the table to give Tesa a hug.

"Be mindful," I said, only somewhat knowing the many

meanings that phrase could entail. Then I turned back to Aggie with a smile.

"And you be mindful of this woman," I warned him. "She's a treasure."

I stepped through the door onto the street and couldn't shake my misgivings about Tesa and what I was nearly sure she had done. There was too much coincidence in the deaths of Olivia and Yavuz, and except for missing the visual of Tesa hiding something in her pocket, I was sure Inspector Indolfo would agree with me. Walking down the street toward the hotel, I replayed the witness examination and cross-exam that I had rolled through my mind earlier. There was nothing to tie Tesa to Hamza's death, not even my own superficial testimony.

Did I think she poisoned him? Yes, I did. Did he deserve it? Yes, but no. He was probably the agent of Oliva's death, but no one deserved to be executed without a trial. Did he steal and hide the coins? No doubt in my mind, but with an emphasis on hide. Now we would never know where they were, but I fully intended to press Corwin to find out what he knew.

I had to be careful, though. If I insisted on tracing Corwin's actions, I might find connections between him and Yavuz. Good enough. And probably find connections between Yavuz and Demir and the Turkish government. That was good too. But if I pressed hard enough, I might uncover details about the dig, including Charlie's paternity regarding Tesa, which she seemed reluctant to bring out.

Worse yet, I might find connections between Corwin, Yavuz, and Demir and the death investigations that were being closed by Rafaela under the claim of *idiopathic* causes—in this case, known as the Curse of Croesus.

I was on my second double espresso and second roll when I got a call from Alana. She said the train was ten minutes out and asked if I could meet her on the platform.

"Italy has security gates at its train stations now," I said, "on the entrance to the platform. I'll find what *binario* your train is pulling into and wait outside the security gate for you."

Last night I had given Alana only the briefest of summaries of what had gone on, and I planned to fill her in more on the details now that we would be together for a couple of days.

I saw her head bobbing above the crowd that disgorged from the train cars and onto the platform. She was of average height but bounced up and down to pick me out. When we made eye contact, she waved her hand and smiled brightly. Slipping through the security turnstile, she dropped the handle of the bag she dragged behind and threw her arms around me.

"About time," she said. "That was the longest train ride ever from Vienna."

I smiled and kissed her warmly on the lips. Her eyes brightened, her smile magnified, and her skin even seemed warmer to the touch.

"I rented a car for the weekend," I told her. "There won't be much use for it in Praiano, but it's Friday now, and we'll need it to get back here on Sunday."

"Just park it around the corner from the market, *Tutto per Tutti*, and we'll just stay in the Villa all weekend."

"Perfect," I replied and hugged her close.

The drive from Naples to Praiano took about two hours, slowed somewhat by the tourists still clogging the streets. But once we hit Castellammare della Stabia, the route hugging the edge of the mountain with views falling off into the Mediterranean below, we felt like we were home again. Just past Vico Equense, the road turned inland, so we lost sight of the sea, but soon we were back on the coastline and approaching Positano. Snaking around the bends and horn-honking tour buses, we descended onto the route that would take us past the sparkling waters of the sea to our right and the looming mountain cliffs to our left.

We talked about the events of the week, me retelling some of the facts that unfolded, and Rafaela's apparent decision to drop the case. I think she knew that Tesa wanted closure on her mother's death but probably also feared that probing too deeply into that might raise questions about why she had visited Yavuz in his jail cell right before he was found dead.

In no time, we arrived at Praiano. I barely knew the route since we had taken a cab here before, but there were only a few roads in the little seaside town. After one or two wrong turns, I found the right street to reach *Tutto per Tutti* and parked the car around the corner as Alana had suggested.

We reached into the trunk for our bags, mine still swollen from a long, lengthy vacation as yet not ended, and Alana's somewhat smaller suitcase planned just for a weekend stay. We walked up the incline from the market past La Moressa, a terrace restaurant overlooking the sea that had become home for us during our week here.

"*Buon giorno!*" shouted the owner from the open doorway. "*Come state!*" he asked warmly. "How are you? You're back so soon!" in halting English.

"Yes, we are. Disappointed?" I asked as Alana smiled back at him.

"No, no! Shall I keep a table for you for this evening?"

"Yes!" Alana said gleefully, anxious to renew the pleasure that we had enjoyed during our holiday here.

It was still many steps up to the Villa Poesia, but the view from the top was worth a million bucks.

We waved to the folks at La Moressa and proceeded down the narrow roadway toward the steps that would lead us between the buildings and up the slope to the Villa. We arrived in mid-afternoon, so the lantern lights and soft lamps on the outside of the Villa were not yet lit, but the view was neverthe-less unforgettably gorgeous.

Julietta met us at the gate that allowed controlled entry onto the property. She smiled and welcomed us back with a warm embrace. Handing me the keys, she said, "I'm sure you know how to use these." Then she departed, leaving us alone just as Alana and I had planned and longed for.

When I went inside to set our bags down in the upstairs bedroom that we had used on our previous stay, I noticed a bottle of Prosecco, a sparkling wine from northern Italy, on the table in the dining room. A card said, "Welcome home," and was signed by Julietta.

We didn't want to waste time unpacking, so we threw the bags on the floor of the bedroom and returned downstairs to the kitchen. Julietta had left a bag of ground coffee, good for the morning, but more importantly, she had put a fresh loaf of bread on the cutting board and some cheese and salami in the refrigerator. While I pulled the cork from the Prosecco, Alana arranged a platter of food and retrieved some wine glasses from the cabinet.

I had not felt this good in a long time. I was with the woman I loved, in a place that was as romantic and beautiful as any place on earth, and I had a bottle of wine and fresh food to nibble on. Once we set our snacks and wine out on the terrazza, the glistening waters of the Mediterranean below and the soft blue of the sky above added to the overall feeling that I had.

Alana smiled at me as we settled into the cushions of the lounge chairs, wordlessly agreeing with the feelings that I was enjoying.

After something to nibble on, a glass of wine and another to be filled, and taking in the breathless views beyond the wall of the Villa, we settled into a conversation.

"So, she's not going to be charged," Alana said, almost as a half question.

"No. Appears not."

"Did she poison Hamza Yavuz?"

"I don't have an opinion on that."

"Come on, Darren. It's me," she said a little impatiently, though her smile allayed any concern I might have of being interrogated by a talented cop from Vienna.

"Yeah, I have an opinion. But it doesn't matter, does it? It's all about what the Italian authorities think."

"I suppose so," she replied. "Would you trust her?"

"Absolutely," I said with confidence. "As long as I didn't poison her mother."

You see, sometimes truth was situational.

Alana's phone rang, and she cast a disappointed look in my direction. Clearly, she didn't want our time interrupted by outside callers. But recognizing the name on the phone, she pushed the green button.

"Hello?"

"Yes, Alana. It's Rafaela. I want to fill you a bit on things that we have been told."

"Yes, and?" Alana said a bit impatiently. I knew that the two women were friends, but the intrusion had caught Alana unawares, and it showed.

"Demir is no longer in Cerveteri," I heard Rafaela say when Alana had turned on the speaker.

"Where is he?" she asked.

"Not sure," Rafaela replied, "but we think he's back in Turkey. Suddenly. And Corwin is nowhere to be found."

"What?" I tried not to participate in the call, but he was my contact.

"Nowhere to be found?" I repeated. "That doesn't sound good."

"As you already know, Yavuz is dead, but Demir and Corwin have disappeared," Rafaela continued. "And now it seems like Peliatis is missing, too."

Antonin Peliatis had only popped onto the radar when Alana went looking, and he showed up as an entrepreneur who traded in bulk metals.

"What does his absence say?" I asked.

"Nothing that I can think of, directly," Rafaela replied. "But Demir, Corwin, and Peliatis entering the conversation just as a cache of ancient coins is found and then goes missing. Makes one wonder."

"Well, thanks, Rafaela," Alana said, and I could tell she was turning her mind back to us. "But seems like this mystery is one that you will have to solve."

"Unless I find out that they turn up in Austria," the Roman inspector said, "and then I have to come visit you."

"Any time," Alana replied with a smile, but then she clicked off.

We held our silence for a few seconds, but Alana and I both knew that we were just trying to mentally revert our attention to our earlier conversation.

"And what about us?" she asked suddenly.

At first, I wasn't sure how to answer. I had decided by the end of our week together here, right here, on the terrazza of Villa Poesia, that I never wanted to let her go.

"Us?" I said with a smile, pretending innocence and ignorance at once. "You know there's a place called Vienna near my home outside of Washington, D.C."

"Vienna? You mean the place in Virginia?"

"Yeah, well..." and I didn't know how to close the statement.

"There is no place like Vienna, Austria," she replied with a smile. "But tell me more about this place Washington."

Dear reader,

We hope you enjoyed reading *The Etruscan Connection*.
Please take a moment to leave a review, even if it's a short one.
Your opinion is important to us.

Discover more books by Dick Rosano at
https://www.nextchapter.pub/authors/author-dick-rosano

Want to know when one of our books is free or discounted?
Join the newsletter at http://eepurl.com/bqqB3H

Best regards,
Dick Rosano and the Next Chapter Team

## ABOUT THE AUTHOR

Dick Rosano's columns have appeared for many years in *The Washington Post* and other national publications. His series of novels set in Italy capture the beauty of the country, the flavors of the cuisine, and the history and traditions of the people. He has traveled the world, but Italy is his ancestral home, and the insights he lends to his books bring the characters to life, the cities and countryside into focus, and the culture into high relief.

Whether it's the historical drama that played out in *The Sicily Chronicles*, the political drama of *The Vienna Connection*, the workings of a family winery in *A Death in Tuscany*, the azure sky and Mediterranean vistas in *A Love Lost in Positano*, the intrigue in *Hunting Truffles*, or the bitter conflict of Nazi occupation in *The Secret Altamura*, Rosano puts the life and times of Italy into your hands.

## ACKNOWLEDGMENTS

Few books can be written with the input of only one person, no matter how hard the writer tries to research the material. For this book, I was supported—as always—by my wife and daughter—but also by professionals whose broad-reaching expertise was critical to me getting the facts straight.

Dr. Barbara Wolff of Montgomery College, a professor of archeology, raised my level of understanding of that discipline, not to her own expertise, but high enough to ensure that I could capably describe the process of physical anthropology. Don Oldenburg, my editor, is a constant encouragement in the process, and his presence is always felt as I write.

Although I don't normally mention the Italian people in a general sense—or the thousands of years of their culture that inspire me—the history and traditions of those people hover as a mystic crowd around me, encouraging the work and insisting on a proper understanding of who they are, where they came from, and what they will be.

And last, but by no means least, is Julietta, the most

engaging and friendly host that a traveler could ever want. She owns and manages the Villa Poesia in Praiano and—together with the unforgettable views—is the greatest reason for us spending time there at the cliffside villa overlooking the Mediterranean.

## OTHER BOOKS BY DICK ROSANO

*Islands of Fire: The Sicily Chronicles, Part I*—An historical novel that captures the settlement of the island of Sicily from ancient times to the Roman era, including the wayfaring invasions and battles fought for domination of the land.

*Crossroads of the Mediterranean: The Sicily Chronicles, Part II*—An historical novel that captures the progress of habitation on the island of Sicily, from the period of Julius Caesar to the present day, including invasions by Greeks, Romans, Goths, Carthaginians, Byzantines, Fatimids, Swabians, Angevins, and many more over the centuries.

*The Vienna Connection*—Darren Priest's hitch in military intelligence is behind him as he plies his new trade as a writer. But when high-ranking officials call up, he realizes that "some things you can't unvolunteer for."

*A Death in Tuscany*—A young man mourns the suspicious death of his grandfather while preparing to take the reins of his family's winery in Tuscany.

*The Secret of Altamura: Nazi Crimes, Italian Treasure*—Secrets hidden from the Nazis in 1943 are still sought by an art collector in modern days. But evil stalks all those who try to reveal it.

*Hunting Truffles*—The slain bodies of truffle hunters show up, but the truffle harvest itself has been stolen.

*Wine Heritage: The Story of Italian American Vintners*—Centuries of Italian immigration to America laid the groundwork for the

American wine revolution of the 20<sup>th</sup> century.

## Other Books by D.P. Rosano

*A Love Lost in Positano*—A war-weary State Department translator falls for a woman under the blue skies of the Mediterranean, then she disappears.

*Vivaldi's Girls*—The young red-haired prodigy could make women swoon with the sweeping grandeur of his violin performances—even more so after he traded in his priest's robes for the dashing attire of a rich and notorious celebrity.

*To Rome, With Love*—Some memories are never forgotten. As Tamara discovers the charms of Rome in the arms of her first love, the sights, food, and wine sweep her away.

The Etruscan Connection
ISBN: 978-4-86747-530-0

Published by
Next Chapter
1-60-20 Minami-Otsuka
170-0005 Toshima-Ku, Tokyo
+818035793528

19th May 2021

Lightning Source UK Ltd.
Milton Keynes UK
UKHW010633040621
384928UK00001B/194